SO-ACV-748

CORRUPTING DR. NICE

By John Kessel from Tom Doherty Associates

Novels
Corrupting Dr. Nice
Good News from Outer Space

Editor
Intersections: The Sycamore Hill Anthology
(with Mark L. Van Name and Richard Butner)

CORRUPTING DR. NICE

John Kessel

TOR®

A Tom Doherty Associates Book

New York

This is a work of fiction. All the characters and events por-
trayed in this novel are either fictitious or are used ficti-
tiously.

CORRUPTING DR. NICE

Copyright © 1997 by John Kessel

All rights reserved, including the right to reproduce this book,
or portions thereof, in any form.

I Don't Know What Kind of Blues I've Got, by Duke Elling-
ton © 1942 (Renewed) EMI Robbins Catalog Inc. All Rights
Reserved. Used by Permission. Warner Bros. Publications
U.S. Inc., Miami, FL 33014.

This book is printed on acid-free paper.

A Tor Book
Published by Tom Doherty Associates, Inc.
175 Fifth Avenue
New York, NY 10010

Tor Books on the World Wide Web:
http://www.tor.com

Tor® is a registered trademark of Tom Doherty Associates, Inc.

Book design by Scott Levine

Library of Congress Cataloging-in-Publication Data

Kessel, John.
    Corrupting Dr. Nice / John Kessel.—1st ed.
        p.   cm.
    "A Tom Doherty Associates book."
    ISBN 0-312-86116-8 (acid-free paper)
    I. Title.
PS3561.E6675C6   1997
813'.54—dc20   96-33020
                                                   CIP

First Edition: February 1997

Printed in the United States of America

0 9 8 7 6 5 4 3 2 1

Dedicated, with affection and gratitude, to
Frank Capra
George Cukor
Howard Hawks
Gregory La Cava
Ernst Lubitsch
Leo McCarey
George Stevens
Billy Wilder

and most especially, in admiration for his genius, to
Preston Sturges

CORRUPTING DR. NICE

PART ONE

Jerusalem, 40 C.E.

Chapter 1

It's a Wonderful Life

As Sloane unlaced the bodice of Genevieve's peasant's dress all she could hear was his breathing, fast and light. It showed how thinly his gentleness lay over his lust, and it was all she could do to keep from running from the room.

"You'll have to excuse me," Sloane said. "I'm not used to these antiquated fastenings."

Genevieve pushed his hands aside and unlaced herself, slowly, turning it into a performance. Sloane tore at his own clothing, hopping up and down on one foot as he tugged at his breeches. Through the tiny latticed window to the courtyard came the smell of rotting vegetables and the voices of the concierge and his wife arguing in eighteenth-century French. Before Genevieve could shrug out of the sleeves of her dress Sloane had launched himself at her and they fell together onto the bed. He reeked of cologne and antibacterial soap. Gen forced a giggle and began to wonder how long she was going to have to keep this up.

At last the door burst open and in rushed August, wearing a dark blue frock coat over knee breeches, black buckled shoes and a cocked hat with tricolor cockade. He flashed the sigil of Saltimbanque Corporation security. "Sloane," he said. "You're under arrest."

Sloane jerked back. Gen acted as if she had never seen such an apparition in all her life. "Who are you, sir?" she asked August. She let a quaver come to her voice.

"Never you mind, madame," said August. He approached the bed as if to soothe her, and she clutched her disarrayed clothes to her breast. Sloane cowered beneath the counterpane.

When August reached the bedside, in a single swift motion he pulled a stunner from his pocket, held it to Genevieve's head and discharged it. The stunner was powerless, but Genevieve collapsed among the bedclothes as if she'd been knocked out. She listened.

"Okay, Sloane. Time to go."

Genevieve felt Sloane stir beside her. "Is she dead?" He sounded terrified.

"Unconscious. She'll be out for a half hour or so. Time enough for me to book you."

"I didn't plan this. It just happened. She came on to me in the restaurant . . ."

"I don't care if she tackled you around the ankles. This isn't an unburned universe. We plan to be here awhile."

"What difference does it make?"

"We have to deal with these people. The Committee of Public Safety's idea of freedom wasn't to have us come in and sleep with their women. You know the rules."

An edge of calculation crept into Sloane's voice. "Give me a break. They've seen plenty of changes. What would it cost to make this right?"

August made him wait. Genevieve wished she could open her eyes. Her father was good. "Can't do it, friend. My movements are logged more tightly than yours, even. If I'm here preventing interference my bosses are going to want to know what happened to the interferer. To say nothing of keeping this girl quiet."

"This tramp? She's nobody. If she disappeared today it wouldn't make a bit of difference."

Gen hoped August would make him pay extra for that. Forget the money—she hoped he'd rip Sloane's lungs out and leave him for dead. Instead August said, "How much cash do you have on you?"

"About seven hundred francs—"

"Not currency, idiot. Eurodollars." Genevieve had reported to August that Sloane typically carried access to more than a hundred thousand in electronic cash on him at all times. He'd sashayed into the 1790s Hyatt like he was going to buy the place, sporting the fashionable rotund physique of 2060s wealth, dropping hundred-dollar tips and expecting to find the Eiffel Tower.

"I can slip you fifty thousand right here," Sloane said.

August snorted. "Pull your pants up and let's get you booked."

"Eighty."

"When is your wife expecting you back at the hotel? Did you tell her you were running down to Notre Dame for a quart of milk?"

"A hundred. A hundred ten!"

Another silence. At last August said, "Let's have it, then."

A rustle of clothes, the tap of code on a wallet keypad.

"All right. You do three things, Sloane. One, you wait here in this room while I dispose of the girl. You don't make a move until I come back. Two, when you get back to the hotel you go to your room and check out immediately, then head back uptime. Three, you keep your mouth shut, and you never try anything like this again."

August was so good when he was playing a cop. Just the right mix of arrogance and corruption.

"Believe me, I will," said Sloane. "You won't regret giving me a break."

"I won't regret it because I'm never going to see you again. Right?"

"Right, right."

Genevieve felt August lean over the bed and pick her up. He grunted. He was getting a little old to lug her around. He carried her out the door, kicked it closed. She opened her eyes and mimed a kiss at him. He scowled. At the head of the stairs he gave up and set her down, winded. "You're no slip of a girl anymore," he said.

They snuck down the back stairs, avoiding the concierge, and out of the Hotel des Balcons. The 1793 Paris lane reeked of piss, horse manure and fresh-baked bread from the pâtisserie on the corner. Outside the shop a couple of Swiss hussars in brilliant blue dress uniforms loitered talking to a girl in a mob-cap. A beggar wearing a tricolor on his filthy hat and a silkscreened T-shirt of Humphrey Bogart clutched after Genevieve's skirts as they passed. "Alms, citizens?"

To the beggar's astonishment, August gave him his frock coat and hat. "*Liberté, égalité, fraternité!*" August said. Gen pulled him away down the street.

She was still upset. "What kept you so long!"

"Nothing kept me. You know as well as I the game works better when the mark's nervous. I don't want him clearheaded. I want him too surprised to see straight."

"And how long did you expect me to keep him off me?"

He patted her arm. "Don't pretend you can't take care of yourself."

She supposed it was the truth, but it was not what she wanted to hear. "I'm tired of being the badger," she told him. "Next time you do it."

"You find me the mark, my dear, and I'll badger her to death."

"We need to get out of this stinking century. Let's do ancient Rome again. We'll sell pieces of the true cross. We'll offer army blankets as the Robe."

"Anything you like," he replied. He stopped, looked directly at her. He had let himself age in recent years; his hair was gray and his brow lined. "You know I wouldn't let anyone hurt you, Genevieve. The man who tries it is history."

Genevieve leaned on his arm, overwhelmed with sudden sadness. It was her day for being emotional, she guessed. "History," she said. History was their business.

A portable plastic sign on solid rubber tires in front of the Odeon Theater proclaimed, *Cette Nuit, Vivant—Edith Piaf!* The historicals were all in a rage for the twentieth-century chanteuse, and for her part, she seemed to like the past better than the future. She was carrying on a famous affair with Danton, who thanks to Saltimbanque had managed not to get himself executed this time, negotiating himself into a position of de facto rule over the city. Though conspirators in coffee shops swore he was in the pocket of the multinationals.

August and Gen ducked down a blind alley across from the theater. A cat, crouching over a mangled rat, watched them warily. At the back of the alley August retrieved his twenty-first-century dress coat. Gen discarded the peasant's dress and threw on her yellow frock and her wristward. They hurried past the Luxembourg Gardens to Montparnasse. As they approached the wall surrounding the time travelers' quarter, historicals in the streets crowded around. "Have pity on my poverty!" a young woman holding a baby to her breast cried. "Chocolate bars, bacteriophage, TV!" a boy shouted. This time August tossed them a handful of coins and they pressed on through the crowd of hangers-on around the Notre Dame des Champs security gate. Saltimbanque security in blue, carrying rifles, manned the checkpoint.

"ID, *s'il vous plaît*," the guard said.

August and Gen ran their wristwards over the reader, which identified them as Mr. and Mrs. Knox Cramer of Hong Kong. The guard passed them through and they headed down the boulevard to the Hyatt Regency, towering over the eighteenth-century French buildings like some glittering glass tumor.

No one in the lobby paid them any attention; for all they knew August and Gen were just some tourists back from the catacombs. They stopped in their room only long enough to pick up their bags, already packed.

"Did you have a pleasant stay?" the desk clerk asked August.

"Most profitable," August replied, paying with Sloane's cash. "There are things to do here we could never find back home."

"Well, you must visit one of our other temporal resorts. We've just settled a new universe at twelfth-century Angkor Wat. You should try it."

"I'm certain we will."

After checking out they headed for the time stage in the hotel's basement, where they purchased tickets, in three jumps, for ancient Athens. The steward took their bags and directed them to the departure lounge. They sat and watched through the window to the chamber. The hotel's Gödel stage was of moderate size, five meters across, surrounded by a field delimiter of stainless steel that looked like a guardrail. In the dim air above the stage hung the subtly warped geometries of the singularity emulator, and off to the side, behind their controls, were the technicians. The lights in the chamber were kept low, though the moments of shot and arrival were accompanied by flares of radiation that their window compensated for. A dark couple and their child—Amerinds, perhaps?—were being helped onto the stage. The woman looked nervous, but the kid was babbling excitedly.

The stage was not busy at that hour, and Gen and August only had to wait twenty minutes. Still, Gen got nervous thinking about Sloane. The secret to this business was giving the mark what he thought he wanted. They'd given Sloane what he wanted: escape from a scandal. But suppose he chafed at August's orders? Suppose, after he calmed down, he figured out he'd been scammed? If he'd hurried, he could already be back at the hotel. He wouldn't want to alert his wife to his playing around, but on the other hand, he was a wealthy man, accustomed to getting his way. He probably did not let social inferiors get the better of him in a deal, and if he ever did figure out what they'd pulled, he'd be a dangerous man.

Gen could still smell a whiff of his cologne on her skin. If they'd had the time, she would have taken a shower. But they didn't. This was the cost of their line of work, and as the window blanked and the Indians disappeared she began to wonder if it was worth it. On the other hand, there was a satisfaction to getting the best of a character like Sloane. She imagined him sitting on four directorships and three committees of public morals, accompanying his virgin daughters to their debuts and cutting anyone whose income was less than his. You could pretty much count on the New Victorians to be the most ready to take advantage of a situation—which made it easy to take advantage of them.

The steward finished locking their baggage down and escorted them into the chamber, through the barrier to the stage. They stood at the center of the pastel bull's-eye. "Have a safe and pleasant trip," the steward said. August handed him a fifty-dollar coin and the man retreated beyond the rail.

At the control panel, the shaven-headed technician played with his keyboard, then looked up at them, smiled and raised his hand to wave. Before he had completed the gesture he and the panel and the walls of the room receded with astonishing speed in all directions. Gen and August fell into a dark space. Then the walls of a similar chamber rushed forward to surround them, and they came to rest on a stage eight hundred years further into the past.

On the wall across from them, beyond the delimiter, "1,000 C.E." was set in an elaborate Byzantine mosaic. The technician at this panel, a woman, was blonde and blue-eyed. Without stopping they made their second jump, to first-century Jerusalem.

Time to throw off any pursuit. Before the technician could set up the third jump to 400 B.C. Athens, August spoke up.

"Excuse me," he said, touching a hand to his head, "but I'm feeling a little indisposed—that last transition was difficult. Might we stop here for a while?"

"Certainly, sir," the tech's voice came back. A steward came from behind the rail to help them off the stage. He gave Genevieve the eye, and she smiled back at him.

"There are vacancies in the hotel?" August asked. The control technician was watching them.

"Yes sir."

"What do you say we stop over for a bit, daughter? Athens will still be there when we choose to go, won't it, young man?"

"Sure. Always was, always will." As the steward started them toward the lounge one of the men at the control board frowned. "Jim, take a look at this." They huddled over the controls.

The room was getting dark. Behind them the Gödel stage hummed. Genevieve turned and watched as, within the delimiter, from a knot of darkness, a man expanded into shape. But instead of arriving stationary, when he reached full size he surged forward off the stage, frantically trying to keep his balance. Flailing his arms like a windmill he fell toward her, his face contorted into a mask of dismay. A metal case he'd carried tumbled forward as if it had been tossed from a moving train. The case bounced and skidded across the tiles. Genevieve danced out of the way and the man flipped over the railing, did a neat tuck-and-roll and ended up crouched on his haunches, fingers touching the floor, nose inches from her legs.

Slender, about thirty years old, he wore a dark green jumpsuit and hideous purple boots. His light brown hair was too long. A label on the front of his case repeated over and over, in red: CAUTION! CONTENTS—LIVE ANIMAL.

One of the transit technicians rushed to help. "Something's wrong with the momentum compensator," his partner behind the board said.

"You made me let go of the case!" the traveler gasped. "Wilma!"

Genevieve righted the carrier. The animal inside thumped against its sides. "The name is Genevieve."

The man looked up toward her in dismay. "Excuse me." After a moment he muttered, "Will you please be quiet? I'm not an idiot."

She couldn't decide whether he was homely or cute, in an ungainly way. She helped him to his feet. "I don't doubt it," she said. "But we have to stop meeting this way."

Chapter 2

Bringing Up Baby

In the evening Owen would walk out onto the plains, carrying the sack of cat food down to the muddy edge of the lake where the young sauropods nested. Careful not to disturb the snoozing adolescents, he would kneel beside their nest and hold out a handful of cat chow. The hatchlings, no more than half a meter long, large-eyed and alert, would nuzzle the food out of his palm with their flexible snouts. They were covered in short down, like pinfeathers, that they would lose as they grew older. One of them, the one he called Betty, would hold the pieces between her teeth, then throw them to her back molars with a toss of her head before grinding them. Betty's short snout, Owen suspected, was an evolutionary adaptation supposed to make her look cute enough that the adult apatosaurs would protect her. Although some of his colleagues disputed the psychological impact of neoteny.

The young had come to expect this snack. Charming and clumsy, remarkably intelligent, their descendants would one day have come to rule the earth, were it not for the unfortunate fact that soon they would all be extinct.

On the day he was due to go back, Owen waited there past the feeding as the sun dipped below the treetops and shadows crept out over the mirror-smooth water, ascending beneath the screw pines and fan palms until the outlines of the trees stood out like black paper cutouts against the orange sky. It still amazed Owen how much the dogwoods, palmettos and magnolias resembled those of seventy million years in the future. The late-Cretaceous wasn't any hotter than Virginia, or except during the rainy season, any wetter. It wasn't the tropical jungle he'd imagined as a boy. He watched a pterosaur far across the lake, circling on the wind, at this distance no bigger than a hawk. It was looking for its home for the night. Owen upended the canvas bag, shook the last crumbs of food out onto the soft brown earth. "All gone," he said.

The larger young poked their snouts at the food, heads bobbing like chickens. One by one they turned away and trotted off toward the lakeshore. Betty snuffled through the last bits, then looked up at him. She was a lot bigger than the three-kilogram hatchling she had been a couple of months before. She must be two-thirds of a meter tall now, and she reached out to gently clutch his wrist with her open mouth. Owen wadded up the bag. "No more," he said. He felt depressed. Betty let go of him, chirped, turned and scampered off into the darkness.

A few minutes later Bill began to pester him. =It's nineteen-twenty,= the voice whispered in his ear. =Time to go.=

"Don't rush me," Owen subvocalized.

=You spend too much time out here alone with these things,= the voice in his head insisted. =One of these days you're going to get eaten by one of your pets.=

"You'd karate chop them into insensibility before they could get a nibble." Owen muttered aloud this time. "Besides, sauropods aren't meat eaters."

=The ones that eat them are. A young fellow like you ought to be chasing other kinds of tail.=

Owen stood up, slung his rifle over his shoulder. His mood boots, currently pea green, had picked up a coating of mud. "All right." He clumped back toward the glow of the research station's lights on the hill.

=You've packed your iguana up nice and tidy?= Bill asked.

"She's no more an iguana than you are."

=I bet she tastes like iguana.=

"Well, we'll never find out, will we."

The wind rustled a copse of fan palms down the watercourse a hundred yards to his right, and despite his bravado Owen hoped a pair of raptors weren't watching him from the cover. He unslung the rifle and slipped off the safety.

But the predators seldom came this close to the station's floodlights. He reached the top of a little swale and followed the jeep track toward the compound's gate.

Vannice Station consisted of five prefabricated buildings, the largest of them housing the labs and the time-travel stage, set down on a leveled hillock. It was the highest ground around in the mosaic of lakes, rivers and the vast floodplain that would one day become the arid Great Basin of Nevada, Arizona and western Utah, but now was a Serengeti-like plain. A great number of ferns, conifers and cycads crowded around the watercourses, and herds of sauropods followed the rains to root out new plant growth. Only in nesting season did they stop long enough to produce a flock of young.

Owen passed through the electrical fence that surrounded the station. Both of the jeeps were in the garage. The lights were on in the abattoir, and Owen detoured over to the opened corrugated-metal door.

The concrete floor was smeared with mud and drying blood from the corpse of the adolescent *Bactrosaurus* Fiona O'Connor had dragged in with the bobcat. Fiona had on a virching helmet and was directing a couple of robot moles she had inserted into the carcass to orbit around the animal's internal organs doing CAT scans. The place reeked of rotting dinosaur, but when it came to devotion to her work the Fiona had a cast-iron stomach.

When Owen tapped her on the shoulder she jumped a foot. She flipped up the helmet's visor and took off the gloves. "Owen! What do you want?"

"I'm leaving now. Did you forget?"

Fiona was a thin woman, her straight dark hair cut very short. She turned from him and picked up an electric saw. She flicked it on and began to assault the back of the dead dinosaur's thigh. "Have you seen these dorsal ligaments?" she said above the saw's whine.

Owen put his hand on her arm. "Don't you have anything to say?"

Fiona turned off the saw. She looked at her shoes. "Owen, it was fun. But I'm a scientist first."

"And I'm not?"

"I didn't say that. You've done excellent work here. Without your support—"

"Without my father's money."

"I didn't say that, either."

"You didn't have to."

"I like you Owen. You *are* a scientist. I look forward to seeing the results of your experiment. When I get back to Boston I'll be sure to look you up."

Owen should have known better than to try to say good-bye; Fiona had more than once made it clear that his leaving was a matter of indifference to her. "Sure," he said. "Well—good-bye, then."

She pecked him on the cheek and turned on the saw again. "Good-bye. Have a safe trip back. Don't forget the shower."

Owen fled the building.

The rest of the place was pretty quiet; most of the others must be testing their own cast-iron stomachs at dinner, which

Owen had skipped in order to prepare Wilma for the trip. And avoid an embarrassing farewell scene at which his colleagues would fawn over him and Dunkenfield would press requests for him to pass on to his father.

In his room Owen sat down at his desk to scrape the mud off his bootsoles. When he turned up the right boot he found a glittering butterfly flattened against his heel. Shining green and gold in the light of his desk lamp, it was of a species he hadn't seen before. It was also quite dead.

=Another species down the tubes.=

"There are probably thousands of these things in a one-kilometer radius."

=If they're smart they'll stay that far away from those killer feet of yours. You're lucky some brontosaurus hasn't returned the favor.=

Owen peeled the insect from his boot.

He was gathering up his suitcase and notebook when Bill whispered in his mind, =I trust naked free screaming obsessive art women!= For perhaps the one-thousandth time Owen cursed his father for implanting the AIde in him. The internal AI had proved useful hundreds of times since Owen had gotten him as a boy, but Owen had long since come to realize it was just another attempt by his parents to protect their investment. It would not do for the only heir to North America's fifth largest private fortune to face the world without a competitive advantage—and a parent-programmed conscience. Bill had been modeled on the bodyguard Owen had until he was seven—William Oakley, head of security at Thornberry, the Vannice estate. Oakley was an ex-spook martial arts specialist with a mysterious past. Bill even had Oakley's voice. Worst of all, in a perceived crisis, for the purposes of protecting his charge, Bill had the power to overrule Owen's voluntary muscles and take control of his body.

His father's picking a spook for the job had been a bad idea. Bill's protectiveness was getting out of hand, and his gruff banter was slipping toward abuse. Of late Bill had taken to generating nonsense sentences that he would project into Owen's ear at arbitrary times. The prevailing sentiments seemed to have something to do with naked women, sex and God. Owen did not see how this in any way applied to him. Add to this Bill's increasing paranoia and the result was Owen was determined to take him into the shop when he got back to the twenty-first century.

From the live animals lab Owen took the lightweight opaque case holding Wilma, another infant *Apatosaurus megacephalos,* and headed for the transit building. It was full night now. Out in the woods his shrewlike ancestors had emerged from burrows to hunt insects. Clouds of moths swarmed in the perimeter lights. He passed between the twin fan palms that marked the edge of the clearing. Down the slope toward the lake a stand of pines obscured the scar where Pike had been stepped on while examining the rhamphorhynchus. They'd planted a dogwood to mark the spot.

Wilma was heavier than Owen expected. Her last weigh-in she'd been only ten kilograms. When she moved about in her carrier he struggled to maintain his balance. He reached the main building and headed toward the transit stage. There he was greeted by a little going-away party: Drs. Marks, Dunkenfield and Bracken. Owen set down the carrier and rubbed his shoulder. The others helped load his suitcase onto the stage. Marks gave Owen a bear hug.

"So long, Owen," he said. "It's been a treat having you work with us. Give our regards to your father."

"Remind him about the new gene chromatographer," said Dr. Bracken.

"And the shower," said Dunkenfield. The others scowled at

him. "Well, somebody has to look out for the common welfare," Dunkenfield protested. "Or the next academic they send back here will find a pile of corpses."

"Don't worry," Owen said. "I won't forget. I want to say—I want to tell you how much it's meant to me to work with a group of thinkers like you, so devoted to knowledge, and nothing else. It's been the most positive experience of my life." He was getting choked up; he ducked his head and stepped onto the Gödel stage.

"The apatosaurus!" Marks said, while Bill shouted the same words in his mind. It created a disconcerting stereo effect.

Owen turned sheepishly. He picked up the case. Through the case's sound baffles, he heard Wilma hiss.

=Moron,= Bill said.

"Sorry," said Owen to Marks.

"Please take the strictest care, my boy," his colleague said. "This is the fourth time we've tried to ship a viable sauroid. You know what happened the first three times."

Owen considered the contretemps at the Stonehenge station. "I remember."

He stepped onto the time stage, was made infinitely dense, shot out of the universe and returned via wormhole to the next stage, identical, thirty million years up the line. This was merely another research outpost, minimally staffed, and Owen didn't even step off the stage before being sent up the line another twenty million years. He wouldn't stop until he reached a historical period. He fell into the nausea-generating disorientation of repeated shot and return. Each leap forward involved a translation over light-years of distance to compensate for the changed position of the earth, and the longer the leap the greater the uncertainties of residual position and momentum. As a result he swayed like a man on the deck of a tossing sailboat.

Owen concentrated on his plans for his arrival. First he'd

check to see that Wilma had managed without serious damage. There would be a lot of reports to make at the university. But eventually he'd have to steel himself for a visit home. He'd have to confront his father, who wanted Owen to keep Wilma at his College of Advanced Thought. It was hard enough for him to be taken seriously as a scientist without having to associate with that circus. And his mother would organize a round of parties and visits to the relatives as a ruse to introduce him to someone's eligible daughter. In the aftermath of his affair with Fiona it was not something he looked forward to.

Owen's parents had converted the family to the New Victorianism when Owen was ten, and at thirteen sent him off to boarding school in Denton, New Hampshire. His father's idea of initiating Owen into sexuality was interactive erotic VR: get a sexual education without compromising your health or reputation. At school, Owen didn't date. The other preppies chased the townies with singleminded attention. Owen disapproved of his classmates' casual treatment of the working-class girls, at the same time he envied their unself-consciousness. They were not shy about wanting to sleep with girls, about the lies they told to do so, or about having contempt for the girls afterward. Perhaps when, awash in hormones, they told some girl they were in love, they believed it. Certainly Owen was awash in the same hormones. But he did little about it.

His first sexual experience was with one of these girls, Dahli Brown. She dated Owen's roommate, Adam Coverdale, whose father was the mayor of Hartford. Adam never ceased telling Owen about his sexual exploits with Dahli, but was sickeningly attentive, in a completely phony way, when he met her at a basketball game or virching party. Owen felt sorry for her. Yet he envied Adam.

One Saturday night Owen was standing outside the Town Mall when Adam screeched up in his Reagan and dumped

Dahli on the sidewalk. Her eye makeup was smeared black but she acted like nothing was wrong. Owen called a cab and took her home. On the way she assessed Adam's character flaws with breathtaking accuracy, and then when they got to her house she took Owen in and seduced him. The next day she was back in Adam's arms, and treated Owen as if nothing had happened.

He thought of her often after that, with longing, regret, rage and confusion. Was Dahli using Adam, or was he using her? Owen could never figure women out. He still hadn't.

After the third time-jump Wilma began a continuous keening. When they hit the stage at the Near Pleistocene station Owen crouched and cleared a window into the case. Wilma was trying to nibble the padding. "Something the matter?" the man at the control board asked.

=What's wrong?= Bill asked.

"She's not taking this too well," Owen subvocalized. "I think she's hungry."

=She ate just before we left.=

"She's a growing girl." Owen turned to the man at the board and said aloud, "Look, I know I was supposed to switch to short hops from here up. But how about shooting me all the way up to 2062 in one jump?"

=Not a good idea,= Bill said. =Naked bed men love screaming wicked God women! We should just stop here for now.=

"Cost a lot more to do a big jump," the controller said. "We're on the edge of the historical periods. There are stations every thousand years, then every hundred. Why waste the energy?"

"I'll pay for it," Owen said.

The man at the board shrugged. "It's your money." He touched the controls and disappeared. Owen, Wilma and their baggage fell away again with a lurch. Owen's stomach turned. Wilma bounced against the side of the case. From falling away they were jerked back to reality in a sudden acceleration. They arrived.

Except something was wrong. The stage they stood on was more elaborate than the ones at the scientific stations. On the window wall behind the board "30 C.E." was displayed in large, stylized figures. A couple of well-dressed tourists, a middle-aged man and a young woman, were being helped by the stewards.

And instead of arriving more or less stationary, Owen came in with a forward momentum, as if he'd been dumped onto his feet from a moving train. When Owen hit he tumbled forward, buckling as he tried to get his resisting legs in motion. Bill took over, sending him into a controlled tumble. Wilma's case shot out of his hands and skidded on its side across the tiles toward the woman, who did a nice two-step to avoid it. Owen did a deft tuck-and-roll and came to rest poised on his haunches, fingertips on the floor, inches away from the hem of the woman's yellow dress.

One of the transit stewards rushed forward to help him. His partner behind the control panel frowned and messed with his keyboard. "Something's wrong with the momentum compensator," he said.

Bill let go. =I think he's trying to kill us.=

"You made me drop the case!" Owen muttered. "Wilma!"

The carrier vibrated with the apatosaur's thrashing.

The young woman righted the animal case. "The name is Genevieve."

"Excuse me," said Owen. She had startling violet eyes.

=Don't tell her about the dinosaur!=

"Will you please be quiet," Owen muttered. "I'm not an idiot."

She took his arm and helped him to his feet. Dizzy already, Owen was fuddled by her perfume. "I don't doubt it," the woman said. "But we have to stop meeting this way."

When Owen started to apologize, she patted him on the shoulder, smiled and left with the older man. The steward asked Owen if they could help him with his bags.

"I don't intend to stop here," Owen said.

"I'm afraid we can't let you continue until we find out what's wrong with the stage," the steward said. "The Saltimbanque Corporation will of course pay for your hotel room. Perhaps you can do some touring while you wait. Meanwhile we'll take your animal to our kennels."

=He's carrying heat. That's a magnum charge dispenser at his hip.=

"I don't care if it's a loaded banana," Owen subvocalized. "Don't take over again."

=His kinesthetic semiotics indicate he's on guard. I'll take care of this.=

"No!" Owen said.

"I assure you we have the best of facilities," the steward said. "We can take care of any sort of animal."

"Not this sort," Owen said. "This is a unique species. It's—"

=A python—=

"—an Andalusian dog," Owen said. He had to get assertive or Bill was going to cause a scene. "A razor-eyed Buñuel, to be precise. And if you are not going to send me forward, you can bloody well allow me to keep this valuable specimen in my rooms." He fumbled for his wallet. "I will be glad to pay any additional cost it takes to secure a suite."

When the steward saw Owen's unlimited e-cash rating, he simmered down immediately. "Of course, sir. Matthias! See that this gentleman—and his dog—get checked in right away."

On the way up in the elevator, Owen calmed down enough to thank Bill for keeping him from getting hurt.

=Believe me, boss. Nobody cares about your body like I do.=

Chapter 3

Roman Holiday

The Palace of Herod the Great had been constructed in 23 B.C., then taken over by the Romans as headquarters for the Prefecture before the time travelers showed up and kicked out the Romans. Now it was a hotel. At first Herod the Great's son Herod Antipas had insisted that the invaders from the future restore him to the palace along with the monarchy, but a few gadgets and the air-conditioned villa they'd built for him on the hills east of the city had won him over. Now he greeted specially honored guests in the King David room. He had a little speech he had learned in English.

The palace was built of freestone, faced with marble. A double portico gave onto the raised courtyard where Pilate had once dispensed justice. It was now the lobby. The futurians had roofed over the space between the three Herodian towers with glass, turning it into a huge atrium. The floor sported an elaborate abstract mosaic, and gold and precious gems gleamed everywhere. The pools that the hellenized Herod had constructed had been expanded and converted into modern swimming pools. Saunas and steam baths had been added to the hypocaust, plus suites of private rooms. At the south end the famous stables remained, where guests could rent horses to ride into the countryside. Onto the old structure the corporation had attached a tower of luxury suites.

In theirs, August found Gen wearing Roman period costume: plaited hair, tunic, stola, sandals. "The Spanish stimstar Antonio Borracho is here," he said. "They say he dropped a megabuck at the blackjack table last night."

"Never mind that. I've already got a line on a hot one," Genevieve told him. "You know that clown we ran into in the transit room? He's rich."

"How rich?"

"Billions." She showed him the hard copies she'd downloaded from the 2062 social register. Dr. Owen Beresford Vannice. Thirty years old. B.S. in biology, Phi Beta Kappa, Dartmouth, 2054. Ph.D., Reconstructive Paleontology, Harvard, 2059. His mother Rosethrush Vannice was the most powerful theatrical agent in Hollywood and head of Vannicom Pix. His father, Ralph Siddhartha Vannice, was CEO of The Harmony Group, a biosoftware empire. A third of the people in the Roman Arms must have had their personalities improved by Harmony programs.

Gen leaned over her father's shoulder, adjusting the strap on her chiton. "I spent some time down in the lounge talking to one of the off-duty transit stewards. Half the women in the hotel are downloading Harmony personalities in the hope of tripping up the young doctor. In ten minutes I spotted four Marilyns and two Garbos. The Marilyns perched at the bar making naive double entendres and falling out of their dresses, while the Garbos sat at tables in the corners, watching the doorway through a haze of cigarette smoke and half-lidded eyes."

August paused to look at her. "No personality from a bottle is going to match up against you, dear."

"I love you too, Dad." Gen tugged at the stola. "The steward tells me the time-travel stage will be out of commission until they check the momentum compensator, but they're still running the tours to unburned M-Us. Dr. Vannice is signed up to see Caesar's assassination. Get dressed."

"Do you have something in particular in mind?"

"According to the steward he was mighty protective of that 'dog' he arrived with. Plus, he's just returning from the Cretaceous. I don't think they had any dogs back then."

They sat among the tourists in the theaterlike lounge, waiting for the Caesar Assassination tour to begin. Gen and August had a good grasp of period Latin and Greek from the Constantine con they had pulled three years before, but looking at the twitchy faces of the others Gen could tell downloaded language mods were fizzing away at the top of their brains like club soda. As usual, despite the numerous amusements offered by the first century—Imperial Rome, bustling Alexandria, exotic India and the rough Americas—the Holy Land was the main attraction. The hotel was crowded with holiday spenders from up and down the timestream, throwing around their money like they owed it to Caesar, besieging the markets for videodisks of the Sermon on the Mount (with subtitles) and after-dinner entertainments in the court of Caligula (without).

Gen wanted nothing to do with the crucifixion. She'd seen plenty of Jesus's talk show back in the twenty-first century. And reports of the older one, the recluse. In a charisma-based society, where anyone with enough money could have himself genetically altered into a duplicate of the famous or dead, she had gotten tired of celebrities a long time ago.

There were only ten people on the Caesar tour. Gen crossed one leg over the other and bounced her foot up and down, holding on to the sandal she wore by the toe, as she watched the door for Vannice's entrance.

The photo they downloaded from the social register showed a man much more handsome than the clown who'd sprawled on the floor of the arrival chamber. At first Genevieve thought it must have been enhanced, but when Vannice entered the briefing room she realized that in person the good looks of his photographs were negated by the prim set of his mouth, the awkward way he carried himself.

He wore a toga and blue robe, his hair disheveled, and muttered in a distracted way as if carrying on a conversation with himself. One of the Marilyns from the bar sashayed conspicuously by, but she might as well have been invisible. He stumbled over another of the tourists on the way to his seat, apologized awkwardly, then sat in silence while the tour directors got organized. He'd lost the mood boots but was no more graceful in an outsized pair of sandals.

"I wonder how much of a tool he really is," Gen muttered.

"A significant one, I'd wager," August said.

"I hope so. I hope he doesn't know a thigh from a drumstick."

"Calm down, my dear. You don't want to appear overeager."

"Don't worry about me, I'll be calm as old smoke. Only I wish we'd get going!"

Finally the tour director climbed to the podium. The room quieted.

"Good afternoon. Welcome to the first century C.E. As you know, from the Herod Palace in our safely settled moment universe we can take you to any of the splendors of Rome, the spiritual glories of the Holy Land, the vital cultures of central Africa and India. From here the more daring can visit virgin moment universes at any time from 100 B.C.E. through 200 C.E., a period that covers the slave rebellion under Spartacus, the last days of the Roman Republic, the emperors from Augustus to Severus, including such illustrious figures as Tiberius, Caligula, Claudius, Nero, Trajan and Hadrian.

"Those of you who've visited a virgin M-U before are perhaps familiar with procedures, but even so we do ask that you give your best attention to what we have to say here today. Here in 30 C.E.-moment-universe Jerusalem we have established a beachhead. The historicals have had ten years to get familiar with visitors from the future and friendly commerce with people of the twenty-first century. Most significantly, they know the consequences should they harm a visitor. But in a virgin moment universe no one will ever have seen a person from the future before.

"The key to safe travel to a virgin M-U is to minimize the contact you have with historicals. First of all, we ask you to remain in character at all times. The biosoftware we have distributed will give you a limited vocabulary in period Latin vernacular, plus a superficial knowledge of local customs and the city's layout. But it's best not to push the limits of that knowledge. Trust your guide.

"Remember that we are visiting a real world, not a virtual reality. A wound from a Roman sword is a real wound, a disease contracted is a real disease. If you are careless, you could be hurt. Those of you interested in a more adventurous past experience are welcome to investigate our 'Intervener Specials': The Battle of Actium, The Siege of Masada, A Night with Messalina—information is available on the videolog in your room. If you want to see what would happen if you turned a machine gun on Brutus and the conspirators, we can arrange that—*but not on this tour!* We don't want to have too much fun, do we?"

The tourists laughed.

Next came a vid about Roman history, with information about Julius Caesar, Marcus Junius Brutus, Gaius Cassius

Longinus and the other principals of the historical incident they were about to witness. Then the attendants checked the tourists' costumes and equipment. They were led through the doors to a dimly lit transfer room. The attendants had them assemble within the circle outlined by a finger-thick cable spread out on the floor. The ends of the cable were plugged into a portable time-travel unit built into what looked like a wooden trunk. The tour guide, his toga falling in folds on the floor, crouched over the keyboard of the unit and typed in some commands. He stood.

"Remember to keep your hands and clothing inside the perimeter," he said. Gen and August nudged themselves closer to Vannice. The tour guide touched a key on the portable unit, and the room disappeared.

They materialized outdoors, in the atrium of a private villa. It was overcast, and a fine mist filtered down through the skies to fall on their heavy woolen winter cloaks. Water drizzled from the roof tiles into the slate gutters of the paved courtyard. "Welcome to 44 B.C.E. Rome," the tour guide said. "This is a private home that will be unoccupied for the duration of our visit. Get in under the eaves while I pack up this equipment."

They moved out of the rain. One of the Marilyns was breathlessly bouncing in front of Vannice, who seemed completely impervious to her simulated charms. She had the genetically altered body, and the software had given her the right ditzy demeanor, but apparently pure sex on the hoof was not his style. A second candidate, this one a gamin Gen could not identify as any specific historical model, shyly asked him for a light, which he gave her with relatively little reaction. Strike two. The tour guide, having put aside the portable unit, hustled over and asked her to put out the cigarette before they left the building.

As they entered the streets the rain began to let up. The villa was in a wealthy quarter of the city; the water coursing through the gutter in the middle of the paved street had washed the air fresh and clean. A matron, her slave holding a shawl above her head to ward off the mist, gave them a glance and passed on. In the distance, the clouds were breaking up and a shaft of sunlight shot down like an image from Michelangelo's heaven.

August made sure they were close to Vannice. "Beastly weather!" he said to Genevieve. "You'd think that with time travel they could at least find us a pleasant morning to arrive. It's pure incompetence."

"They must have their reasons, Daddy."

The opportunity to explain something, apparently, was the right bait. "Excuse me, sir," Vannice interrupted. "They can't take us to another time. Not if we're here to see Caesar assassinated, since it happened on this particular rainy day."

August turned to him, squinting. "Of course, of course, young man. How foolish of me."

Genevieve smiled at Vannice. "This is our first tour. Have you traveled in time before?"

"I guess you might say I'm an expert on time travel."

"That's right! You're the gentleman we met at the time stage. When you . . . arrived."

Vannice blushed.

"My name is Genevieve Faison." She touched August's arm. "My father, August."

"I'm Owen Vannice."

"A pleasure, son," August said. He appraised the cloudy skies. "I wish it were warmer."

"It will be, sir. It's due to be a very nice afternoon."

The guide broke them into twos and threes so as to attract less attention. They walked through the muddy streets of mid-morning Rome. Genevieve and August got themselves paired with Owen.

"What I don't understand," Genevieve asked him, "is, with all these tourists going back to see the same assassination, why aren't there hundreds of us gathered here? Tours have been going on for years, haven't they? By now most of the people in the Roman Senate chamber ought to be from the future."

"It would be that way if time weren't quantized," Owen said. "But every instant of time is discrete, separated from every other instant. If we affect a single instant, by coming here for example, it does change the future proceeding from that instant. But the adjoining instants have entirely separate futures, which are unaffected."

Gen played the innocent. "I'm afraid I don't follow you."

"Okay, suppose we arrive in Rome at exactly ten A.M. local time. We go out on our tour and see the assassination, come back and return to the hotel in Jerusalem of the settled moment universe. Another tour group comes tomorrow, and they arrive at exactly one minute after ten. Because ten oh-one is an entirely separate time quantum from ten o'clock, they don't even see us. In our stream we're still standing around the rainy atrium; in theirs the place is empty except for them. So they go to the senate and see the assassination too, but in a way it's a different assassination than the one we saw."

"How clever!"

Vannice became more excited the more he got into his explanation, and his awkwardness faded. Or didn't fade exactly, but changed from a detriment to an asset.

"Each moment of time is connected to an entirely different time continuum. In practice the size of the quanta depend on the reciprocal of the fine structure constant—137.04 moment universes are packed into every second. So in a way there are 137 separate worlds per second, and simply by sending each tour group to a slightly different arrival moment, we in effect send them to a different—but identical—past. So we never meet any of the other tour groups."

"But doesn't this mean that we can do anything we want without affecting the future?"

"In a lot of ways we do. Even more so in a settled M-U. Look at how changed our Jerusalem is."

"So why do the chronological protection people make such a fuss?"

"Well, some are worried that if we effect too many changes in adjacent timestreams we'll cumulatively degrade the whole period. The number of timestreams isn't infinite, just very large. We can get away with changing individual streams for a while, but if time travel is done irresponsibly we will ultimately affect the entire time environment. That's what the protectionists think, anyway."

They reached a street of multistory apartments with shops at the street level. On the mezzanine of one a pair of girls were playing, singing a song. Within a market colonnade cooks haggled with vendors while their slaves waited, carrying baskets of figs, vegetables, freshly slaughtered poultry. Even the tallest of the Roman men, like most historicals, were half a foot shorter than Owen Vannice, and his height alone was attracting attention, to say nothing of his babbling on in some strange tongue. Owen was so intent on his explanation he noticed none of this. He stepped on the tail of a dog that was lapping water from a mudhole in the middle of the street. The dog squealed and ran off, and Owen tromped into the mud, splashing August's calves. "I'm sorry, sir!"

Genevieve watched August repress his annoyance. "Quite all right, son. You seem to be more scholar than dancer."

"Actually, Mother sent me to ballet classes for five years. I had to wear tights."

"But no one ever mistook you for Nijinski."

"No." He smiled ruefully. "The only thing they ever mistook was my name."

"Your name?" Genevieve asked.

"Yes. The thing that drives me crazy is when people mistake my name. You wouldn't believe how many people think 'Van' is my middle name. So they think my last name is 'Nice.' " He looked morosely at the pavement. "The others in my Ph.D. program called me 'Dr. Nice.' "

"Dr. Nice," said Genevieve. She touched his arm. "I think that's cute."

"That's easy for you to say."

"Aren't you nice, Doctor?"

"Oh, I suppose so. That's for other people to determine, not me."

"I'm conducting my investigation at this very minute."

"I take it, Owen, that your doctorate isn't in ballet," August said.

"No. Mother gave up on ballet after I dropped the teacher. Compound fracture." He shook his head. "I'm a paleontologist. I've just spent two years in the Cretaceous."

"So, is that dog you're traveling with *camarasauridae, diplodocidae* or *titanosauridae*?" Genevieve asked.

"*Apatosa*—you know sauropod taxonomy!"

"Only a little." The Marilyn, ahead of them, turned to give Gen a withering gaze.

"A dinosaur?" August asked. "This must be a rare specimen, eh?"

"Unique. Wilma's a new species: *Apatosaurus megacephalos*. She's the smartest sauropod ever discovered."

The dark girl who'd asked Owen for a light spat in the street.

"Isn't it dangerous, dealing with those huge animals?"

"Wilma's just a baby. She won't be able to crush you to death for months yet."

"Better watch out for thieves, son," August said.

Owen looked surprised. "Thieves? What could they possibly do with a biological specimen?"

"There are a lot of exotiphagists around. Who knows what some eccentric might pay for a dinosaur steak?"

"Oh, Father," Genevieve said, "don't be melodramatic. Who's taking care of Wilma while you're here, Owen?"

"She's resting in my rooms. Time travel doesn't agree with her. I gave her a sedative."

She pointed out another puddle to keep Owen from stepping in it. "So, Dr. Nice, didn't you miss human companionship back in the Cretaceous?"

"Not really. Dinosaurs are my life."

"Well, you may not be worried about this specimen," August said, "but we're going to take care that you get back safe and sound."

The tour guide came back. "Please keep your conversation to a minimum, or speak in the vernacular. We're almost there."

They emerged from the street into the Forum, crossed the tiled agora past the temple of Castor and Pollux. Above them on the Capitoline Hill the temple of Jupiter shone dramatically in the sunlight, against dispersing gray clouds. The Senate was meeting in Pompey's Theater instead of its regular building. The tour guide, having been through this dozens of times before, was able to sneak them in while avoiding anyone who might notice. From behind an arras embroidered with the suckling of Romulus and Remus by the wolf, they watched Cassius, Brutus and Casca plunge daggers into the stunned Caesar, who fell at the foot of Pompey's statue. He muttered something in Greek, and died. There was not as much blood as Genevieve had envisioned. As with so much of the real history she had witnessed, it was over too fast, and nowhere near as striking as the later dramatizations. A good performance of *Julius Caesar* would blow it off the stage.

Brutus and Cassius shouted for attention. About half the senators fled, others stayed to hear the conspirators justify their actions. Brutus made a short speech calling for a return to the Republic that his illustrious ancestor had helped found almost five hundred years before. Over the bleeding corpse of the man who had once stood as the Republic's defender, it was more than a little ironic. Before he finished, the guide had pulled the tourists aside. "We need to leave now. Soldiers will be here soon. We don't want to have to explain our presence."

The news had preceded them to the streets, and as they headed back to the villa they found the crowds were electrified and fearful. Gen saw her chance. She slowed until they were bringing up the rear of the tour group. They entered a crowded square. When a soldier on horseback galloped by, a troop of legionaries double-timing behind him, Gen stumbled. Owen caught her and pulled her away, but by the time she gathered herself she had managed to separate them from the group.

A gust of rain slanted down between the tall apartment buildings. Though she pulled her cloak over her head, Gen made sure she got good and wet before they ducked under an awning. When she shivered Owen took off his own cloak and threw it around her shoulders. He started rubbing her arms, blushed furiously and stopped.

"Do you know the way back?" Gen asked.

"I'm not sure."

She leaned against him.

"That market looks familiar," he said, pointing.

As the news of the assassination spread the city was in turmoil. Gen and Owen ducked into the covered market to hide out until the crush in the streets dissipated. They walked down the market nave, past vendors gone suddenly quiet. Flies hovered over displays of cheese and vegetables. In the doorway of a wine shop sat a weeping barmaid, who no doubt served other appetites in the back rooms. Everywhere shocked citizens whispered in twos and threes. At a barber's three shabby men discussed the implications of the assassination: who was responsible, who would take power, would the Republic be restored . . . The barber set aside the hot iron with which he was curling the fringe of a balding man, and said darkly, "Let those conspirators only set foot in my shop, and I'll give them a shave they'll not forget."

"Who's to say you haven't shaved the lot of them already?"

"They might well have learned their bloodletting from lead-handed Lucius!" another said.

No one laughed.

"This is fascinating, isn't it?" Gen asked.

Owen was staring at her shoulders and neck. "Yes, I haven't seen . . . anything like it . . . for some time."

"We've just witnessed one of the signal events of history, Owen."

"I'm sorry. It's just that I've been in the Cretaceous . . . for two years."

"There aren't any girls in the Cretaceous?"

"Most are sauropods."

The barber looked up at them standing by his doorway. "Who's that lanky oaf?" He pointed at Owen. "I haven't seen you before. Why are you lurking around here?"

Owen fumbled with the language. "Pardon me—"

Gen took him by the arm. They retreated to the end of the market. "Owen," she said. "At least try to look like you belong here. You stand out like a telephone pole."

"But how would I know how a Roman's supposed to act?"

"Pretend. Act like you know what you're doing even when you don't. Make it up. Haven't you ever pretended before?"

"I don't like to lie. We should get back to the villa. They must be worried about us."

"What's the matter, Dr. Nice? Afraid to be seen with me?"

And just because he was so sober, she ran off through the crowd, down the length of the market, dodging through the gossiping Romans, and out the other side.

Behind her she heard Owen's cry for her to stop. She felt exhilarated. She danced down the steps, through a plaza where worried citizens, huddled in doorways, discussed the uncertain future. Down a narrow side street reeking of rotting food. In the next twisting side street she saw the entrance of some public building where women came and went—a bath.

Hesitating only a moment, she strode inside. She paid a quadrans and proceeded to the dressing rooms, where she left her pala, stola, loincloth and sandals. In the tepidarium she sat with a dozen matrons and young women. A red-haired woman came in and announced the news, and several of the others immediately left. An old lady, face painted into a mask of white lead above her sagging breasts, watched Gen. Gen smiled back. From the tepidarium she moved on to the caldarium. The floor, inlaid with an image of the goddess Diana dispensing laurels, was heated from the chambers beneath its pavement. In the center of the room a huge bronze cauldron, heated by the subterranean furnace, billowed clouds of steam. The steam escaped through a hole in the rotunda that admitted the watery sunlight that was the dim room's only illumination.

Gen sat on a limestone bench and sweated. It felt good. After fifteen or twenty minutes she passed back through the tepidarium to the pool on its other side, open to the afternoon sky. She lowered herself into the chilly water.

Nothing, she thought, could feel more invigorating. She felt clean for the first time in weeks.

She wondered what Owen was doing. Did he wander the streets looking for her? Had he returned to the villa in a panic to alert the tour guides? She supposed this was the end of the scam, but what the hell. They didn't need the money that badly. But August would worry whether this erratic behavior meant Gen was going sour as a grifter. As she floated beneath the pre-Christian sky Gen wondered if that was right. She couldn't tell why she'd run from Owen Vannice, except for his goofy earnestness. He had no business being so dumb. But it was good to enjoy the bath.

After a while she returned to the dressing rooms, put on her clothes. She would have to hurry back. Even on ordinary nights the streets were prey to bands of young men who beat up passersby, manhandled women and smashed shops; in the aftermath of Caesar's assassination who knew what might happen? Just outside the entrance she found a number of citizens crowded around someone in the street, arguing. The man in the middle was Owen. He looked damp and miserable. As she drew closer, she heard him mutter in English, "I'm not going to leave until I make sure she's all right, so you might as well accommodate yourself to the prospect."

"He's mad," one of the Romans said. "He's talking to himself."

"What language is that?" said a small man with a cap of curly black hair. "He must be a barbarian."

"I'll warrant he's involved in this assassination," said a self-important man, some cousin of an oligarch with a purple hem to his robe.

Gen pushed her way into their midst. "Why are you bothering my slave?" she asked in Latin.

The man with the purple hem turned to her. "He was sitting outside the baths talking to himself. We thought he might be a madman."

"He's my manservant, waiting for me to come out. And this is none of your business."

"He talks to himself," said the little man.

"He's a Teuton—you know how they are." She turned to Owen, who looked confused, and grabbed his arm. "Hrothgar! Let us go!"

She tugged him down the street. While the Romans stood gawking, Gen hurried them around the corner.

"Your language mod must be more thorough than mine," Owen said. "What did you say to them?"

"You're my slave, Vannice. What were you doing out there?"

"I was worried about you," he said. "You may be wealthy, Genevieve, but wealth won't keep you out of trouble in a place like this."

Genevieve stifled her laughter. "I'll keep that in mind." Owen looked forlorn. "I'm sorry I ran away, Owen. I was just teasing."

He flashed a brief, dark smile, so grateful she wanted to run away again. "There's going to be a dance at the hotel tomorrow night," he said. "Will you go with me?"

Chapter 4

Simon at Work

As Simon ascended the hill into west Jerusalem, past the Hasmonean toward Herod's Palace, he was startled by a noise from behind him. He stumbled to the side of the street in time to avoid the sport limousine that shot past, jouncing over the cobbles. The windows were opaque, but the seal of Herod Antipas was painted on the door. Though the narrow steep streets of Jerusalem were unsuited to wheeled vehicles, that didn't stop Herod from going everywhere in the abomination the invaders had given him. He was even having a road built from the time travelers' compound to the new palace they had built for him.

Jerusalem's upper market bustled. Those who had not already bought lambs for sacrifice or food for the sabbath meal were busy making last-minute purchases. The smell of roast lamb and fried eggplant wafted from the booths of vendors. A couple of disreputable-looking men stood in the shade of a wooden awning, whispering political conversations under the cover of whining liturgical music from a hammerbox. A troop of Roman mercenaries wearing leather skirts, plumed helmets and carrying assault rifles hustled down the street toward the Antonia. A colorful bird sat forlornly in an animal dealer's wooden cage, eyed by a cat from the alley.

A Pharisee, phylacteries wrapped around his arm and forehead, stopped in the street, praying aloud, his voice challeng-ing the roar of the air-conditioning compressor that disfigured the wall of the shop next door. He draped his robes carefully, bowed so deeply that every vertebra in his back might be sep-arated. Simon stopped, bowed his own head, as did some of the workers in the street and people in the shops. Not as many paid respect to the holy man's ritual as might have even a year be-fore. Simon himself did not respect the Pharisaic ritual as much as he once had: on the one hand, his master had ques-tioned the sincerity of those who prayed ostentatiously in the street, on the other, such displays of piety did little to move Israel toward freedom. Behind him, below the Hasmonean colonnade, he heard a couple of kids continuing to hawk boot-legged vids.

It was ten minutes before the Pharisee rose and moved on. Simon brushed off his tunic, adjusted his girdle and headed for the hotel. He passed the grand entrance between the Hippicus and Mariamme towers and entered through the loading docks at the south end of the enclosure around Herod's Palace. At the security booth guarding the dock he stopped and showed his credentials. On the platform a purchaser in the uncouth clothes the future people fancied haggled with a dealer in exotic ani-mals who held two surly camels by a short halter. The guard, a thick, humorous man named Hans Bauer, smirked. "Late again, Simon. Callahan will be pleased."

Simon entered the hotel. The staff entrance was on the basement level. The guts of Herod's Palace had been ripped out and replaced by an extensive substructure containing a ware-house for trade goods to be shipped back and forth in time, a large industrial time-travel stage, the hotel laundry, a kennel for livestock and trade animals, kitchens, security offices and the power plant. Simon headed through the main corridor to the trans-shipment warehouse and hurried down the aisle between stacks of loot waiting to be shipped forward in time—amphorae of the finest Greek wine, crates of scrolls from the Alexandrian library, perfumed oils in alabaster jars from the East, bas-reliefs from Babylon, figs from Galilee, statuary from Egypt. And other heaps of goods meant for the locals. Weapons for the Roman collaborators. Televisions. Chocolate bars. Crates of gin. Simon thought about the destruction represented by those rows of pallets. His world was being drugged like a whore, bled like a sacrificial lamb.

He reached the glassed-in office in the corner of the warehouse. Two men sat there, amid bills of lading, drinking coffee and munching dried apricots. On the window wall music pix played.

"You're late," said Patrick Callahan, the operations manager. "Haven't you learned to read a clock yet?"

Simon bowed his head. "I am sorry," he said.

"Sorry is the word for you, that's right. I can't get a decent shift's work out of any of you towelheads."

"Cut him some slack, Pat. The guy's out of his depth."

"Simon? No, Simon here's deep. Used to be an apostle, didn't you, boy?"

"I believe you are mistaken, sir. Are we shipping the rest of that wine tonight?"

"Listen to this guy, Arnie. Let me decide what gets shipped or not shipped."

"Certainly, sir."

"The transit stage is out of order," Arnie offered.

Simon tried not to show any reaction. "Is that so?"

"Yeah. An arrival came in with sideways em-vee. An order of magnitude larger and he'd have been pulped against the wall."

"He doesn't know momentum from shinola, Arnie," Callahan said. "Do you, Simon?"

Callahan's mood seemed to improve the lower Simon's got. "No, sir."

"Well, anyway, our bad luck's your good fortune. No heavy lifting tonight. It's down to the kennel for you, Simon old chap. They need you to clean it up. I know you people haven't invented the mop yet, but we've spent a lot of money training you. You remember how to use it, don't you?"

Simon nodded.

"Then get out of those filthy rags and get to work." Callahan turned his back on him.

Simon headed to the historicals' lockers, segregated from the lockers kept for staff from the future. He wondered whether the out-of-commission transit stage was a coincidence or part of the plan. He had heard nothing. Should he try to contact Jephthah? But if he left the hotel in the middle of his shift, at the very least he would lose his job, and at worst he'd arouse suspicions.

On the shelf of his locker he found a note. Written in bad Hebrew, it told him to look into the closet outside the laundry. He changed from his tunic, robe and sandals into the dark blue coveralls the invaders insisted on, then headed down to the kennel. The dogs started barking as soon as he showed up. A devout Jew could not even own the representation of a beast, but these future people had an obsession with animals; apparently it was a considerable coup to own a pet from an earlier era.

From the closet he got out the wheeled bucket, the mop, the cleaner. He filled the bucket from the hose at the sink, and squirted in some cleaner. The pungent ammonia scoured his nose. He rolled the bucket down to the aisle of cages. Some of the dogs stood on their hind legs, their paws against the front of their cages, noses against the glass. Others lay curled up, eyeing him miserably. He dunked the mop in the bucket, squeezed it out in the wringer and began to work his way down the aisle, sweeping side to side, not hurrying, his mind on his plans for the night.

At first Simon's passivity in the face of the futurians' insults had been an act, a veil over his fury. Ten years had complicated that. He looked at the future dwellers with a combination of awe and resentment, and could not accord their ordinariness—they seemed to be people just like him—with their power. Just when he had gained enough knowledge to have contempt for them, they would do something that revealed anew how alien they were. He could not imagine the world they lived in. A world without God, apparently, although they were obsessed with Yeshu and had stolen him away.

A decade before, when Simon and Alma had first come to Jerusalem from Galilee, he had been mocked as a rustic who did not pronounce his alephs at the front of words. The city was in a queer state of shock. The Sadducees, living fat off the money they stole from the tithes meant for the support of the Temple, strolled through the streets with bland assurance. The Pharisees were more interested in following the Law than expelling these strangers from the future.

The troops of the time travelers had taken the Roman garrison in Jerusalem in a single hour, had defeated the Roman legion from Caesarea in an afternoon. They had had to do remarkably little fighting. They brought Herod Antipas back from Galilee to nominally rule Judaea. The Romans and their Syrian troops now collaborated, and the Roman Prefect and the Legate were mere puppets. Though Simon took some satisfaction in seeing the Romans reduced to servility to the invaders, it was cold comfort. Jews were one step further removed from ruling their own nation.

So he mopped the kennel in a basement room of what had once been the great Herod's Palace. As a boy he had envisioned this place with awe. The sight of Herod wearing his spandex jacket and sunglasses as he walked through the upper market with one of his whores turned Simon's stomach. It was easy to have contempt for Herod. But what if you felt *yourself* slipping away?

Simon put the mop in the bucket, wrung it out and began swabbing down the floor along the second row of cages. At six P.M.—the invaders had given him a wristwatch, and he could indeed read it—he left his mopping. He took the canvas cart of laundry, filled it with old towels and pushed it down the corridor. The hallway was empty. He wheeled past the laundry to a closet, took his keys and unlocked it. Inside were two cases marked TRANSTEMPORAL MUSIC IMPORTS.

Quickly, he loaded the cases into the cart and covered them with dirty towels. He then ran the cart over to Trash and transferred the cases into plastic bags of refuse that were bound for the Gehenna landfill. He made an aleph on the bags with masking tape and wheeled the cart back to the laundry. One of the other custodial staff, Jacob, was unloading sheets from an industrial dryer.

"Shalom, Simon. How are you?" Jacob asked.

"I am fine." Simon began unloading the dirty towels.

"I did not hear you singing tonight. Usually you sing while you work."

"I have been in the kennel. The dogs do all the singing there."

Jacob touched the music bead in his ear. "I have a new song for your son. One of the tourists gave it to me. It's called 'Don't Get Around Much Anymore.' " He pronounced the English with a thick accent. Simon had worked hard on eliminating his own.

They shared an interest in the futurians' music. It was one of the few changes Simon could accept, one of the still fewer he and his son Samuel could share. But his own liking for the music troubled him. How could such infidels create such heart-felt music? Perhaps Simon's love for it was a sign that he was being corrupted.

"I don't care about music," Simon said. "I have work."

Simon went back to the kennel and finished cleaning. At the end of his shift he washed up, hung his uniform in the locker room and put on his tunic, robe and sandals. He paused to run his thumb over the close-woven cloth of the uniform. The weave was as fine as that of the clothes of Herod himself, in-humanly regular. They said that this cloth was made by a ma-chine. The metal of the uniform's belt shone like silver, but was much harder.

He drew his hand back, felt the cloth of his own robe. His father, a weaver, had made it for him. It brought back memo-ries of the shop in Capernaum, his father bent over his loom. The boys in town had mocked Simon's father behind his back. To be a weaver, associating with women, was the lowest of pro-fessions. Simon had told himself that those who scorned his father could not live without his skill. But now these men from out of time, with bolts of cloth made by machines, had driven weavers out of business. He closed his locker.

At the security booth he was searched, then left through the staff exit. The streets of west Jerusalem were quiet.

He hurried from the time travelers' quarter, under the harsh sodium lights, and down the hill into the dark second quarter of the city, where the only illumination came from occasional oil lamps in hanging baskets. Few Jews were abroad so late. He met his friends in a large house in the northeast, beneath the wall near the Damascus Gate. The house belonged to Asher of Carmel, a merchant who supported their cause. The others greeted him with excitement, and they went up to the roof and knelt in prayer.

"O God of Israel, grant that we may establish again Your holy kingdom on earth," Jephthah chanted. Jephthah's dark beard shone with oil, his voice cracked with harsh emotion. He was young, handsome, a man of action. In the background, Simon listened to the rustling of hot desert winds in the palms of the courtyard.

When they sat back, Simon told them about the malfunction of the time-travel stage. Was this part of the plan? Jephthah and the others didn't know. Simon was to meet with Serge Halam the following afternoon, and undoubtedly the agent from the future would know something about it. Jephthah ordered Simon to pay close attention to the goings-on inside the hotel to see if he could pick up any useful information.

"Make sure you give no sign of what is to happen," Jephthah said.

"What makes you think that I would do so?"

"Ask your son, who wears their clothes and sings their music."

Simon bit back his urge to reply. Where had Jephthah been ten years before, when Simon had been the most zealous of them all?

They retreated to a room below, where Asher provided wine and bread. The others, like men hoeing over the same field for the one-hundredth time, discussed their situation. Simon had once contributed to these obsessive complaints, these fervent oaths; now he sat silent, wondering whether he deserved Jephthah's suspicion.

"Perhaps once we begin, the Sadducees will turn our way," said Joset.

"As long as they get their penicillin, microwaves and frozen dinners, the Sadducees are lap dogs," Asher said. "The Essenes—"

"—are of no use to us," Jephthah said. The Zealots had once pinned considerable hope on the assistance of the Essenes. Yeshu's brother James was one of these deeply religious mystics—but after the departure of Yeshu the Essenes advocated complete withdrawal from contact with the futurians. They had retreated to the dry hills south of the city. That left only the Zealots, and those Pharisees they could goad into joining them, to try to sway the confused citizens into revolt.

Jephthah played with the blade of his curved dagger, speaking as much to it as to his fellows. "These dogs do not understand the power of faith. Their silk stockings and perfumed soap are not proof against faith."

It was Jephthah's theory that as the presence of the invaders caused more and more changes, so that even the simple could not fail to see how their lives were being irrevocably changed, the situation was turning their way. Obscene music blared out of the loudspeakers in the market, boorish tourists in scanty clothing, complaining about the heat, poked their cameras into sacred tombs, young men abandoned the scriptures for comic books, young women learned foreign slang and chewed gum. Just last autumn a film crew from the future had insisted on shooting a musical in the Temple, and only with difficulty had been kept out of the Holy of Holies. Then the star of this film, this gentile singer Elvis, accosted a young girl in the market. A riot started. The time invaders had had to call in a Roman legion to put down the uprising. Most of Simon's fellow conspirators felt a crucial point had been turned.

Simon hoped they were right. But he had had more contact with the futurians. Even Jephthah ought to be able to see that Halam, though he was helping their cause, was not a holy man.

Late in the night, with a feel of morning in the air, Joshua and Elam returned from the landfill with the boxes. They carried them to the downstairs room just off the courtyard, behind a hemp curtain, where the other cases Simon had smuggled out of the hotel over the last month were unpacked.

Black rifle parts gleamed in the guttering light from the oil lamp. Cases of ammunition were stacked in the corner.

Jephthah picked up one of the rifles and ran his hand lovingly down its side. "The days of the invader are numbered. We shall slaughter them to the last man and his whorish concubine, and Israel in the light of God and the heart of faith will be free at last!

"God will deliver them into our hands."

Chapter 5

The Connecticut Oatmeal Bath Treatment

When Owen opened the door to his room a stench assaulted him. Wilma had abandoned her carrier and defecated on the floor.

That was not the worst: She'd eaten the potted plants down to the soil. He found her contentedly peeling away the veneer from the coffee table, having already dismantled the credenza and pulled most of the stuffing out of the sofa.

=Cherry credenza, manufactured in Hickory, North Carolina,= Bill said. =Sofa by de Leon, wool-acrylic blend. Sixteen hundred dollars damage, minimum.=

Wilma looked up at Owen placidly, then turned her snake-like neck back, muzzled her nose among the debris on the floor, and swallowed a glass egg. He didn't know how her digestive system would handle the foam sofa stuffing, but the egg would do service as a gastrolith.

Owen hustled in and tried to pull her away from the table. He got her front legs off the floor, but her hind legs stayed planted. She stretched her neck out farther between his arms and kept munching. He tried to pull her backwards and stepped in the dinosaur droppings, his foot skidding out from under him until he fell on his butt in the mess. Through the bedroom door he could see a half-eaten bedspread and the mattress pulled off onto the floor.

=Make that twenty-five hundred,= Bill said.

Owen let Wilma go. It wasn't as if pulling her away was going to save the already ruined table. But he didn't like the idea of her eating finished wood. There was no telling what effect the resins would have on her. He would have to check her feces.

=If you want to get her to move, lure her.=

Owen picked up the end of the table and dragged it into the bedroom. Wilma followed, still nibbling at the corner. Once he had her in the bedroom he changed into some clean clothes. He had not planned to be so long getting back to the future, and so had not taken a supply of dinosaur food. Back in the Cretaceous, where grasses and flowering plants had not come into being, Wilma lived on a diet of ferns, protoconifers and cycads. He called down to room service.

"This is Owen Vannice, in room 224. Doesn't the hotel have some sort of fern bar?"

"Well, sir, we like to think of our King David Room in more refined terms."

"Yes. Do you suppose you could send up a supply of potted ferns for me?"

=This ain't going to work,= Bill whispered.

"If you find you room's accoutrements unsatisfactory, sir, I'm sure we can move you to a more suitable one."

Owen would have to hazard a change in diet. Whatever he came up with would be better than cherry veneer. "How about hay? Do you have any hay?"

"Hay?"

"Yes, you know. Dried grass?"

"I don't think hay would do much for your room's decorating scheme, sir."

"This isn't about decorating," Owen said.

=Raw oats,= Bill whispered.

"How about oats?" Owen asked.

"If you will check your screen, sir, you'll find we have oatmeal on our room-service menu, with strawberries."

"Good. Send up about twenty liters. You can skip the strawberries."

"Twenty liters, sir?"

"Yes."

"We tend to measure by the bowl."

"How much is in a bowl?"

=She needs a wheelbarrow,= Bill said.

"Be quiet, Bill," Owen muttered.

"Excuse me, sir?"

"I said, it'll be quite a bill, I'm sure. For room service, I mean. How much oatmeal is in a bowl?"

"I don't know—maybe 250 milliliters."

"Okay, then, send me up one hundred bowls of oatmeal."

"One hundred bowls."

"Yes. And it doesn't matter if it's cooked or not."

=Maybe you should get bananas on it,= Bill said sarcastically.

"Do you want bananas on it?" the room-service operator asked.

"Yes. Send up a couple of bunches."

"Bunches. Are you going to eat this yourself, sir?"

"Oh no. It's for—"

=Don't tell him you've got a dinosaur!= Bill hissed.

"—uh," Owen stalled, his mind working furiously. What was it Gen had said about pretending?

=The bathtub.=

"—it's for bathing," Owen said. "A skin condition. You've never heard of the Connecticut Oatmeal Bath treatment—for *Apatosaurus dermastentoritis*?"

The operator was silent for a moment. "I guess I did see

something about that—in *Modern Disease?*"

"That's it," Owen said.

"I'll see what I can do, sir." The operator rang off.

After he hung up Owen realized he'd forgotten the dinosaur droppings. Of course he'd have to get a sample for the coprophology exam, but there was definitely more here than he needed. He punched room service again.

"Yes sir," it was the same voice.

"I forgot to mention, can you also send up a shovel?"

"Is this for the oatmeal?"

"No. It has nothing to do with the oatmeal. Well, it has a little to do with it, but not much."

"I'll see if I can locate one, sir. Anything else? You wouldn't want a jackhammer, or perhaps a parachute?"

"No, thank you. Just a shovel."

Ten minutes later a small dark man in custodial coveralls arrived pushing a cart laden with four stainless-steel pans full of steaming oatmeal, three bunches of bananas and, on the bottom shelf, a square-bladed shovel. His name badge read "Simon." Owen blocked the doorway.

"Thank you, Simon," Owen said. "I can serve myself."

"I'm not here to serve," the man said. "I am here to clean." He pushed forward, and Owen relented. Simon took in the broken furniture, wrinkled his nose at the smell.

"I had a little accident," Owen said. "I'm not feeling well at all."

"I will prepare your bath," Simon said, wheeling the cart toward the closed bedroom door.

=Do you want him to see Wilma?= Bill asked.

Owen threw himself between the cart and the door. "That's okay. I can take it from here." He fumbled in his pocket for a tip, but he had left his money in the other pants.

Simon made a face like a steamroller. "My boss insists I am helpful in every way. I was told this is for your bath."

Owen leaned against the door. "This condition makes me very sensitive. I will take care of it myself."

"My boss will want to know how I did."

"I will give them the best report. I'm afraid this room's kind of a mess." Owen slapped his palm a couple of times against the door.

From the other side came a couple of answering thumps.

Simon's eyes narrowed. "Do you have someone in there?"

"It's just an echo," Owen said.

Wilma butted her head against the door again, harder this time. The door rattled in its frame. She must be up on her hind legs, forefeet against the wood.

"Is this perhaps one of my people you are keeping captive? A woman?"

"Certainly not. It's just my—"

=Your Andalusian dog.=

"—my Irish setter, Cuchulain."

Wilma trumpeted, an eerie bleat, and slammed the door so hard the latch splintered, throwing Owen forward. She shoved her head around the door's edge and, holding her face sideways, peered at Simon with her right eye.

Simon yelped and fell backwards. He grabbed for the shovel. When Wilma advanced on the cart he scrambled out of the suite on his hands and knees.

Wilma stretched her neck over the top of the cart and shoved her head into the top pan of oatmeal.

=I told you oatmeal was the answer,= Bill said.

A woman in a burgundy collarless jacket stood in the hall. She radiated as much personal warmth as a spreadsheet. "Mr. Nice, I am Eustacia Toppknocker, the hotel manager."

"The name is Vannice," Owen said. "Dr. Owen Vannice."

Ms. Toppknocker ignored him and cruised into the room.

Wilma was locked in the bathroom with the oatmeal and bananas. Owen had cleaned up the dinosaur droppings as best he could, and moved most of the wreckage out of the way, but the hotel manager's calm survey of her debilitated luxury suite made him cringe anyway. "I have checked your credit rating and am sure you will cover these damages," she said. "It does not concern us at the Herod Palace how you spend your spare time. But we cannot tolerate an animal in the guests' rooms."

"This isn't an animal, exactly. It's a valuable specimen."

"What, exactly, is it?"

"It's an *Apatosaurus megacephalos*."

"Which is . . . ?"

"A dinosaur."

For a moment she looked impressed. But the veil of the hotelier dropped immediately into place. "We operate an extensive kennel service. You can keep this creature in the kennel and we'll guarantee its safety. We are used to transporting livestock."

"This is not livestock. It is the rarest of dinosaurs."

=Perfect, Dr. Einstein.= Bill sighed.

Owen ignored him. "Is the time-travel stage back in service?"

"Technicians are still testing the momentum compensator."

He thought for a moment. "I'm not about to let this creature be endangered."

=Tell her that we don't wanna see fillet of dinosaur on the menu tonight.=

"—and I don't want to see fillet of dinosaur on the menu tonight."

"This is a four-star hotel, Dr. Vannice. It's true we serve *dodo au vin*, but I'm sure we would not know how to prepare a dinosaur."

Owen pondered. "Do you have any atmosphere-controlled cages in this kennel?"

"We do."

"If you'll make one available and ensure security, I'll bring Wilma down there."

"I'll have the hotel AI programmed to keep a twenty-four-hour watch on her," Ms. Toppknocker said. "But these room damages—"

"Will be paid in full. You've heard of my family?"

"Of course—assuming you are really Owen Vannice. We've seen plenty of genetically altered impostors before."

"I'm aware of such impersonators. I can supply my genetic bona fides."

The manager's tone improved markedly. "Of course, Dr. Vannice, we trust you to do the responsible thing."

"I'll move Wilma down within the hour, Ms. Toppknocker."

=Wait a minute, boss.=

"Good day, Dr. Vannice."

"Good day." Owen closed the door before Bill could protest. "I'll take her down to the kennel myself," he said. "She may be better off there anyway."

=So we're going to stay longer?=

"Do you want to take a chance on a faulty momentum compensator? We could take the next jump and end up in outer space. We'll wait a couple of days. Meanwhile, the hotel room isn't doing her any good. In a controlled atmosphere cage I can boost the carbon dioxide level to Cretaceous levels, control the temperature. Wilma'll be feeling better in a day or so."

=Something's fishy here. Yesterday you couldn't wait to get her back uptime. Now you want to be a tourist. Something tells me this change of heart has something to do with that microwave soufflé you chased around Rome.=

"I wish you wouldn't use that kind of language."

=I don't know any other languages. This Faison woman figured out you had a dinosaur mighty quick. Given the fact that your father invested a billion dollars in setting up your dinosaur station, you ought at least to protect his investment. I told you not to admit anything to her.=

"Yes. You almost shouted a hole in my cerebrum. My ears are still ringing."

=I can't make your ears ring. I'm in your head.=

"Well what was I supposed to do, lie?"

=Yes. You don't even know what her game is.=

"She doesn't have any game. She's just interested in pale-ontology."

=Spelled M-O-N-E-Y.=

"You know that's not true. Her father owns a villa in Provence and a plastic farm in southeast Asia."

=To hear her tell it.=

"Bill, I can take care of myself. Not that I'm going to need to, with Genevieve. You ought to give me more credit."

=Just as long as you don't give her any. Naked bed men love screaming wicked sex women!=

"Which makes about as much sense as everything else you've told me today. Oatmeal in the bathtub!"

Owen cleaned out the animal carrier in preparation for the move. The batteries on the lightweight controlled atmosphere case still carried most of their charge. The message board and security alarm tested out. He turned to the bathroom.

Wilma lifted her head as soon as he entered. Owen sat down on the ledge of the bathtub, leaned forward and examined her. Why was she so ravenous? He'd expected her appetite to decline as she adapted to the more intense regime of care he was giving her. Perhaps the strangeness of her surroundings made her anxious. In the bright bathroom light the dappled yellow and green markings of her back took on a bluish tinge. As she aged the pattern would darken to a green indistinguishable from that of the conifers and tree ferns that lined the watercourses of her home. From below she was almost pinkish white.

Wilma sat back on her rump, tail stretched out to curl behind the toilet, her hind legs bent and forelegs stretched out to hold up her shoulders. Her large eyes gleamed up at him, and she lowered her head to focus both of them forward, which emphasized the characteristic higher-domed brain case of the *megacephalos*.

Owen could see his own reflection in her eyes. He wondered how he appeared to her. From being her benefactor back in the Cretaceous, had he become her enemy? It was foolish to project such thoughts on an animal hardly as intelligent as a rabbit. Still, he could not help feeling his own betrayal of Wilma, jerking her out of her own time to imprison in this strange space.

He thought about Genevieve. The excursion with her had left him in confusion. Why had she run away from him? Did she think him a fool? He suspected she did, nattering on about time travel like some grad student. Yet she had not laughed. Even when she had to pull him from the midst of the suspicious Romans, she did not make him feel any less competent for it. She treated him like a complete equal, with no awareness of his money or self-consciousness about her beauty. Owen found that powerfully attractive. He cursed Bill for his paranoia. It was like carrying his parents around in his head, questioning his every instinct.

Owen went to his bag, hauled out his logbook, plugged it into the hotel's system and punched in "Genevieve Faison." She and her father were listed as guests; no further information came up on the screen. But they were wealthy people. They had no doubt paid a great deal for their privacy. He ran his hand through his hair, went back into the bathroom and coaxed Wilma into the carrier.

"Can you stand a day or two more, Wilma?" he asked.

The *Apatosaurus* thumped the side of her box. Owen hoisted it and headed for the door.

Owen lugged Wilma in the titanium carrier down to the service elevator. A floor down the car stopped and another hotel guest got on. He was a slender man with round face and fair hair, pushing a cart with a couple of boxes on it. The boxes were labeled TRANSTEMPORAL MUSIC IMPORTS.

=I know this guy!= Bill said. =He ran guns out of Malaysia during the Micronesian revolt! Women think obsessive wicked men are therefore dysfunctional!=

"Give it a rest, Bill," Owen subvocalized.

=I'm not making this up. He's a ruthless character. His name is Serge Halam.=

Genevieve was a gold digger, this man was a spook. There was only one way Owen was going to get Bill to shut up. "Are you a trader in musical instruments?" he asked the man.

"I beg your pardon?"

"Owen Vannice," Owen said.

The man looked Owen over, then extended his hand. "Serge Halam."

Owen tried not to drop his teeth. Bill didn't say anything. If an AI could be smugly silent, Bill was being smugly silent.

"Are—uh—the historicals interested in modern instruments?" Owen asked.

"You'd be surprised what they're interested in."

"What are these?"

Halam acted completely calm. "These are harmonicas."

"Harmonicas?"

"Harmonicas have certain advantages to the trader with historicals. It's a low-tech instrument. It's easy to learn. It's portable."

"Gosh," Owen said. "That's a clever product to try out in the first century."

"Thanks. These are very hot items," Halam said quietly.

When the elevator stopped in the lobby, the acceleration shifted Wilma and she began thumping the carrier. A couple of guests looked in. "Going up?" they asked.

"Down," said Owen.

The doors slid closed. Halam looked over. "What do you have in that carrier?"

=I hope I don't have to remind you— = Bill started.

"An iguana," said Owen.

"That's a new one. Why bring an iguana to ancient Jerusalem?"

Another opportunity to pretend. Owen launched into it without hesitating. "I'm headed for Central America. I'm going to breed this one with historical iguanas. I'm an iguana breeder."

"I didn't know iguanas had breeds."

"Oh, yes. There are all sorts. There's the highland iguana, the mutant blue iguana and of course the Malibu Max. This one here's a Nice."

"A Nice?"

"Well, it's not really very nice. Your true Nice is prone to losing his tail in moments of anxiety. That's not a show-quality iguana."

=For a guy who wouldn't lie to that dame, you're developing a disturbing flair for this.=

"You can imagine how bad it looks when your iguana loses its tail in the middle of a judging," Owen continued. "Because an iguana show is really quite anxiety-provoking, for the iguana as much as for the owner."

"I don't doubt it," Halam said.

"That's why we're hoping to breed with the historical Central American iguana, to see if we can eliminate this undesirable trait."

The doors slid open.

=Please get us out of here,= Bill said. =But don't run.=

"Good luck," Halam said.

"Yes. Well—good luck on your harmonica imports."

"I hardly need it," Halam said. "Business is booming."

Chapter 6

A Day at the Pet Store

A lot of tourists made no concessions to local customs, but in order to fit in with first-century Jerusalem, Genevieve had downloaded Aramaic. It made her brain itch as if an ant colony had taken up residence in her head. Although she did not plait or oil her auburn hair in the fashion of the wealthy women of the times, she wore the traditional shawl to conceal it. Her white linen shift fell to her heels, and over it she draped a rich purple robe. Her sandals were simple soles strapped to her feet. On first glance, someone spotting her in the street might take her for a young Judaean wife.

Her father hummed a tune as he oiled the beard he had grown overnight. Over his own shift he wore an embroidered white robe, with a curiously chased silver belt. Add gloves to keep him from touching anything unholy and he would look every bit the wealthy patriarch.

"You will dazzle him senseless at the dance tonight," August said. "And tomorrow—tomorrow I will dazzle him dinosaurless."

Smuggling a dinosaur uptime would be tricky, but aside from the fact that it was alive, it was something they had done many times before. There were the gold artifacts they'd lifted from the Inca sun temple in Cuzco from under the eye of the

Conquistadors, Charlemagne's sword they'd sold to that meat packer in Des Moines, the Hemingway manuscripts they'd stolen from the Gare de Lyon in Paris.

"Where are we going to sell it?" Genevieve asked him. "A thing like this has got to be next to impossible to fence."

"This is the beauty of it, my beauty. We're not going to fence it. Do you remember Lance Thrillkiller?"

"I thought he went down with the *Titanic.*"

"Yes. Well, he's up again. He has a new scam going back home, a phony committee to protect the past. When we return to the twenty-first century, we will donate Wilma to Lance's committee, for her own protection. Think of the contributions a dinosaur will raise for the cause."

"But she'll be stolen property. Won't that draw a lot of heat?"

"She's already stolen property. Our friend Dr. Nice had no leave to draw such a specimen from an unsettled moment universe. The audacity of his snatching the first dinosaur out of the Cretaceous will draw the ire of every protect-the-past radical in the Northern Hemisphere. Out of that will arise enough of a legal smokescreen to keep Vannice from reclaiming her. Plus contributions in the millions to Lance's cause—of which we will take our percentage."

"Seems risky to me."

"Life is risky. Nothing ventured—"

"—nothing lost."

He looked at her, as if trying to make up his mind about something. "Come now, it's time to go," he said abruptly. "We need to buy a dog. A valuable Egyptian saluki. Did you know I was a member of the Westminster Kennel Club?"

August adjusted his shawl so that the ends dangled down his back and they headed down to the hotel kennel. The kennel was in the basement, next to a large warehouse of stalls and cages that held livestock waiting to be shipped uptime. A window wall in the office opened onto a view of a Galilean valley. A young woman, whose name tag read MAUREEN, greeted them at the desk.

"Good morning," August said. "Can we purchase a dog here?"

"I'm afraid we aren't in the business of sales. But I can give you the addresses of several reputable dealers in the city."

"How about an animal carrier?"

"You can purchase that there as well. Here at the kennel we only take care of animals prior to shipment."

"Very good," August said. Under the pretext of getting a look at the kennel where they intended to keep this valuable dog they were planning to buy, August made the woman show them down the aisles of cages in back. Gen examined the security setup. The usual camera midges, hooked into the hotel's AI, hovered in the corners of the rooms. There were ways of disabling them. But they needed some information on the hotel personnel routines.

"Father, do you think we could get someone to come with us to purchase this dog?" Gen asked.

"If you're worried about security in the city, it's really not that dangerous," the woman said.

"Don't a lot of the historicals resent us?"

"Only a radical minority. Most of them are happy we're here. Here's Simon, for instance. Excuse me, Simon?" the woman called to a man wheeling a cart of food down one of the aisles.

"Yes?"

"Simon, I want you to help these guests go out and purchase a dog."

The man's brow furrowed. "Mr. Callahan told me to clean out the large cages."

"I'll speak to Mr. Callahan," Maureen said. "Go now."

"We will pay you handsomely for your help," August said.

"There's no need for that," Maureen said. "We pay you quite enough already, don't we, Simon?"

Simon was silent. He looked at Gen for the first time, then did a barely noticeable double take. "I will take you," he said.

Despite Maureen's assurances, Gen had no doubt that Simon had seen enough of tourists to get tired of them. Working in the hotel, he would have become familiar with their condescension. The very fact that he had to take orders from a woman must at the very least gall any man of this time period, and at worst humiliate him.

"Shalom, Simon," Gen said, bowing her head.

The historical looked at her for a moment with open astonishment, then ducked his head and began to set out a bowl of food for the mewling cat inside the next cage. "Go to the hotel lobby. I will meet you there in five minutes."

A moment after they got to the hotel entrance, Simon approached from a service door, still in his hotel coverall but wearing a shawl and headband. The day was bright and hot, the cloudless sky above the busy plaza a depthless blue. The upper market filled the area just outside the palace walls below Mariamme's tower. Since the upper city had largely been taken over by the time travelers, most of the shops were electrified and bore signs in English as well as Hebrew. It was the hottest spot in Judaea for legal trade. Shadier dealings tended to go on in the lower city: the plaza near the Hippodrome was a notorious black market for currency, condoms and antibiotics.

A fishmonger hawked his wares from a polyfoam cooler. Outside a wine merchant's shop hung skins of wine like the bellies of pregnant women. An old man with a barrow scraped up the leavings of donkeys and horses to keep the pavements clean for the tourists. Simon led August and Genevieve across the plaza and down a narrow side street. The street climbed up a hill between two-story stone buildings. They turned a couple of times and ended up in a still narrower street of shops close to what had once been Herod the Great's magnificent stables. From down the way Gen smelled fresh bread from a bakery, heard the barking of dogs from an animal wholesaler's.

Genevieve had owned a pet only once in her life. She and her mother were living in a run-down house west of Dufferin Grove, in what had been an Indian section of Toronto. Her mother worked a doubles scam above a microorganic cleaners on Bloor Street, selling bereaved people the chance to retrieve their loved ones by stealing their doubles from recent moment universes. Most of their marks were retirees or parents who had lost children. To kidnap a real duplicate required access to a time machine; about the only ones who could do that were the mob. The outfit Ivy Faison worked for had no time machine, so they just sold the promise.

Ivy didn't seem too worried about crossing the mob, or the cops. At nights she would come home with one or another of her men friends, or lie on the sofa in her VR suit embracing phantom lovers, picking up objects that weren't there. Gen was alone a lot. She got the idea that if they had a dog, it would give her somebody to talk to, and keep her safe. One of her friends at school got her a full-grown German shepherd named Max. Max's right ear had a notch in it from some old fight, and he had fleas and smelled bad. A bath got rid of the fleas, but Max never was much of a watchdog because he never, under any circumstances, would bark. Gen loved him immediately.

Eventually her mother started coming home later and later. She would wobble into the room after twelve, push some Snooze into her arm to get herself to sleep and some Focus in the morning to get her up. Sometimes she wouldn't come home at all for a day or more. Finally she didn't come back at all. Gen didn't know what to do. She couldn't call the police. Even if they found Ivy, she would end up in jail, and Gen in some foster home. So Gen kept going to school, hoping each day that her mother would be there when she came back. Instead she had Max. For a month she lived alone in the apartment with her German shepherd, rent unpaid, the bills collecting and the food dwindling.

One day at recess she saw a man watching her from outside the chain-link fence of the schoolyard. At first she thought it might be a cop or one of her mother's boyfriends, and she tried to ignore him. But there was something familiar about the way he stood, and when he finally called out to her, "Genevieve!" she knew it was her father.

She had never seen her mother again. Two years and a dozen scams later, Max died.

Simon had said little to them since they'd left the palace, but Gen caught him giving her an occasional wary look. The awed expression on his face was out of keeping with his brusque manner. Was he attracted to her? But at times he seemed almost afraid. He took them down the street to a shop under a big painted sign:

Fiery Furnace Sale!
HONEST ABEDNEGO'S DISCOUNT ANIMALS
Why Waste Time? Why Pay More?

The building was one of the new sandfoam prefabs with a stucco front and a high tin roof that must drum like a demon when it rained. Simon nodded at the entrance but did not follow them inside.

Both sides of the front room were lined with cages of animals: birds, snakes, lizards, cats, dogs. The place smelled of wood shavings, a trace of urine. Incense burned in an iron lampstand. The HVAC system hummed above them. An open doorway in back led to a sunlit courtyard and a glimpse of paddocks containing horses, camels, oxen. The rear wall held racks of animal carriers. Most had wire-mesh windows, but on display was a pearl-gray metal quarantine carrier identical to the one Vannice had brought from the Cretaceous, hermetically sealed with an environmental readout on top.

On the corner of the service counter rested a green lava lamp and a flatscreen playing the 2062 *Sporting News*. Though it was turned upside down to her, Gen recognized a clip of Babe Ruth swatting his latest homer for the Vancouver Sea Lions. A clean-shaven man in a stained brown tunic came up to speak to them. "Yes, sir?"

"I would like to purchase a dog," August said.

August went off with the owner to examine a selection of Egyptian dogs, and Gen went back to where Simon stood under the shadow of the entrance.

Outside, a man had stopped in front of the baker's shop to pray. Several passersby stopped to join him. The baker came to his door to scowl at this impediment to his business, but did nothing to chase the man away. Simon watched, a sober expression on his face. The praying man wore a blue-and-tan shawl, a brown robe. On his left arm he wore a leather strap wound seven times around his biceps, from which dangled a leather cube. Another cube hung from a band around his forehead.

"Coming with us must have disrupted your schedule," Gen said. "Will you have extra work to do when you return?"

Simon turned his attention from the praying man. "There are more people who need work than jobs to do."

"When does your shift normally end?"

He only stared at her. He was shorter than she, and his dark brown eyes worked with powerful emotion. Despite herself, Gen stopped thinking of him as a source of information and saw him as a man. "You don't like to deal with us," she said.

"I am a poor man. I do what I must."

"What did you do before the people came from the future?"

"I was a weaver."

"That is a difficult work, as I understand it."

He looked at her as if trying to detect some insult. "Men call it women's work. Yet they would be without a cloak in the cold of winter were it not for weavers."

"An injustice. Doesn't the change that we have brought offer you some hope?"

He looked away.

A band of teenaged boys came dashing up the street, shouting and hurling sticks. While one of them decoyed the owner's attention by throwing a fistful of pebbles onto the awning over the shopfront, another of them snatched a loaf of bread from the baker's table. Simon stepped forward. "Samuel!" he shouted.

One of the boys turned to them, while his companion ran off with the loaf. The boy saw Simon and Gen, hesitated, then dashed off down an alley. Simon took another step toward him. The baker glared. When Simon retreated, the baker turned on the Pharisee, and yelled at the man to move along. An argument started.

"Who was that boy?" Gen asked.

"That was my son. Running with thieves."

"Why did he look at us like that?"

Simon paused. "You carry yourself like his mother."

Gen tried to think of something to say. "You must wish that she could keep him out of trouble."

"His mother is dead. So while I spend my day working for foreigners, he slips away from me."

Gen stood there in the shadow of Honest Abednego's sign, at a loss for words. Simon still would not look at her. In order to live, Gen and August often had to impersonate historicals. It was a small step from impersonating to sympathizing. In the scant hour she'd known him, Simon had slipped from being a prop in their con game to a man with a dead wife and a troubled son.

"Genevieve?" It was August.

"Come, help us," she said to Simon, and reentered the shop.

August held a slender silky-haired dog by a leash while the shopkeeper prepared the carrier. Gen knelt down next to the dog and scratched behind its long and delicately formed ears; it whipped its tail and sniffed her hand. "This is Pharaoh," August said.

The Saluki slipped readily into the carrier and they sealed the door. While August paid the proprietor, Gen made Simon haul the carrier to the front. She could not estimate the degree of his resentment, and she tried not to think of it. The baker had given up trying to get the praying Pharisee to move, but now the life of the street went on around him, oblivious.

Chapter 7

A Night at the Hippodrome

In the evening three trumpet calls from the heralds at the Temple summoned the faithful to prayer, while the magic light of sunset turned the narrow streets soft gold. Serge Halam could understand how, to the Jews, Jerusalem seemed the center of God's universe. It was little wonder that they hated the futurians who so casually told them this was only a backwater moment in an incomprehensible universe.

He walked down the white stone street of the lower market, through crowds of pilgrims, priests, traders, thieves, anchorites. Jews, Greeks, Romans. A line of chanting Levites in white robes filed upward to the Temple. The smoke of the evening offering would soon rise. He passed a tailor, a worker in brass and copper, a shoemaker's shop. The shoemaker knelt before a low table in the shade of his wooden awning, pounding a piece of leather, a brass mortar in his deft hands. A letter writer with a reed pen stuck behind his ear crouched over an old-fashioned portable computer. Behind him a boy, no doubt his son, practiced writing Hebrew characters with a second reed pen.

Outside the entrance to the Hippodrome a couple of Greek touts were taking bets on that night's baseball game between Jerusalem and Capernaum. Halam paid five asses for a ticket and headed through the turnstile. The Jerusalem squad was pathetic, the Capernaum team not much better. The players were all captives taken in war, slaves or criminals, with a couple of impoverished freemen, coached by a retired major leaguer hired by the Saltimbanque Corporation's Cultural Improvement Office. The historicals were miserably awkward batters. The concept of the curve ball was beyond them. The heat vibrating off the artificial turf turned day games into an oven, and quite regularly somebody had to be hauled off the outfield in a dead faint. Now that the lights had been installed most games were played in the evenings. Since devout Jews would not go near such sports, let alone bet, the crowds were mostly Romans, Greeks and Syrians, but that didn't keep the Pharisees from protesting the corruption it was causing.

It was probably a bad idea to try to introduce a modern sport into ancient Judaea, the brainchild of some PR flack with a newly minted social-engineering degree who didn't bother to learn about the people he was trying to persuade. Or maybe the company wanted to cause friction, as an excuse to continue military rule.

Halam bought a basket of fried locusts from a vendor and found his seat. His contact had not arrived, so he sat watching as the ground crew laid down the chalk around the batter's box. Behind the home team's dugout, just opposite first base, Pilate and his son were settling into their reserved box. The Roman Prefect had taken to baseball and was a regular at most home games. His son wore an absurdly large Jerusalem Scholars cap, under which his ears stuck out like two open doors on a cab.

The game started and right away the Scholars fell behind. The pitcher walked the first two batters. The next hitter skidded a single into right center which the center fielder kicked to the wall; in the ensuing Marx Brothers routine between him and the right fielder both runners scored. The batter ended up on third. The crowd did not seem to mind, cheering every mishap wildly.

In the top of the third, score 6–2 Capernaum, a man sat down next to Halam.

"When we drive you invaders away we will have this place torn down."

"It's just a game, Simon," Halam said. "Save your indignation for something that matters."

Above the walls of the stadium, up on Herod's magnificent platform, the wall of the temple gleamed gold beneath a purple sky. "When I was a boy," Simon said, "I dreamed of escaping Galilee for Jerusalem. I longed to become a Levite, have my lot chosen to be the one, once in my life, to make the offering of incense. To walk before the great temple, to be vouchsafed a single glimpse of the Holy of Holies. That was before I saw the palaces the Sadducees built for themselves with the money collected from the poor."

"Money draws corruption. You shouldn't expect otherwise. That's the way the world works."

"Judaism is about purity."

"You're not going to get rid of your conquerors by being pure."

Simon spat onto the stone bench. "I don't know why I speak with you."

"You speak with me because I get you assault rifles."

"Once all you invaders are gone we'll destroy those rifles, and fling the pieces into the desert."

Halam laughed.

"Why do you laugh?"

"You remind me of something the inventor of these weapons said. He was an immigrant to a country in the future, a place called the United States."

"What do I care about this mythical country?"

"It was an important place. It lasted a couple hundred years."

"Israel has lasted a thousand. It will be here long after you have been driven away."

"Perhaps. Anyway, this inventor said his family emigrated 'so they could worship God according to the dictates of their own conscience, and prevent others from doing the same.' " Halam finished the last of his locusts. "Better hold on to those rifles, Simon," he said. "You'll need them."

A chant arose from the crowd as the Scholars mounted a rally. The Capernaum pitcher, a lanky Syrian who advertised his free-born status with an impressive black beard, had already worn himself out and was lobbing gopherballs. The Jerusalem batter took a furious cut at a pitch, popping a high fly into foul territory outside first. The first baseman, a look of terror on his face, circled under it for what seemed like a full minute, then muffed the catch. The crowd cheered. Halam set down the empty paper dish and leaned forward. "Don't overswing!" he shouted.

"There's nothing in the Torah against virtual reality," he said to Simon. "Or about microwaves, or radio, or electricity. These things are just machines. They don't have any moral content."

"You are worse than the Romans. You force your blasphemous images into everything."

"We call it advertising."

" 'Wives, be subject to your husbands as you are to the Lord.' Yet your women talk openly in public, and wear scandalous clothing, and fornicate. They should be stoned."

" 'Let he who is without sin cast the first stone.' "

Simon clenched his fists and glared at the ballfield. "Yes, he said that. But he left us. You stole him away."

"Save your money, take a tour to an unburned M-U. He's still there. Or visit the future. We've got several versions."

"Yeshu is everywhere but here, where he's needed the most."

"Why do you think he went? If he had stayed here he would be dead."

"His death would have been our victory. In his name we would have ripped Herod from his throne, stuck Pilate's head on a pike and swept the Romans into the sea."

"My understanding is that he did not advocate violence. Perhaps you disagreed with him on this?"

Simon said nothing. He was acting as hysterical as Jephthah.

"Has something gone wrong?" Halam asked.

The Zealot looked up at the Temple again before answering. "My superiors at the hotel have been treating me as if I'm the only employee there. The sent me up to a room where one of your tourists had some kind of demonic lizard."

"You sure it wasn't a VR setup?"

"I could smell it."

"It was probably an iguana. Is that all that's bothering you?"

Simon looked him in the eye. "I don't know where my son is."

Halam sighed. This was more personal information than any one of the revolutionaries had ever trusted him with, and he didn't much like it. "You want my help?"

"What I want is for you all to leave." There was more weariness than rage in Simon's voice.

"Understand this," Halam said. "Your supporters in the future hired me because I like Jerusalem, but I think they're as deluded as you are. Even if you throw the corporations out, the time travelers will be here. I can give you self-rule, but not keep them away forever."

"What good is self-rule if you tear us apart? Your drugs and your music and your games?"

"Simon, your faith is immortal. But you can't stop change."

A foul ball screamed off the bat, curling right at them. Simon, oblivious, would have been beaned had not Halam surged up and snagged it. Simon looked befuddled. Halam sat back down, tossed the ball up and caught it. "Hey, how about that! I've never caught one before in my whole life! All right now, straighten it out!" he yelled.

"When can we attack?" Simon said.

"Calm down." Halam saw that Simon was not going to be reasonable. Maybe the Zealots could scour the effects of the time travelers out of Jerusalem, but then they'd only be back in the Roman world. But there was no point in his trying to explain it all again.

The Jerusalem batter laced the next pitch into the left-field corner. The man on second came around to score. The left fielder chased down the ball and came up throwing, a mile over the cutoff man and halfway up the first-base line. The batter, arms flailing, rounded second and steamed toward third. The Capernaum first baseman kept the throw from going into the dugout, thought about throwing to third but held up. The batter ran through the stop sign at third and steamed toward the plate. The sparse crowd was up and screaming, Halam with them. As the catcher blocked the plate, the first baseman threw home. The ball and the base runner got there simultaneously. There was a huge collision.

When the dust settled the umpire, leaning over, yelled, "You're out!"

The crowd hurled curses down on him. The Jerusalem manager rushed out of the dugout and jawed with the ump, throwing his arms about like a madman. The ump turned purple and told him to shut up. The catcher and the base runner lay on the ground groaning. The Capernaum manager barged in to launch a few choice epithets. The crowd hurled refuse onto the field. They began to chant, "Prefect! Prefect! Prefect!" Finally the umpire threw up his hands and turned to the Roman's box.

Pilate stood from his seat, pulled his fine blue robe around him. He held out his hand, thumb parallel to the ground, and let the moment draw out. The crowd hushed. Then, with a little grin, he turned thumbs up. Safe.

The crowd cheered, the Jerusalem manager helped up his player, the ump wiped his brow and the Capernaum skipper, muttering, stalked back to the dugout. The pitcher raised his arms to the heavens, then rent the neck of his uniform shirt, which looked to have been torn and resewn a dozen times already.

Halam checked his watch. "I've seen enough," he said. "Let's go."

Night was coming on and the streets lay in shadow. Simon led him down a narrow street to the river, then turned south down an even narrower street. Where it passed below the old wall of the City of David, near the Pool of Siloam, they loitered in the shadows. Halam lit a cigarette; Simon turned away in alarm, and Halam smoked quietly. Eventually a very handsome man in a brown cloak approached them.

"Hello, Jephthah," Halam said. "Howya doing?"

Jephthah stared at Halam's hand as if it were a cloven hoof; Simon grimaced, shifting from foot to foot. The instant the younger man appeared Simon had got even stiffer than before. Apparently it wasn't just the Saltimbanque staff that was bossing Simon around.

"Okay, let's get down to cases," Halam said. "You've distributed those Model 25s?"

"Model 25s?" Jephthah said, watching for passersby.

"The Czech submachine guns."

"We haven't been able to fire them near the city. The noise draws attention. But our men in Salim are getting some experience with these weapons right now."

"What do you mean?"

Jephthah looked suspicious. Simon broke in. "They're taking over the garrison there tonight."

Halam shook his head. "That's foolish, you know. You should keep quiet until the time comes. This way you're only going to waste ammunition and get everyone jumpy."

Jephthah protested, "You said we should create a diversion."

"Not until just before you move on the hotel."

"I cannot see that it is a disadvantage if the time travelers send their Roman hirelings to Salim."

Maybe he was right. The Zealots were quite resourceful when they put their minds to it. They would have been a success at terrorism in any century. "Fine," Halam said. "You need any more ammunition?"

"We have husbanded our cartridges," Jephthah said. "What we need from you is a time when we can attack."

"I've got a worm program working on the time-travel system's finder. So far they assume the problem's only with the hotel time-travel stage. In order to fix their momentum compensator they're going to have to calibrate it against the main travel stage at the Antonia fortress. My worm will infect the Saltimbanque computer. When they power up the system again, it will trigger the worm and in twenty minutes both time-travel stages will go out. They'll be helpless for at least an hour, maybe two."

"What about the hotel's security system?"

"A separate subroutine in the AI will knock out all the camera midges; meanwhile we'll feed recorded footage into the security system. To anybody checking the monitors it will look like everything's normal. The staff you'll have to take care of yourself."

"We will grind them into the dust."

"Just be ready. Sometime after ten in the morning the travel stages will crash, and at ten-thirty the midges go blind."

Simon and Jephthah wanted to discuss the details of the raid. Halam didn't want to know about it; it really wasn't his responsibility. They would have to control the hotel before reinforcements could be brought in from uptime, and at the same time keep the Roman garrison in the city from coming to the futurians' aid. Timing would be everything.

Jephthah prepared to leave. "Deliver me from workers of iniquity," he said to Simon.

"And save me from bloodthirsty men," Simon replied.

With that Jephthah slipped off into the darkness. As Simon started to do likewise, Halam said, "If I should hear anything about your son I'll let you know."

Simon stopped. "You know something?"

"Nothing for certain."

Simon left, and Halam went back into the Second Quarter, to a club called Adam's Garden. He paid the cover and entered the back of the smoky room, lit only by oil lamps on iron stands and the glow of the charcoal fire from the pit in its center. A few of the patrons were tourists—two Germans in safari jackets, some prosperous Vietnamese in brand-new first-century garb—but mostly this was a hangout for historicals into cultural mixing and revolutionary politics. On a low stage in what once had been the atrium of the private residence, Simon's son Samuel, locks greased into a pompadour, wearing a lavender polyester jumpsuit stenciled with the words BUY DARWIN MOLES, played the blues on one of Halam's harmonicas. Behind him was a band on electrified lute, pipe and bass.

Halam found a table and ordered some Galilean wine. The boy's version of "Terraplane Blues"—he had never seen a Hudson, and could not imagine the Mississippi Delta—was weirdly skewed by the whine of Chasidic temple music. But it had a certain soulful originality. Halam made a note to remind himself to get the kid down on disk. A demo might lead to something.

Chapter 8

Dancing in Jerusalem

The hotel casino was packed. Palestinian servants moved swiftly between the tables, bringing chips, setting up drinks, extending credit. Women in extravagant hair styles and low-cut gowns leaned over tables to exchange fragrant whispers with men in tuxedos.

Owen did not understand why people traveled two thousand years into the past in order to do something they could do in Atlantic City. But gambling he grasped. It was an expression of biological élan, a fundamental quality of all life, the opposite of self-preservation yet genetically linked to it. A bet was a test of the statistical nature of reality. The longer the odds, the more the chance of losing, of course. But life was long odds, anyway. As Wilma could attest, most species in history lost, and so in the end did all individuals. A gaming table was only a metaphor for that evolutionary bet. Some people, without even knowing it, were drawn to try to recoup in the casino what the DNA in each of their cells knew they would lose outside of it. If you won, you could feel you had beaten time's arrow back a few ticks of the clock.

But in the end nobody ever beat the house.

He searched for Genevieve and found her and her father

playing cards, at one of the pavilion tables adjoining the dance floor, outside the casino.

"Good evening, Mr. Faison."

"Good evening—Owen, is it?"

"That's right, sir. May I join you?"

"Certainly. Champagne?"

=It's probably drugged,= Bill said.

"Thank you."

"Would you like to join us in some three-handed bridge?" Gen asked.

=Right. And get pauperized?=

"No, thank you, I don't gamble." He was going to have to do something about Bill. He had a strategy which sometimes worked. "Let me get a glass for myself, and another bottle of champagne," he said. On the way to the bar he spoke to the AIde. "Look, Bill, you remember that hotel employee with the oatmeal? Why do you think he was so intent on getting into our bedroom? Do you suppose he might be after Wilma?"

=He ran away as soon as he saw her.=

"Very conveniently, I might add. Before we could ask him any questions."

=You're right. We should probably hide.=

"No. I want you to think about what he might be planning. The Saltimbanque Corporation's in heavy competition with Mother's conglomerate for the entertainment dollar. What could be his connection to them? Have a report ready for me by tomorrow morning."

=Will do.=

That ought to occupy Bill for the evening—at least reduce the frequency of his interruptions. Of course, if the ruse worked the way it had in the past, Owen would have to pay the price in Bill's increased suspicions for the remainder of his hotel visit.

When he got back to the table August said, "Well, here's

your opportunity. My daughter here wants to dance. Despite your unfortunate dance history, you could do us both a very big favor by escorting her tonight."

"It would be my pleasure, sir."

The palace hotel had two main wings, surrounded by gardens. Inside the portico between the wings a pavilion and dance floor had been set up. Under soft area lights historicals tended bar. Beyond the portico couples strolled down paths through the groves and fountains, along reflecting canals lined with exotic plants, and above on the western wall, looking over the valley and the orchards. The throb of dance music stirred the dust of the tombs below the city. Above, in a violet sky of surpassing lucidity, the stars were coming out, and in the west Venus hung like a beacon above Mercury, her pale reflection.

The bass played figures on Owen's endocrine system. His chest tingled with the rhythm, and he watched the women in twenty-first-century knockoffs of biblical gowns sway to the music. Too much thigh and bosom for authentic clothing, but they reveled in this opportunity to dress in a way not condoned by the straitlaced rules of 2062. They were in a totally disposable world, and the rush of freedom was written in their flushed faces. Owen guided Gen to a secluded spot just inside the portico. The champagne he'd already drunk had left him delightfully elevated, and he went to the bar to refill their glasses.

The bartender, a young historical, looked miserably uncomfortable in his starched white jacket. Sweat glistened on his face. Owen felt a moment's curiosity—who was this man? What might he have been in authentic history? Owen's habitual dismay at the exploitation of history swept over him. He returned to Gen, beside the dance floor.

"A thousand dinari for your thoughts," Gen said.

"Actually, I was thinking—how beautiful you look."

"You've just spent two years in the Cretaceous."

Owen smiled. "That has nothing to do with it."

"Dr. Nice prefers cold-blooded animals."

"Dinosaurs aren't cold-blooded."

"Some women are."

He sipped champagne. "I wouldn't know about that."

"But you're a scientist. You're prepared to find out."

He set down his drink, took her hand. "Let's dance."

The band was starting up a neo-quadrille. The couples formed two diamond patterns across the open flagstones. Owen remembered the figure from his class; he had never been any good at it. But something different was at work tonight. He seemed to understand the rhythm of the changes for the first time. What had seemed an arbitrary set of transformations was now the most natural development in the world. Maybe it was Gen's eyes. He twirled her in his arms, he stepped once, twice, forward and back; they glided, joined, separated and rejoined.

His mind whirled, the throb of bass in his heart. He was graceful.

"You dance well for a dinosaur hunter," she said.

"I'm not a hunter."

"Not a hunter, Professor? I think you are."

"Oh, no. Actually, I'm investigating sauropod heterochrony."

"Ah, heterochrony." She twirled away from him, showing him a lethal length of calf, then back. "What's heterochrony?"

"Heterochrony comprises phylogenetic changes in the expression rate of an organism's particular features."

"I see." The couples slid into two lines. The line of women retreated, curtsied. Owen's line of men bowed. They came forward and joined hands. In pairs, they began to circle the floor.

"Despite the fact that it's been proven for years that all basal sauropods, including *Apatosaurus megacephalos,* had fibro-lamellar primary bone—just like us—still, the alteration of somatic growth relative to maturation has remained a fundamental question."

"A real puzzler."

"For instance, is their sexual maturity in synch with physical maturity?"

"A question I have pondered for many years." Gen kept her eyes forward.

Owen was entranced by her clean profile. "I mean," he said, "just because they're grown up doesn't mean they're ready for sex."

"A truth universally acknowledged."

"It's a vital determinant of reproductive policies."

"I find honesty is the best policy." Gen stepped forward, measured pace by pace, delicately and precisely. Her toenails were painted red.

Owen felt exhilarated. The dance came so naturally, and he felt eloquent. "Plus, do they care for their young as we do?"

"Better, I hope."

"Fibrolamellar primary bone in basal sauropods usually indicates elevated growth rates. They get big fast. Ontogenetic studies taken before the advent of time travel indicated proportionately higher growth rates among juvenile individuals. The young grow faster than the old."

"And suffer for it, I'm sure."

"Were the sauropoda R- or K-reproductive strategists? I intend to prove that the speed at which they attain maturity is dependent on their environment. A coddled specimen will stay an adolescent a lot longer than one exposed to a harsh struggle for survival."

"Which explains a lot, doesn't it?"

"With the proper care, diet and ready availability of food, I'm sure Wilma will grow more slowly than they think."

"Some individuals never grow up." Gen looked up at him, smiling. Her eyes were the most remarkable shade of violet. The quadrille ended, the couples laughed and leaned together, and the band began a slow jazz tune. Feeling flushed, Owen took Gen in his arms.

He had never realized before what a beautiful custom dancing was. Men and women who not long before had been separate, now held each other in their arms. The embrace was a way station of intimacy. Each, afraid but willing, risked exposure. Genevieve let him hold her, and he kept a formal space between them, but as they turned he felt her hair brush his cheek.

Did she really like him, or was her teasing pure mockery? Owen had no aptitude for women. He dreaded that his mother was right, that anyone who liked him was only interested in the fifth-largest private fortune in North America.

But Genevieve was different. She made no attempt to put him at ease, but when he blathered on about dinosaurs she pretended not to notice how absurd he was. Her warm hand on his shoulder seemed connected right to his racing heart.

His mind ran ahead. After the dance they would walk beneath fragrant olive trees, warm breeze laden with the scent of spices, the old moon like a ruin in the sky. He'd lean close in the night, her breath fragrant on his cheek, and describe for her the brilliant blue-and-gold of the archaeopteryx. She'd laugh. He'd take her in his arms. Her lips would part . . .

The song ended. The dancers applauded, and Gen whirled away, as if she hadn't noticed he wanted to kiss her. He felt his face flush. He followed her to one of the paths. "Ms. Faison, I didn't mean—"

In the shadows beneath an olive tree, she turned to him. "Don't kid me, Owen. You men are only after one thing."

Owen panicked. "I don't—"

"All you want is a wedding ring. A woman who doesn't drag

you into bed before you trick her to the altar is asking for trouble. You marry us—and the next thing we know you've stayed with us forever. It's tragic."

"But I'm different!" Owen protested. "I don't want to marry you."

"You say that now, Dr. Nice. But you'll be singing a different tune in the morning."

"I'm afraid I don't follow you."

"Just hold on to my hand. I'll lead."

Dizzied by her zigzag conversation, he let himself be led by her along a reflecting pool. "Besides," she said, "how do I know you're who you say you are? You could be a twanked imposter posing as Dr. Owen Vannice, the wealthy paleontologist. How do I know you even *have* a dinosaur?"

"Meet me for breakfast. I'll take you down to see her."

"Perhaps," Gen said quietly. "Look—" She pointed at the sky. "There's Venus. Isn't it beautiful? It looks exactly the same as it does back home." She locked her arm in Owen's and they followed the path in a wide circle until they found themselves back at the pavilion, and August's table.

"A beautiful evening," August said. "Have you been enjoying yourselves?"

"Owen has been telling me about his life of crime."

"You've lived a life of crime?"

"Your daughter seems to think so. I confess her definition seems a little odd to me."

Gen looked him in the eyes, then turned to her father. "But what does a life of crime amount to today? Just a few lines on his resumé. Owen might as well have been an honest man his entire life. Father, do you think you could take me to that club we heard about?"

"I'm feeling a little tired, dear. I want to check on Pharaoh in the kennel early tomorrow."

"But the night is so beautiful."

"Perhaps Owen here would consider taking you."

"Owen, the master criminal? Would you? I've heard there's wonderful music there."

=Forget it,= Bill whispered. =How many risks are you going to take in one night? Do you think your father purchased me for nothing?=

"You won't stay too late?" August said.

"We'll be careful," Gen replied.

=This city is rife with hostile historicals.= An edge of hysteria crept into Bill's voice. =Do you think they admire us? That hotel guy is plotting to kill you. What do you know about this crazy dame? You're a scientist, not a dancer!=

"We'll be very careful," Owen said.

Owen and Gen passed through hotel security into the streets of the upper city. It was full night, perfumed by flowers and a hot desert wind. Away from the hotel, this Jerusalem resembled that of the unburned universes, with differences. Instead of oil lamps in the windows, he saw battery lamps. A restaurant displayed its name in blue neon. Here and there the roar of a portable air conditioner disturbed the night. From rooftop sleeping terraces came the gabble of Aramaic on portable radios.

Historicals, seeing they were from the hotel, followed them. "Mister, mister, you want the videodisk? Got the authentic miracle from Egypt! Got the John the Baptist execute! You buy!"

Owen flung a handful of coins at them and he and Gen broke away down toward the palaces of the high priests. He looked over his shoulder to see the beggars hurrying back to the hotel to await other tourists. From the south wall of the city they looked out at the Valley of Hinnom, over the glare of lights from the Holy Land amusement park, where young historicals cruised for girls and tourists rode Moses's Snake and the Deluge Waterslide. Beyond, under the moon, fields and olive orchards spread to the south. A flock of sleeping sheep lay scattered across the hill opposite like dirty white ottomans. But any sound they might make was drowned out by the roar of tinny music from the park.

Afraid to look at her, but feeling bold, Owen tried to explain the thicket of his emotions. "Genevieve, I know I've only known you a day, but there's something that I need to say to you."

"You're drunk, Owen."

"Not so much that I don't know what I feel. I—"

She put her hand on his lips. "Come on! While we stand here there are people in this city having fun."

Owen let her lead him away past the amphitheater and into the Second Quarter. She seemed to know where she was going. A neon sign above the entrance to the club read *Adam's Garden.*

The club was a Hellenized residence turned into a restaurant. Walls between the inside rooms and the central courtyard had been ripped out, and a low stage had been set up in place of a fountain in the middle. Though the club was electrified, the lighting was still provided by smoking oil lamps on iron stands. The place was crowded with historicals, Romans, Syrians, Greeks, a scattering of tourists from the future. A four-piece band of historicals on electrified lute, pipe, bass and harmonica played some queer variation of twentieth-century blues. Just as Gen and Owen were being served their drinks, the teenaged historical playing the harmonica, locks greased into a pompadour, wearing a hideous polyester jumpsuit, stepped to a microphone and began to sing,

> *"There's two kind of woman,*
> *there's two kind of man,*

> *there's two kind of romance*
> *since time began:*
> *there's the real true love,*
> *and that good old jive;*
> *one tries to kill you,*
> *one helps to keep you alive.*
> *I don't know—what kind of blues I've got."*

Eyes squinted shut, head cocked sideways, he slid into a discordant harp solo. Owen had never heard the song before, but he knew there was something twisted in the boy's performance of it. The boy did not know how ludicrous he looked. He probably thought he was making himself into a modern man by adopting the time travelers' clothes and music and language. Instead he had made himself into a joke. Despite the champagne and the evening and the woman beside him, Owen felt a wave of sadness.

The song ended and a few patrons applauded. "Isn't this flagrant?" Gen asked him.

"It's a car wreck. He's singing in the ruins of his own culture, and doesn't know it."

"But it's a music that never existed before, could not have existed before the invention of time travel."

"Doesn't it bother you a little?" Owen said. "Once these people had their own future."

"A lot of that future was misery. For all we know that boy—his name is Samuel—might not be alive without us."

"You *know* him?"

"I ran into him in the street earlier today."

Owen tried to judge the smile on her face. Was she pulling his leg? "Well, I'll bet you he can't read the words stenciled on his shirt. He doesn't understand the song he's singing. It's from another world."

"He sings it well."

"If we weren't here he'd be singing his own song, not something written two thousand years after he was born."

"Culture is miscegenation," Gen said. "That's how progress happens. Monocultures are vulnerable; they're too easily destroyed."

"Is rape better than virginity?"

"Those aren't the only options. Those are the extremes."

"This situation is extreme."

"We come from an extreme age," Gen said.

"The people we're exploiting think the age we come from is heaven. All that boy wants is to get to our time. He doesn't know he'd be fatally out-of-place there, and the things that he otherwise would have happily devoted his life to—his family, his work, his god—are devalued into nothing."

"Maybe," Gen said, "but in 70 A.D. this city would have been sacked and destroyed by the Romans. The temple would be demolished, not one stone left on a stone. The Jews would be dispersed in a hostile world. Because we came here, that's not going to happen, at least in this universe."

"You don't think there's anything wrong with the way we're treating them?" he said.

"If you're a chronological protectionist, why are you stealing a dinosaur from the Cretaceous?"

It was, Owen realized, a good question. Before he could think of an answer there was a commotion in the back of the room. A troop of Roman soldiers, carrying rifles, had entered the club. They fanned out, scanning the tables. The manager hustled up to them and an argument began.

"What's going on?" Gen asked a passing waiter.

"Uprising in Salim," the man whispered in a thick accent. "They're looking for Zealots."

Already a few of the patrons had headed for the rear exit. Up on the platform, the harmonica boy slipped his harp into his pocket and faded off the back of the stage. One of the soldiers collared him before he could reach the men's room. When the boy resisted the soldier whipped the butt of his rifle across the boy's shoulder fast enough to make an audible crack. The boy fell against a table. Without thinking, Owen found himself coming to his feet.

He went up to the soldier. "Hold on there, friend. What do you think you're doing?"

The soldier turned, knuckles white on the rifle, then realized Owen was not a historical. He would not make eye contact. "This boy is wanted for questioning."

"You've made a mistake. He's not a native. He works for me." Samuel had gotten to his feet, holding his shoulder, eyes blazing in the dim light. "His name is Thor."

"And who are you?"

"Owen Vannice, Miracle Optivideo Productions. We're shooting a movie. Thor's an actor from the future. From Cincinnati." The soldier looked skeptical. Owen tried not to sweat. This was exactly the kind of situation Bill was programmed for. Owen expected him to take over at any second, turn Owen into a whirling dervish of cross kicks and lethal martial-arts chops. Probably break every bone in Owen's hands, and get them shot in the process. He tried to sound sure of himself. "What's your name, soldier?"

The soldier's brows knit. "You will show me your passport," he said to Samuel.

The boy looked confused. "I have his papers," Gen said, fumbling in her purse. "I hope you haven't damaged that costume, Thor."

From across the room came the explosive slam of a fist on a table. Owen and the soldier jerked around. A slender, fair-haired man was arguing with two of the other soldiers. Owen recognized him as the man from the hotel elevator, Serge Halam. Halam shouted something at the soldiers about thuggery; when one of them grabbed his shoulder he shrugged it off. In the midst of his apparent fury he glanced over at Owen and winked.

"You should spend your time on the real troublemakers," Owen said, gesturing. "If we lose any shooting days because you've hurt this boy, you'll have some explaining to do. Thor, come with me! Genevieve?" Owen put his hand on Samuel's shoulder and pushed him toward the door. He tried to hold his back straight and walk as calmly as possible. Behind them, the soldier hesitated for a moment, then went to help his compatriots with Halam.

As soon as they got outside, before Owen could ask any questions, Samuel dashed off down the street.

"Who was he?" Owen asked Gen.

"The son of a historical I met earlier."

"How do you know he wasn't involved in this uprising?"

"I don't. But if they took him in for questioning it's not likely he'd come out again in one piece."

"He probably *is* a terrorist."

"Maybe. Why did you go to help him?"

Owen felt embarrassed. "I couldn't help it."

"That was some pretty good pretending. Interfering with the past is easy, is it?"

"Entirely too easy. Which proves my point." Up the street the lights of a jeep flared. "We'd better get back to the hotel."

=Good idea,= said Bill.

"Where have *you* been?" Owen subvocalized. "I could have used some insurance back there."

=I've been thinking. Are those Roman soldiers paranoid, or what?=

They wound their way back to the hotel as quickly as possible. Owen was shaking after the confrontation. But at the same time he felt exhilarated. He could actually *do* things. Gen *liked* him.

He imagined what it would be like to introduce her to his parents. It wouldn't have to be a long engagement, and he would insist that Mother not turn the wedding into a production. They could live in the town house in Cambridge, and he could lecture at MIT. The more he thought about it, the more feasible it became.

Back inside the hotel complex the dance was over and the white awning of the empty pavilion snapped in the warm breeze. They walked through the gardens to the western wall. He drew her aside. "Genevieve, I won't be put off anymore. I don't think our meeting was an accident. I can't tell you how much fun I've had with you."

On the plain outside the city, the glare of floodlights from a hovercraft field obliterated the night sky. A squad of troops was being lifted out of the city.

"You're awfully sure of yourself, Owen. Suppose that little game back there had gotten you shot—it might have, you know."

"That's a chance I was willing to take."

"Yes." Gen looked at him, more soberly than she had all that evening. Owen had never seen anyone more beautiful. "You always try to do the right thing, don't you," she said.

"I know you well enough to see you do, too."

"What if we don't agree what's right? It's hard to change the bad habits of a lifetime, Owen. There's a difference between you and me."

"You're against marriage."

"That was just a tease. But let me give you an example. Suppose you fall in love with a young woman. But she's not the right sort of girl. Your family would never approve of your marrying her. What do you do?"

His heart leapt. "If I love her, I don't care what my family says."

"That's because you're honorable. Me, I don't get into that

fix in the first place. I find me the richest, homeliest man in the room and seduce him."

Owen was instantly deflated. "I see," he said. "You're smarter than I am."

"Just remember that," she said, touching his cheek. "I'm smarter than you are."

Chapter 9

Simon at Home

It was late before Simon returned to his home in the lower city. A small mud-brick building around the corner from a tannery, it stank with the reek of the tannin vats. He walked by the hut of the old woman who lived next door, who had helped Simon when Samuel was small, then through the door of his home.

He lit the oil lamp and put the leftover beef he had brought from the hotel aside for the morning, not without guilt. He had not kept the dietary laws for a long time. He located a piece of hard greasy bread and gnawed at it, sitting cross-legged on the floor, wondering where his son was.

Samuel had fought back when Simon scolded Samuel for running with thieves: hadn't Simon himself kept company with tax collectors and prostitutes when he had followed Yeshu? The question only fueled Simon's rage.

He knew that he was not as good a father as he might have been. He had tried to set a good example, teach his son to respect God, learning and tradition. They had gone to the temple on the feast days, and despite Simon's poverty, he always bought a spotless lamb for the Passover sacrifice. But he had not been able to keep Samuel away from the time travelers and their seductive ways. What was tradition compared to television? Samuel was no doubt out at that very moment begging at the hotel entrance, joyriding in some stolen vehicle, indulging in a virtual-reality dream at some arcade.

Simon put aside the bread and crawled over to Samuel's pallet in the corner. He searched among the boy's possessions: a music bead for his ear, an English/Aramaic dictionary, a copper bracelet that had been his mother's. Underneath the rolled-up robe that served Samuel for a pillow Simon found, to his surprise, the sling that Simon had made for Samuel from bull's hide when he was only six. Perhaps Samuel's keeping it meant that he was not yet completely beyond reach.

Simon slid the sling back into its place, sat by the fire pit. Halam was right: the uprising in Salim would only put the hotel security staff on alert. If so, Simon, as the point man in the assault, was not likely to survive the day. And if that happened, what would become of his son?

He thought about those people in the hotel. They would be swept away. They deserved to die. But he wondered what their future world was like. Halam said that in the future the Jews had been driven from Israel and lived under the rule of Gentiles for two thousand years. They were persecuted for killing Yeshu, by a new religion sprung from Yeshu's teachings. Flocks of the tourists who visited Jerusalem were these "Christians." Simon could not imagine what connection the divine being they spoke of had to do with the wise and passionate man who had been his teacher. Some of these had even established a mission in the upper city to convert followers of Yeshu like Simon to Christianity.

Halam had outlined for Simon an entire history, none of which would take place since the futurians had arrived. Yet in his own time, Halam claimed, it *had* happened. Holding these thoughts in one head was too painful—assuming that anything Halam said was true.

Simon had met people in the hotel who claimed to be Jews

from the future, dressed more outlandishly even than the Greeks. Their women were without shame. Simon believed in the one God, without doubt, and had felt that His commandments were clear, if not easy to follow. Now, on the eve of the assault his heart told him would bring them freedom, he was racked by doubt.

He knelt on his hemp mat, bowed his head and prayed. *Lord, your enemies shall lick the dust! I would rather be a doorkeeper in the house of my God, than to dwell in the tents of wickedness.* Head touching the hard earthen floor, he tried to hear the word of God.

Faintly, from the distance, riotous music drifted from the amusement park.

He was drawn from his prayer by the sound of a footstep at the door. Samuel came in, his robe pulled loosely across hunched shoulders.

Simon straightened. "Where have you been?"

Saying nothing, Samuel went past his father to his pallet. The boy lay down on his side, rubbing his shoulder. The garish suit he wore was torn.

"What happened to your arm?"

"Nothing."

Simon knelt beside him, drew down the zipper and pulled back the sleeve. The corner of Samuel's collarbone was bruised, swollen and turning purple. Simon fetched a basin of water and a cloth. "What happened?"

Samuel flinched at the cloth's touch. "Some soldiers came into the club. When I tried to sneak out they hit me."

"How did you get away?"

"That woman I saw you with. She was there, with a man, and they helped me."

Simon put aside the cloth. "Why did she help you?"

"Does she really look like my mother?" Samuel drew the sleeve awkwardly back over his shoulder.

"She's not your mother. Under that woman's shawl her hair is cut as short as that of an adulteress." Simon paused. He had never told Samuel how rebellious Alma had been. How she had run away from her parents; how if Simon had not married her it was likely no one would have. "When your mother died you were too young to remember her."

"If they had not helped me, the soldiers would have taken me to the Antonia, and you would never have seen me again."

Simon stood, feeling the stiffness of his own joints. "If you did not waste your time in illicit places, they never would have found you. Playing their music, wearing their clothes. Don't you understand that to them you are nothing more than a toy?"

"They have things we don't have!"

"They have *nothing* that we need. They have *nothing* that comes without a cost."

"What about the cost we pay by not having those things?"

"Don't speak like a child."

The boy struggled to his feet. "If you had used their medicine, Mother would be alive!"

Simon slapped him.

Samuel looked up at him. In the dim light his cheek was pale from the blow. Without a word he turned and left the house.

"Samuel! Don't go!" Simon followed into the street, but his son was a retreating figure against the glare of the mercury vapor lights at the top of the hill. Simon took a few steps, then stopped. From the direction of the Essene's Gate he heard the sound of trucks shifting gears.

Simon stormed back into the house, kicked over the lampstand, crushed Samuel's ear bead beneath his foot. He raged around the room, cursing until he was out of breath, then fell to the floor, tears in his eyes. Every year of his life weighed on his shoulders like ten. The world was tied into a knot. He could neither forgive Samuel's disrespect nor feel righteous in punishing him.

After a time he forced himself to move, stirred the fire in the pit and in the flickering light found the box that held his most valuable possessions. As a boy he had carved the top himself from a single piece of olive wood. He remembered hearing one of the tourists say that some of the olive trees in the Garden of Gethsemane would still be alive two thousand years from now. By tomorrow afternoon, Simon might be dead. Samuel could be dead before the night was done.

Sick at heart, from the box Simon took a photograph of himself and Alma, a still from a digital recording taken soon after the advent of the futurians. No devout Jew was supposed to keep an image of man or beast, yet Simon could not part with this relic. In the picture Simon and Alma stood among a crowd of Yeshu's followers on a hill outside Capernaum. Simon wore the same red robe, worn and faded now, that Samuel had used to cover his wounded shoulder.

When Samuel was three, a few years after Yeshu had gone and the men from the future were solidifying their rule over Judaea, Alma had taken ill. The strangers had medicines proof against all sickness, the promise of which was enough to bend the weak of Jerusalem to their will. But in that day Simon had not considered himself weak. He did not believe the time travelers' promises when they had lied so many times before, and he refused to give in.

So Alma had withered and died in a year, falling into a sleep from which she would not wake, and soon after breathed her last. Yeshu's magic might have saved her, but Yeshu was gone. At the time Simon told himself it was because of the theft of Yeshu that she had died, but since then he had wondered if it had been because of his own stubbornness. Either way, she was gone.

In the photograph Alma stood at Simon's side, young and

strong. He looked into the face of the woman who was now dead, into that of a young man rigid with certainty, untouched by grief. These strangers had control over time, and he did not. Everything was possible for them, nothing for him. Nothing he could do would give him back the feeling that had filled his breast that morning on that hill, as he listened to the *nabi* speak of the poor and the kingdom of heaven, while he held his wife's hand. Nothing could bring Alma back.

Samuel might not understand, but in order to give his son his own life, Simon would have to act. He put the photograph back into the box and from beneath it took out the pistol. He had learned enough from the strangers to accept this fact: the future was not something irrevocably written. Tomorrow he would begin its change.

Chapter 10

That Uncertain Feeling

Genevieve awoke, stretched, watched the sunlight stream across the bedclothes. From the living room of their suite she heard her father humming a tune.

She got out of bed, pulled on her robe. August was programming a sequence of words into the animal carrier he had bought. He tested it. CAUTION: LIVE ANIMAL . . . The words flowed from right to left across the display strip, over and over. He looked up as Gen entered, and smiled.

"Just remember, daughter. The poor may pass away, but the rich we have always with us."

"You're in high spirits this morning," she said.

"Always a good morning when there's work to be done."

His good humor disquieted her. Gen retreated to the bedroom and began to brush her hair, put down the hairbrush and stared at her reflection. It was a beautiful face. She stuck her tongue out at herself.

She remembered Owen's warm, dry hand on hers, trembling slightly as they danced. How he had stood at the edge of the pavilion before he spotted her, feet together, head tilted a little forward and to the side as if he were trying to find her by ear. She imagined him standing like that in whatever godforsaken prep school his parents had consigned him to, listening to the headmaster tell them about their moral obligations as children of wealth.

Yet he treated everyone the same, with no hint of arrogance. Difference made no difference to him. She had delighted to watch Owen confront the Roman soldier, with his lame story about Thor from Cincinnati.

On the way back to her room, Owen had babbled like a boy, so cheerful that his shoes hardly touched the floor. He'd insisted on opening the door for her, fumbling with her key. He blushed when she turned and kissed him on the lips. Her last glimpse of him through the closing door was of his astonished blue eyes.

She had told Owen that she was smarter than he was, and it was true that she could think rings around him. Yet he had put his arm around her waist and guided her away as if he were the one in control! Classic mark behavior—but instead of feeling contempt, Gen wanted to protect him from his own naiveté. To protect him from *her*.

She watched her father over her shoulder in the mirror. August was tapping some code into the pad on the top of the metal carrier. He finished and came into her room. "Did he tell you last night that the hotel made him move his dinosaur down to the kennel? This is going to be absurdly easy: forget the gypsy switch. We simply go down for our dog, you distract the staff person at the desk, and I'll get Wilma."

Without turning, she said, "August, I don't want to do this."

He sat on the corner of her bed. "There's no real risk, Genevieve. I'll be in and out in a minute, and Dr. Nice none the wiser."

"I'm not worried about you."

He took a file from her table, and began to file his nails. "I notice you came back pretty late last night."

"Yes, I did."

"I assume he's primed for a fall."

"I assume you're right."

"And why shouldn't he be? I hate to see the most enchanting woman in this moment universe wasted on a man who doesn't know what to do with a trillion dollars except spend it on dinosaurs."

"There's something extraordinary about that, isn't there?"

"One might say so."

She turned to the window, looked out over the city dawn. She had played her father's wife more than once, had acted as bait for his scams even more often, but she wasn't his wife, or some tart he kept on a string—she was his daughter. "Why do we always have to be so smart?"

August put down the file, came over to her, sat down on the sill. "Is something wrong, Genevieve?"

"I don't know. I just don't like the idea of taking the guy, I guess. He's too innocent."

"They're all innocent. It's just that some of them think they aren't. I'll give this one credit for being more obviously naive, but that's to our advantage."

"I'm tired of thinking about advantages."

"Owen Vannice was brought up in the world of advantages."

"He's not like that."

"Well, if he didn't learn to be mercenary from his father then he learned to be superior from his mother. You've seen enough of the rich. Don't forget his five years of dancing school."

She remembered Owen's trembling hand. "I haven't."

"They use their innocence as a shield, when they're not using it as a club."

"He's not like that."

"That remains to be seen."

"Regardless, I don't want to go through with this."

He took her hands in his, made her look into his eyes. The

beard was gone this morning. He looked to be in his fifties, almost as old as he really was. She remembered how tall and handsome he'd seemed to her when, as a little girl, she'd watched him and her mother dress for work. "You're telling me you're falling in love," he said.

"Doesn't it ever bother you to be making our living by tricking people? It's sordid."

He let go of her hands.

"What's the matter?" she asked.

"Your mother said the same thing to me when she took you and ran off."

Gen put her hand on his. "I'm not running anywhere."

"How long has our life seemed sordid to you?"

"It's not sordid when we're dealing with the Sloanes of the world. But Owen is different. I'm not going to abandon you, Father. If I marry him, we'll have enough money to swim in."

"Marry him?" August got off the sill. "This is worse than I thought. Has he asked you?"

"Not yet. But he will. Then there'll be no need for us to bilk people."

He stared at her, silent for a moment. "Do you actually think I do this for the money?"

"What are we in it for, then?"

"For the thrill of the hunt." August sounded hurt.

But he was her father, not her lover. He had no right to feel hurt. He had brought her into this way of life when she was too young to imagine any other. "That gets old, Dad. I'm getting old."

August went back to the carrier. "I don't think it's old that you're getting. It's something more disturbing." He crouched, checked the lock code again. "Why do I do it?" he said without turning his head. "You *know* why. I do it for the look on their faces when they figure out they've been taken. For the thought that they go back to their corrupt lives and never even *realize* they've been taken. I do it because I'm not one of them. They tell lies all their lives and never see it. Well, I know the difference between a lie and the truth. When I tell a lie, I know I'm lying."

"Owen can't lie. It isn't in him."

"He's a chronological protectionist yet he's carrying around a dinosaur."

"So? Is Lance Thrillkiller going to take better care of this dinosaur than Owen?"

August drew himself up. "You may do whatever you please in your love life, but I have no wish to sit around listening to my arteries harden. I've got business to transact. Today my business, sordid as it may seem, is liberating this dinosaur—with or without you."

Gen stood up. "If you can do it."

"Just how do you propose to stop me, short of finking on me?"

"I'd never do that. But you're not the only operator in this family."

"Why, you little sprout! I taught you everything you know. Don't tell me you expect to beat me in this game."

"I'm not your daughter for nothing," Gen said.

Chapter 11

Mad Wednesday

The lead story of the *Intertemporal Herald Tribune* concerned a riot at a Las Vegas rhetoric conference in the 1956 moment universe. The trouble started when the old Saint Augustine took offense at the young Saint Augustine's bringing a showgirl to a session on "Sex and Religion: (Re)dressing the Naked Truth." Young Augustine ("Call me Augie") branded his older self a hypocrite and ran a video of their sex life. Old Augustine wore a traditional fourth-century Roman scholar's garb; Augie wore skintight leather pants and an egg-yolk-yellow silk shirt. In the ensuing melee three sophists were trampled to death; the report included a video of Frank Sinatra's bodyguard beating up the Greek philosopher Protagoras.

=They ought to know better than to try to hold an academic meeting in the twentieth century,= Bill said.

"We mustn't judge the past by the standards of the present," Owen said. "If we had lived then we might have been crazy, too."

He switched off the paper and checked his wristward. It was after nine. The atrium restaurant, morning sunlight filtering down through the fronds of fan palms, was filled with the discreet murmur of breakfast conversations and the clink of china. He scanned the entrance hoping to find Gen. Had she changed her mind about meeting him?

=I suppose you're never going to ask about that report you ordered.=

"What report?" Owen replied impatiently.

=On that hotel employee, Simon. It's possible he is Simon the Zealot who was an apostle of Jesus.=

"But Jesus is gone. There are no apostles in this moment universe."

=Right. But in this M-U we didn't snatch Jesus until he was already preaching, so this Simon already had the career of the apostle before we arrived. He's a fanatic religious revolutionary.=

"Even if this is the same Simon, which I doubt, you haven't thought it through. He *was* a fanatic. Then he became an apostle of a man who preached nonviolence. And it's been ten years since Jesus left. Now he's a hotel employee."

=How about Halam? I *know* that man is a gunrunner.=

"If I can trust your memory."

=What you ought to trust is my judgment. I don't expect you noticed, but it was Halam who raised that ruckus at the restaurant last night in order to let the boy escape.=

Owen was nonplussed. "So?" he said. "You don't know why he made a fuss."

=Here's why: it's a conspiracy to steal Wilma. Listen. The Zealot shows up in your suite, creates a disturbance! He gets your dinosaur transferred down to the kennel! Women think obsessive wicked men are therefore dysfunctional! There's a known smuggler in the hotel! Genevieve Faison knows the boy! The boy is Simon's son! What more do you need?=

"I knew you'd have to work Genevieve in here somewhere."

=I've got a theory about her. 'Faison' is close to *faiseur*, which means 'quack' in French. Now if you assign each of the letters in her first name a numerical value according to the pitch of the phoneme in aramaic pronunciation, then— =

"Bill, I don't want you to think any more about this."

=As a precaution, I've already take steps to secure— =

Just then Genevieve stepped into the light of the restaurant's atrium, and all thought flew from Owen's mind. "Shut up, Bill."

Genevieve wore a striped blouse and a broad straw hat. The sunlight brought out the light spray of freckles on her forearms; the shadow of the hat's brim fell across her mouth. When she saw him wave, she came toward him, smiling. Her white teeth were bright between her painted red lips. From her shoulders wafted the faintest scent of her perfume. She kissed him on the cheek.

"Good morning, Dr. Nice."

"Hello," he said, uncertainly. Damn Bill. He needed to shake off the dust of the ALde's paranoia. "Are you ready to come see my dinosaur?"

"It's not necessary."

"No. I want to prove to you I'm not some impostor."

"Who can say what constitutes proof, in these modern times?" She looked at him steadily, a trace of a smile. Then she took his arm and they left the restaurant.

"You have a way of keeping a man off-balance," he said as they got on the elevator.

"Balance is overrated. You have to learn how to fall."

The window wall in the kennel office showed a bright alpine valley. The young woman behind the desk greeted them pleasantly. "Hello, Ms. Faison," she said. "That's a beautiful dog your father bought."

"Yes, he is."

Owen was confused. "Your father bought a dog?"

"Yesterday. We're here to see Dr. Vannice's dinosaur," Gen said.

Maureen checked Owen's identification from his wristward. "I'll show you right back."

She led Owen and Genevieve to the rows of cages. Behind the glass of a large sealed compartment lay Wilma, curled up in a twilit corner. When she saw Owen she lifted her head, then came forward to press her snout against the glass. "Here she is," Owen said to Gen. "An *Apatosaurus megacephalos*."

Gen leaned forward. After a moment she said quietly, "She's beautiful."

Maureen unlocked the cage. Owen examined Wilma. Her breathing was more normal, her heart rate nominal. Her eyes looked clear. All in all, though she was acting a little surly, it seemed that her stay in the controlled atmosphere had done her good.

"Can we take her for a walk?" Gen asked.

"You'll have to use a carrier if you want to take her through the hotel to the outside," the attendant said. She led Owen to the storeroom where he got the carrier, then returned to the front office. Owen went back to Gen at the cage. It took some time for him to coax Wilma into the carrier.

As he was lugging her out he heard a spate of barking from the adjacent aisle. At the end of the row August was bending over an animal carrier. He looked up. He did not seem surprised to see Gen there.

"Good morning, Father," Gen said.

"Mr. Faison!" Owen said. "Hello. Your daughter just told me you bought a dog."

August Faison brought over his carrier, set it beside Owen's and pumped his hand. "Good to see you, Owen. Yes, this is my Saluki. This breed is at the head of its gene line, very rare item."

=A Saluki, named after an ancient Arabian city, is a dog of the greyhound family, with long ears and— =

"I *know*, Bill."

"Excuse me?" August said.

"A *noble* animal," Owen said. He was impressed by the force of the old man's enthusiasm. "Gen, you didn't say anything about your father being a dog fancier."

"Didn't I?" Gen said.

"You know women, Owen. They keep all sorts of secrets."

=Finally, the guy tells the truth.=

"Yes," said Gen. "How is Pharaoh?"

"He's fine. I was just making sure his environment is stable."

"We wouldn't want him to get into an unstable environment, would we?"

"Where are you going with him?" Owen asked.

"Pharoah needs to be walked daily. They won't let me take him on a leash through the hotel, though," August said. He picked up the carrier and started to go.

=He's taking the wrong carrier!= Bill screamed.

"Mr. Faison. You've got my *Apatosaurus*!"

"What? No, my boy. This is my Saluki."

Owen stepped toward him. "I don't think so."

"My lord, I believe you're right! What could I have been thinking?" He gave Owen the case he carried and went to retrieve the one Owen had left. "I'm so glad you noticed."

"What an embarrassment!" Gen said.

"It's not a problem, sir. These things happen."

"Yes, but I don't want to lose that dog, which in its own way is as important to me as your dinosaur is to you."

"Owen is going to let me take Wilma for a walk around the gardens."

"How agreeable of Owen," August said quietly. "That must

be why they call him Dr. Nice." He looked over Owen's shoulder. "Have you seen that young woman? She was supposed to get me some dog food."

The chair behind the office desk was empty. The only person in the office was some canned shepherd in lederhosen hiking the Swiss landscape on the wall. "I don't know what happened to her," Owen said. "I'll go back and look."

"Father can help himself, Owen," Gen said.

"No. I'd like to help," Owen said.

"Ask for a container of canine lab chow," August said.

"Surely." Owen went back into the kennel. He was glad for the chance to get away from Gen for a moment to collect his thoughts. While they walked in the garden he wanted to tell her how he felt about her. He began to rehearse a little speech.

Maureen was not in sight, but he found a worker crouched over a locker in the staff room between the kennel and the animal warehouse. "Excuse me," Owen said.

The man threw something back into the locker with a clunk, then slammed the door. "Yes sir?" He looked vaguely familiar.

=It's him! Simon! I never eat a naked screaming God bed!=

Owen winced. "I'm looking for some canine lab chow. Actually, my friend is, but we can't seem to find it. Can you help us?"

Simon gave him a nervous look, then dashed into a storage closet.

=If you don't get us out of here I'm going to have to kill him.=

"Will you *shut up*, Bill? Let me handle this."

Simon emerged carrying a sack of food, shoved it into Owen's hands, then hurried back to the lockers. "See?" Owen subvocalized. "He doesn't give a damn about us."

The discussion Gen and her father were having ended the moment Owen returned. Owen set down the bag of food. "Shall I open it, sir?"

"Please." As Owen bent to undo the lacings, August leaned toward Gen and whispered something in her ear. When Owen turned back, August was standing on the opposite side of his carrier.

"Here you go."

"Let me help you with that," Gen said, bending over. Owen got a spectacular view down the neck of her blouse. He felt his face color. "That can't be another dinosaur over there?" Gen said.

"Where?" Owen turned. "No, I think that's an iguana," he said. When he turned back now Gen had the handle of August's carrier.

"I didn't realize they had iguanas in the Middle East," August said grumpily. As he bent to open the bag of food he stepped forward and kicked it over. Owen tried to catch it, but missed, and it sprayed across the concrete floor.

"How clumsy of me," said August, lifting Wilma's carrier away from the mess.

"Yes," said Gen. "You could get into trouble, Father, being so careless."

"Only if someone reports me," he chuckled.

Owen scooped as much of the dog food as he could back into the bag. "No harm done," he said. "At least mistakes aren't illegal, yet."

They gathered up their cases and left the kennel for the elevators. No one was staffing the desk in the kennel office. Owen hit the call button for the elevator.

"Still, mistakes happen," Gen said. "Father, before we go, why don't you show Pharaoh to Owen?"

"He's seen a dog before."

"Not like this one."

Owen did not care for dogs, but just to be polite he said, "Certainly, sir. I'd like to see him."

August frowned. "He's not partial to strangers; I'm not sure—"

The elevator doors opened. Just then Owen stepped on something that crunched. It was a small mechanical device. He crouched to examine it.

"What is it, Owen?" Gen asked.

"A security midge. It seems to have gone dead."

=Of course it's dead. You stepped on it.=

"Why was it lying on the floor?" August asked.

Samuel did not return that night. Heart full of misgivings, Simon arrived at the hotel at seven A.M. "On time for once," Bauer commented. "I heard Callahan was on your ass about that."

"Mr. Callahan does not miss anything."

"Nothing except a conscience, a heart and a little brains. He has a good strong voice, though."

Simon reported in to the custodial office and was assigned to the time-transit warehouse. The transit stage was running double shifts to make up for time lost when it was being re-calibrated. He spent an hour lugging crates of Galilean wine onto the stage, observing them shot off, waiting for it to fail. He kept watching the crates to see whether they were shifting as they left. But shipment after shipment departed and arrived with not so much as a sloshing of wine in the amphorae.

McLarty checked off the invoice numbers on his list and they loaded pallets onto the forklifts and out to Aisle 6 of the warehouse. Simon helped bring in a string of horses from the animal warehouse in preparation for sending them uptime.

About ten o'clock, while they were bringing in the last of a shipment of truck tires before sending the horses, a stack came in sideways, tipping, tipping, then toppling. The technician shouted from his booth and the warehouse crew fled. The middle stack hit the waiting forklift and scattered. Tires bounced crazily and rolled in every direction, the crew dodging them like soccer players. The horses reared in panic, but were held by their lead ropes.

No one was hurt. Callahan came out to survey the damage. "Son. Of. A. Bitch," he said. "Shut it down, boys. Alert the passenger stage. And somebody tell the kennel to get these damn horses out of here."

"I will do it," Simon said.

While the crew set to gathering the tires, Simon hurried down the main corridor to the kennel office. "The time-travel stage has malfunctioned again," he told Maureen. "Can you come and help move some frightened horses? I'll be along soon."

When Maureen left he went to his locker in the staff room and got out his pistol. Simon had had little chance to practice with it. The pistol, which Halam called a "M1951 nine-millimeter Beretta" radiated an unholy aura—it was another of those objects that announced by its very strangeness that it was from another world. Yet it was entirely material, weighing heavily in his hand, black, smooth, compact.

It was 10:23. The Zealots were going to hit in seven minutes.

"Excuse me," a voice said from behind him.

Simon tossed the pistol back into the locker and slammed the door. He turned. It was the man from the future who kept the monstrous snake thing in his hotel room. "Yes sir?"

"I'm looking for some canine lab chow. Actually, my friend is, but we can't seem to find it. Can you help us?"

Simon had to get rid of him before Maureen returned.

Shaken, he dashed into the storage closet, grabbed a sack of food off a pallet and shoved it into the man's hands. Simon's watch read 10:31.

He rushed back to his locker, got the pistol. He hurried back to the warehouse and checked to see that the time-travel stage was still out of commission. Before Callahan could spot him, he ducked out and hustled down to the employees' entrance. Bauer had a newspaper turned on at his desk, but was ignoring it as he peered at something on the floor. It was one of the security midges.

Simon slipped into the booth and pressed the pistol up against the back of Bauer's neck. "Don't move."

Bauer stiffened. "Simon? What the fuck do you think you're doing?"

"Come away from the desk. We're going to wait here. Just a few minutes."

Bauer jerked back from the desk. A minute later a van pulled up to the loading dock. Simon waved through the window and Jephthah and the others jumped out. "You are going to be in a world of shit," Bauer muttered. Simon buzzed the security doors and the Zealots, hauling their rifles from beneath their robes, rushed in.

"God will honor you, Simon," Jephthah said.

So far they had not been noticed. Most of the staff were preoccupied with the downed transit stage. The security AI, fed with Halam's canned images, must not have realized the midges were out. Zebediah put on Bauer's uniform and sat in the security checkpoint. They hauled Bauer down the corridor, tied him up and dumped him in a supply closet.

Before they reached the kennel an alarm started sounding. The buzz was ear-splitting; several of the Zealots were so surprised they dropped their rifles and covered their ears. "Pick up your guns!" Jephthah shouted. "Hurry!"

They raced down the hall to the cross-corridor, but the security doors had slammed and locked before they got there.

"There's a service elevator near the kennel!" Simon shouted over the din of the alarm.

He led them to the side corridor, through the double doors. The tourist with the creature, plus a couple of others, were at the elevator. The doors were open. The younger of the two men turned toward the Zealots, and Simon realized with dismay that he was going to put up a fight. But the woman yanked him back, and before the man could react Jephthah slammed the butt of his rifle against his head, shoved the others aside and hit the elevator button for the lobby level. Nothing happened.

It wasn't working. Somehow the hotel's security system had been tripped. They were trapped.

He watched Jephthah as this sank in. He could read Jephthah's thoughts: the only thing they had now was the tourists—if he couldn't hurt the hotel, he could at least hurt them. The woman was trying to help the dazed man on the elevator floor. With dismay, Simon recognized her and the older man as the father and daughter he had taken to Honest Abednego's.

The Lord was playing some game with him.

Jephthah poked the muzzle of his rifle into the older man's ribs and herded him and the others back to the kennel. He picked up the phone and waved it at Simon. "Call them," he said in Aramaic.

Simon took the phone from his hand, stared at the blank screen. He wished he could get a message out to Samuel. He hoped the boy had not gone back home that day. He wondered if he'd ever see him again.

Genevieve had beaten August. There was no way he could get out of this situation without opening the animal case. As his tight expression slipped into a rueful smile, she felt triumph—but sadness too. She had never crossed her dad before.

Gen watched Owen poke at the crushed security midge. An alarm shrieked, and she jumped. From down the hall came the sound of slamming security doors. A band of dark men carrying rifles burst through the double doors at the opposite end of the corridor. "Stop!" the lead one yelled.

Owen turned toward the men, crouched as if he were about to take them on. It was suicide. Gen grabbed his collar and yanked him into the elevator, but by then the attackers were on them. The tall one in front whipped his rifle butt across Owen's face, knocking him to the floor. He shoved August aside and hit the elevator button. The doors would not close.

Among the invading men was Simon.

Maybe Owen was right about the risks of getting involved with historicals. Gen knelt beside him. The blow had opened a gash over his eyebrow that bled profusely, but she did not think he was badly hurt. He touched a hand to his head, then stared, dazed, at the blood that came away on it. Gen gave him her scarf to hold against the cut.

The Zealot leader, an extremely handsome man with dark eyes and a brooding profile, poked the muzzle of his rifle into August's ribs. Face glistening, he pushed them back into the kennel office, made them sit in a corner. On the window wall, the man in lederhosen had reached the top of the ridge and had turned back to wave.

The leader picked a phone off a desk and waved it at Simon. "Call them," he said in Aramaic. Simon took it from his hand. Turning, the Zealot leader seized Gen's shoulder. "You like to have men pay attention to you, whore? We will find out how much your rulers value your painted face."

"Leave her alone," August said.

The man spat in August's face. Gen, her hand on Owen's

chest, felt him try to get up, and she held him down. Simon pulled the man away from August. "Jephthah, listen. We can't harm them. These people are our only chance to get out of here alive." Jephthah shrugged off Simon's hand, but stepped back. Simon took Gen's, August's and Owen's wrist cuffs and gave them to one of the other Zealots. "Take these to some other room. Let the hotel AI think we are somewhere else."

Jephthah scowled. He pointed to the phone. "I told you to call them. Tell them only what I say."

Before Simon could even touch the phone's keys a window opened in the middle of the alpine scene on the wall and a man in a Saltimbanque security uniform appeared on the screen. "You are trapped in the basement of the hotel," the officer said. "There is no way out. You must surrender. If you harm any-one you will pay a heavy price."

Jephthah cursed. He took a step toward the wall and smashed the butt of his weapon into the face on the window. The wall went blank gray, with a nice dent where the rifle had struck.

Gen began to think this was going to be a long day.

The other Zealots looked worried. "Joset, Elam—take this furniture and make a barricade in the corridor," Jephthah said. "Make sure you have a clear shot at both the cross-corridor doors and the elevator. Get those carriers these infidels were carrying and bring them back here."

"Tell them to retrieve the guard," Simon said.

The other men looked at Jephthah without moving. "Yes. Get that other one." The men moved, and Jephthah turned on Simon. "Call them and tell them we have four of their peo-ple," he said.

Gen, August and Owen sat on a couple of quilts in a corner of the office. The cut on Owen's brow stopped bleeding, but not before Gen's scarf was dark with blood. Owen's eyes were bloodshot but he seemed otherwise okay. He leaned against his animal carrier, and Gen sat beside him, holding his hand.

Jephthah directed Simon's negotiations. "Tell them that they must surrender the hotel to us or we will kill the hostages," Jephthah said.

Simon relayed the demands over the hotel phone. While he spoke, Jephthah took a portable phone from his pocket and spoke in rapid Aramaic with someone outside the hotel. A couple of the Zealots returned to the office dragging a blunt-looking man wearing only his underwear. As soon as he saw Simon he tried to speak, but the guards dumped him in the corner with Gen and the others.

"August Faison," August said to the man. "My daughter Genevieve. Dr. Owen Vannice."

The man looked them over. "Hans Bauer," he said, eyeing the skinny young man who sat guard over them. The boy could not have been more than fifteen. He did not look like he knew which end of his antiquated rifle was which.

Jephthah folded up the portable phone. "The others have taken one of the towers at the Antonia, but the Romans are keeping them from the courtyard and the Temple. The mercenaries were so surprised we should have been able to take the hotel before anyone realized what was happening."

Simon looked unhappy. "God is against us," he muttered. "We should not be here."

"How did they know we were in the building? We have been betrayed."

"Perhaps Halam's computer worm failed."

Jephthah stared at Simon. "Why did you linger with Halam after we met the other night? What did you talk to him about?"

"Nothing."

"One does not talk when there is nothing to say." He pulled out his dagger.

The room was swept with a sudden silence. The air-conditioning had stopped. Until it stopped Gen had not noticed the rush of the air. Simon looked up at the vents, and got back on the phone to hotel security.

An hour after the stalemate started, the Zealots' portable phone went dead. Over the hotel phone, the Saltimbanque negotiators informed them that the raid on the Antonia had been squelched and the Zealots taken captive.

Jephthah said nothing; he played with his dagger. Gen watched the dynamics of power among the Zealots shifting. Jephthah only grew more angry as time passed and nothing happened. Simon seemed to be the only one able to grasp the bind they were in. But most of the men still looked to Jephthah for orders. It was not a reassuring situation.

They demanded that the hotel turn the air-conditioning back on. The Saltimbanque negotiators blamed the shutdown on the mess that had been made of their computer system. The hours stretched, and the basement got hotter. Whenever Jephthah lost patience with the slow pace of Simon's negotiations he would seize the phone and take over, but soon enough after doing so he would get frustrated by his tangled attempts at English and thrust the receiver back into Simon's hands.

After it became clear the futurians were not going to surrender the hotel, Simon and Jephthah got into a debate over whether they should kill one of the hostages and send the body back up on the elevator to show they meant business. Simon persuaded Jephthah, at least for the moment, that they should hold off on such a suicidal move. "We must live to fight again," he insisted. He convinced Jephthah to ask for a vehicle and safe conduct out of Jerusalem. Saltimbanque security promised as soon as possible to provide an armored hovercraft.

But nothing happened. More hours passed. The Zealots crouched behind the barricade in the corridor, discussed the situation in low conversations freighted with fear, or searched the kennel for something to eat.

The hostages sat in silence for a long time. Bauer actually

fell asleep, and began to snore. Owen occasionally touched a hand to his swollen eyebrow. "I hope you're proud of yourself, daughter," August said.

"What do you mean, sir?" Owen asked.

"He means that if I hadn't come down here I'd be safe," Gen said.

"What else could I mean?" August said.

Owen looked distracted. Gen wondered if he was entirely clear from the blow on his head.

"You know, when we do get out I could still probably get the wrong case—by mistake," August said to no one in particular. "I'm sure the confusion will be great."

"I'll make sure you keep them straight," said Gen.

"I hope Wilma is all right," Owen said. "But if I open her case they'll no doubt kill her."

"Owen, as long as we're waiting here, why don't you tell us some more about your work? How long before you know whether your theory about dinosaur growth is correct?"

"I should know within a year."

"Assuming we're not still down here a year from now," August said.

"We're going to get out," said Owen, tight-lipped. "You will, anyway."

"I admire your optimism," August said. "But I think you're being a trifle unrealistic. These are desperate men."

At the desk, Simon hung up the phone and turned to Jephthah. "They say they have the hovercraft. It will be piloted by a historical, but it will take another hour to get here from the company oil field."

"They are stalling."

"We cannot know that. What else are we going to do?"

"Do they think we won't kill these people? You may not, but I will. Make that clear to them." Jephthah twisted the rifle in his hands. "Tell them if it isn't here in half an hour we start killing the hostages."

"No, Bill," Owen whispered. Gen watched his face. His lips moved, ever so slightly, with a faint stir of breath.

"Owen, are you all right?" Gen asked.

"Uh—I'm fine."

Gen whispered in Owen's ear, "You're subvocalizing. Do you have an AIde?"

Owen looked at her, a sober expression on his face. "You figured it out."

"What's it telling you? Does it see a way out of this?"

"Bill got us *into* it—Bill's his name. Last night, while I was asleep, he took me over and called the hotel AI. He had extra monitoring set up. He was afraid Wilma would be stolen."

"How paranoid," August said.

"Yes. He doesn't trust people."

"Took you over?" Gen whispered. "Bill can take over your body?"

Owen nodded. "Right now he's blasting Wagner into my mind. *Sigfried.* He wants to get me in the mood."

"Mood for what?"

"He's looking for a chance for me to overpower them."

"For god's sake, stop him! He'll get us all killed."

The boy guard surged toward them, clutching his rifle. "What are you speaking? You will say out loud! Say or I will kill you!"

Simon came over. "Go over there," he said to the boy. "Be quiet," he told the hostages gruffly. He sat down on one of the carriers, and after a moment added, "Some of these men would rather kill you than get out of here alive."

Gen watched Simon, who was watching Jephthah. She laid a hand on Owen's side, hoping to keep him from doing anything. Simon did not look happy. After some time he turned to the hostages, his rifle across his knees. He said to Genevieve, "Why did you save Samuel last night?"

"We did not want to see him hurt."

Simon's brow furrowed. "I do not understand you people. This is not some game. You push us aside like animals, step on us like weeds. Do you expect me to be grateful to you for saving him from your own thugs?"

"I expect nothing," Genevieve said.

"Nothing is what you will get." But he did not seem to rest easy in that threat. In agitation he continued. "You dragged Yeshu away to your insane future so we could never see him again. Then you come back here for pleasure, to see Yeshu crucified. Is this sanity?"

"I'm not here to see him crucified," Owen said. "I think that's sick."

Simon looked down at his gun. "I would go, if only to see him again. Perhaps he could explain you to me. At least I could see a Jerusalem where you haven't ruined everything."

The phone beeped. Jephthah picked it up. "Yes," he said. Simon looked over at him, seemed about to go take the phone. Gen felt Owen's thigh tense under her hand. If Simon took his attention off Owen, that might be just the cue for Bill to attack.

"Where is your son now?" Gen asked Simon hastily.

Simon turned back to them. "I don't know. He was not a part of this, and I hope he is keeping himself hidden."

Across the room, Jephthah's voice was rising. He gripped the phone in his fist, shouting into the mouthpiece, then threw it against the wall.

"What's the matter?" Simon asked.

Jephthah scowled at him. "They say the hovercraft has broken down. The functioning craft were all sent to Salim, they say. The assault on the field left all of them damaged. They ask if we will take a van."

"A van?"

Jephthah stormed over to Simon. "Why are you surprised? They are toying with us, setting us up. When they attack, at whom will you be aiming that rifle? What will you be doing?"

"I will be dying, like you."

Jephthah cursed. "I saw you talking with this whore. Do you want her?"

"Do not insult me."

"You are the one who associates with these scum." He stormed back and forth in the room. "How did they know we were in here! You bungled it."

"It was Halam's job to wreck their security system. But the hotel AI must have a source of information not connected to the system."

"*You* are their source of information!"

"I am not."

"Prove it to me." He pointed at Gen. "Shoot her."

Simon said nothing. In the corner, the nervous Zealot boy watched. Bauer, awake now, raised his sleepy head. Owen shook off Gen's hand. She saw his eyes flick back and forth, measuring distances.

"This is mad," Simon said. "They will exterminate us."

With a whir, the air-conditioning came on again, and cool air blasted down from the vents in the ceiling. In the cool air came a pungent mist. Jephthah exclaimed and ducked, as if he could evade the gas by crouching. From the corridor a shout, and a dull concussion.

With her first whiff of the gas, Gen felt her mind sway. She grabbed for Owen. Instead Owen evaded her and grabbed the animal carrier. "Kill them. Kill them all!" Jephthah shouted.

Simon turned to the hostages. Owen swung the case toward him, skidding it across the floor, and Simon stumbled. Jephthah squeezed off a rifle-burst that riddled the carrier. Owen leapt forward, twisted, kicked the rifle from Jephthah's hands, whipped around and, graceful as a dancer, snapped his fiery red mood boot into Jephthah's kneecap. Jephthah's leg bucked and he fell.

More concussions from the corridor, and the lights went out. In the eerie glare of red emergency lamps, a couple of the Zealots straggled back into the room, falling to their knees as the sleep gas took hold. Owen whirled, swaying. Simon, facing Gen, raised his rifle.

Owen stood frozen for a second, his face contorted. Gen lost her balance and went down, feeling the heaviness in her limbs increase. Her cheek touched the cold tile floor. In slow motion, Owen lurched toward Simon. This time it looked like Bill was finally going to get someone killed. "Shoot her, shoot!" Jephthah, on the floor, gasped.

Simon raised his rifle, slipped his finger inside the trigger guard. His eyes glinted in the darkness, and Gen wondered who he saw when he looked at her. Owen threw himself between Gen and the rifle.

Simon let the gun drop, turned, took a step and fell over. Owen sprawled on the floor behind him. Gen noticed the blood, black in the red emergency light, seeping from the riddled carrier. Then she closed her heavy eyelids and fell asleep.

She was wakened by a gas-masked man in a hotel security uniform. It must have only been minutes later. He held his thumb on the inside of her elbow where he had just given her some injection. She was lying in the hallway. The lights were back on. The doors at the end of the corridor had been blown open and men in masks and mesh body armor were dragging the handcuffed terrorists aside, lining them up on the floor like cordwood. "Are you okay, ma'am?"

Owen pushed past the man. He bent over her. "Gen!"

"I'm okay. But your dinosaur!"

Owen looked sick.

"I'm so sorry. Maybe she's not hurt too badly," Gen said.

"That case looks pretty shot up," the security man said. Owen looked at the carrier. The pool of blood was larger. The sign, LIVE ANIMAL, scrolled around the top.

They heard a faint rustle from inside. "She's still alive!" Owen said. He stumbled over, opened the case.

Inside was a dying dog.

Chapter 12

Hail the Conquering Hero

The time stage was up again, for special purposes only. A curfew was imposed and tourists were confined to the hotel. Squads of Saltimbanque mercenaries from twelfth-century Spain, wearing desert uniforms, arrived and were posted to key spots in the city.

Right after the troops came a horde of media reps. Bauer, Gen, August and Owen were mobbed. August and Gen asserted their rights as privateers to remain unharassed by any electronic data-transmission system. The Saltimbanque Corporation, only too eager to minimize the negative publicity, backed them up. But they could not avoid scheduling a press conference.

Fortunately, they had Owen to take the heat. It turned out that, thanks to Bill's warning, the hotel had installed a video bug in Wilma's carrying case. The entire hostage crisis, including Owen's heroics, was captured on disk, and had already been released to the media. Once they found out he was the son of Ralph Siddhartha and Rosethrush Vannice, the hype doubled. When they discovered he was carrying with him the first live dinosaur to be retrieved from the past, the hype went exponential. The net hawks were ecstatic.

The afternoon edition of the *Herald Tribune* ran the vid of Owen shattering Jephthah's knee on the first page. A feature *Hollywood Grapevine* already had in the pipeline about Owen's mother was ripped apart to turn him into the lead. The Saltimbanque lawyers subpoenaed Owen's testimony for the trial of the Zealots. *Fiberoptic Life* wanted to re-create the hostage situation for their wireheads. The university frantically messaged him to find out whether the specimen was all right, and when Owen returned the call his v-mail log recorded 8,916 messages.

That evening's debate on "Historical Equivocators of the Future" degenerated into a shouting match between those who wanted to ship all the Zealots to some particularly unpleasant M-U, and defenders who called for stricter regulations on settlement of the past. Back in 2062 the twenty-three-year-old version of Jesus, contacted during a public-appearance tour about his knowledge of Simon and Jephthah, claimed he had never met the men. From his retreat in Costa Rica, the older version, Yeshu, would not comment.

Fresh out of the infirmary, Owen, the simulflesh bandage over his eye still a little tender, faced the press corps.

"How did it *feel* to be threatened with death?" a stringer from *Alternative Decay* asked him.

"Perhaps the Zealots were not really revolting," the reporter from *Moral Quietus* suggested to the head of Saltimbanque security. "After all, they could have been after Dr. Vannice's dinosaur."

"Isn't it true," the woman from *Secrets!* asked hotel manager Eustacia Toppknocker, "that one of the historicals on the hotel staff had seen the creature the previous day?"

"Sure, nobody was killed," the munitions editor from *Hour of Carnage* remarked wistfully, "but several of the Zealots were seriously wounded, and the hostages were put at risk."

"Was the counterassault even *necessary*?" asked Rupert Bignose of the *Times* op-ed page. "I blame the permissive policies of the 1960s."

The crime reporter from *PMLA* pressed Owen further. "If they were so intent on harming you, why didn't this Zealot Simon pull the trigger when he had the chance?"

When Owen got fuddled Bill whispered plausible answers in his ear and reminded him of the names of the reporters. He survived the tidal wave of attention, but somewhere in this madness lost track of Genevieve and August. Ms. Toppknocker agreed to let Owen keep Wilma in his rooms for the remainder of his stay, offered to wipe out his hotel bill and provide him with daily security.

Finally, exhausted, Owen made it back to his suite. He identified himself to the security guard, went inside and locked the door. Loosening his tie, he went to the bedroom reserved for Wilma. She was snoozing on a pallet of satin quilts. She had polished off several tubs of oatmeal. Owen crouched over her, and she lifted her head and nuzzled his neck. Her eyes looked clear. The pebbly scales of her head were warm and dry. He patted her until she settled down again, then closed the door and went to his own room.

For one thing, he had to change his boots. It seemed that in the assault on the kennel, some of the cages had come open. Dazed after his recovery from the sleep gas, Owen had stepped on a gerbil.

When he checked his logbook there was a message from his mother.

WHATEVER YOU DO, OWEN, DO <u>NOT</u> SELL YOUR STORY TO ANY MEDIA REPRESENTATIVE. TELL THEM FULL RIGHTS TO ANY MULTISENSUAL SIMULATION, REPRESENTATION, RECREATION, WORDS, PICTURES, EPIC POETRY, SUGGESTIONS, SPECULA-

TIONS OR THOUGHTS ABOUT OWEN BERESFORD VANNICE OR
ANY CREATURE IN HIS POSSESSION ARE THE SOLE PROPERTY
OF ATD PIX LTD.
NICE CROSS-KICK. FATHER SENDS HIS REGARDS.

ALWAYS YOUR AGENT,
MOM

Owen filed the message and hooked into the hotel system
to try to find out what had happened to Gen. This time the
Faisons were not even listed as guests.

"I wonder where they are?" he muttered.

=Skipped town as soon as they could.=

Owen remembered staring down the barrel of Simon's rifle,
unable to do anything more than watch helplessly as Bill
jerked him around like a puppet, believing that Wilma was shot
full of holes, that he would never get to see whether his experiment would work out, that he was going to die in a few
seconds—and all he could regret was that he would never kiss
Genevieve Faison again. Gen wouldn't leave without talking
to him; they had too much unfinished business. Her bravery
under the hostage ordeal was something he would never forget. A man and a woman who had gone through what they had
gone through together *couldn't* be kept apart. They could overcome any obstacle.

Besides, she had shown him how to dance.

How could he ever get back to normal? Prepare himself to
meet his parents, end the media circus and get back to work?
He took a shower to wash away any bugs the reporters might
have sprayed on him. He put on his pajamas, brushed his
teeth. The man in the mirror looked pretty much like the same
person he'd been the day before. He cursed himself for not
sticking with her after their rescue. But he knew he was going

to see her again. He'd spend whatever it took to find her.

When he went back out to the bedroom, Genevieve stood in the doorway.

"Gen!"

=Don't panic,= Bill said. =I'll alert security.=

"No!" Owen said.

"Is that no for me or for Bill?" Gen asked.

Owen pushed past her to look out into the suite's living room. How had she gotten in? "What happened? Where did you go? What are you doing here?"

Genevieve waited for him to calm down. Her auburn hair was down around her shoulders, and in the sideways light from the bedside lamp, Owen had never seen a more beautiful woman. "Did you think I could leave without seeing you again?" she asked.

"I was afraid so."

"Well, you were mistaken."

Owen kissed her. She melted in his arms. After some time she pulled herself away.

"Owen, I have one question," she said softly. "When Simon was about to shoot me, you threw yourself between me and him. An AIde would never do that, would he?"

=She's got *that* right, anyway.=

"No. That was my doing."

"What were you thinking?"

"I wasn't." He kissed her again. He couldn't tell how long this one lasted. His head spun, and he wondered if he was suffering some aftereffects of the sleep gas. Just before he passed out entirely, he forced himself to be responsible. He was not just some guy: he was Dr. Owen Vannice. He put his hands on Gen's shoulders, and held her at arm's length. "Genevieve, Genevieve—I want you to listen to what I've been trying to say to you since the dance."

=Good idea. Keep this in the talking stage.=

"First, I'm glad you're here," Owen said.

"I certainly *hope* so."

"Though it's unseemly—if anyone knew, it might ruin your reputation—"

=What reputation?=

"—and though we've known each other such a short time, I have felt an instinctive understanding between us from the first moment I saw you."

"Falling off the time-travel stage?"

"Well, right after, anyway. I'm a scientist, Genevieve, and I know about evolution. In their time, dinosaurs like Wilma were the highest expression of the biological tropism toward complexity. Some things are hardwired into our natures, and individuals can't go against them. We act out these scientific truths whether we are aware of them or not."

"You're talking about instincts."

=Don't say anything that could be construed as a legal commitment.=

Owen held her shoulders, looked deep within her eyes. "I'm talking about love, Gen. A kinship exists between us that may be young and undeveloped, like little Wilma, but like Wilma, it has in it the programming to become very large."

"And strong."

"Yes—very strong. Stronger than custom, or family, or thought itself. In the end, thinking doesn't have much to do with it."

=Thinking doesn't have much to do with *this,* at least. Your endocrine system's in a meltdown.=

"Be quiet, Bill."

=Marry in haste, repent at leisure.=

Owen found it hard to look into Gen's beautiful face and keep talking. Her perfume was faint but intoxicating. He imagined the lake and the *Apatosaurus* nests outside Vannice Station, and the words came back to him. "In this case, instinct brought me to an inescapable conclusion. We were meant to be together. So you're right. When I threw myself in front of that rifle I *wasn't* thinking. I haven't been thinking for the last three days! The best three days of my life."

There, he had said it. Now he had only to wait for her reaction.

Genevieve reached up and took his hands from her shoulders. His heart sank.

Without letting go, she pulled them around her waist. She pushed him toward the bed. "Maybe you should try not thinking more often."

"I—I like to think."

=I wouldn't brag too much about your ratiocination right now.=

"Thinking has its time and place." The backs of Owen's legs hit the bed and they fell over onto it. She pulled his pajama shirt off his shoulder.

"Then—you understand?" Owen asked.

"I *think* so."

"I'm—I'm sorry about your father's dog."

Gen propped herself up on her elbows to look him in the eyes. "Yes. That was sad, wasn't it? Now I have some things I want to say."

=I could have her in a half-nelson in a second, boss!=

"Don't do that," Owen said.

"You can't stop the eternal conversation, Owen." She kissed his cheek. Her hips pressed against his, the fabric of her dress rough against his chest, and he felt her warm breath against his cheek. "The conversation that's been going on between men and women since the beginning of time." She kissed the nape of his neck. "And we're part of it." She unbuttoned his shirt and kissed his chest. "Don't you feel like you're part of that conversation, now?"

"Conversation? I—I suppose so. Though I don't feel much like talking."

=I don't like your blood-pressure readings, boss! Heterosexual relationships that begin with high-intensity physical encounters inevitably face an early crisis.=

"Neither do I. But there's just one more thing I have to say, Owen."

Her perfume made his head spin. He wondered if she could feel his heart race against hers. "What's that?"

=I'm not kidding. Forty-seven percent of such encounters— =

She leaned still closer, and whispered in his ear. "Bill. Go away."

She reached out and turned off the light.

Chapter 13

The Awful Truth

When Genevieve came back to her room early the next morning, August was out. Humming to herself, she showered and dressed. She decided to wear her white dress with the broad hat. Why not white? She felt like a new woman.

August came in while she was adjusting the hat. "I don't suppose I ought to ask where you were last night."

She tugged the brim a little lower over her eye. "You know where I was."

"It's a lucky thing that he's drawn most of the media attention. But if you spend much time with him, some is going to rub off on us. I think we ought to leave as soon as they open up the time-travel stage for tourists."

Telling her father was something she had not planned out. It was harder than she imagined. "That makes a lot of sense," she said.

"You know I ought to be angry with you," August said. "For twenty years, nobody has crossed me as badly as you did yesterday."

Still she could think of nothing to say. August watched her. Finally he spoke. "You really love him, don't you."

Surprised, she said, "Yes, Dad, I really do."

August sat down on the dressing-table chair. He looked tired. "You know it will be hard, loving that young man."

"He's just naive. He hasn't seen much of the real world."

"He's too old to be naive. These permanently innocent types can have a nasty side."

She turned. "What do you mean?"

"How do you think he's going to react when he finds out your profession?"

"I'm not going to keep any secrets. I'm meeting him for breakfast, and I'm going to tell him."

"I hope he loves you as much as you love him."

"Oh, August, stop fretting. I want you to have dinner with us tonight. We'll talk it all over. There's no need for you to continue living this way, you know. You're going to end up all alone, in some hotel, practicing three-card monte."

August stood, tugged his jacket straight, turned away from her. "What makes you think, just because you've gone soft-headed, that I want to give up my career? I was conning marks before you were a gleam in your mother's eye, and I'll be doing it after you've been buried under a pile of Junior Leaguers—a fate, I might add, that strikes me as rather worse than death."

She came over to him, made him look at her. "I'm sorry. I had no right to say that to you. But I'm going to tell him, nonetheless."

August wouldn't meet her eyes. "I knew this day would come, but I didn't think it would come like this. All I can say is, I hope he understands how lucky he is. And for you—I hope it's a hell of a ride."

He smiled. "And I suppose that after I give the bride away, I can sell his relatives some stock in our fifth-century platinum mine."

"I'd like that." She kissed him on the cheek, squared her

shoulders and headed for the restaurant, trying hard not to run.

In the lobby soldiers guarded the entrance. A trooper stood conspicuously beside the main desk. Gen hurried out to the atrium restaurant. It was another beautiful day. The morning sun was bright and the air cool.

She found Owen at a secluded table in the plaza, screened by foliage, reading a newspaper. He wore dark glasses, as if that would keep the media away. Watching him from the doorway, she had to smile. The skin above his damaged eyebrow was pulled tight. She could not get over the fact that Owen had thrown himself in front of a rifle for her. Not that it had much to do with her. It had more to do with his absurd romantic notion of who she was. It made her both nervous and giddy. How much fun it was to knock him over and jump on him, tease him out of his coma, wake him into himself. What an enthusiastic amateur he had been in bed.

When he saw her coming he jumped up. He took her hand, kissed her cheek. "How are you?"

"It's not every day I get to have breakfast with a spy."

Owen looked puzzled, then smiled and took off the glasses. "A dumb idea, huh?"

"You look handsome in them. Mysterious."

He stared at her. "The mystery is that you're with me."

Gen smiled. They ordered breakfast. While they waited for it, Gen stared at the tablecloth. She played with her fork against the fabric, trying to get up her nerve. How much harder this was than almost anything she had had to do before. She knew Owen was watching.

"What's the matter, Genevieve? Have I done something wrong?"

She looked up at him, smiled. "No. Excuse me, I need to freshen up."

"You look wonderful already."

"Now don't you be fresh. I'll be right back." Gen fled toward the ladies' room.

=We taking odds on whether she comes back?=

"Of course she's coming back," Owen said. "Why wouldn't she?"

=She showed every physical sign of concealed stress.=

"That's two of us, then." Owen was relieved to think Gen might be as nervous around him as he was around her.

=You're nervous because you like her. We don't know what she's hiding.=

"Why can't you accept that she's attracted to me for who I am?" he said. "You're supposed to be an advisor, not a lead weight tied around my self-confidence."

=I'm supposed to watch out for you.=

"I'm not eight years old anymore. If I can't look out for myself now, I never will."

At the next table, watching Owen, sat a stout man with dark hair. Probably some reporter hoping to eavesdrop his way into an exclusive. Owen tried to ignore him, but the man kept staring. Had Owen been talking to Bill aloud again?

Finally Owen decided he might as well face him. "Is this your first time-travel vacation?" Owen asked.

The man did not seem taken aback. "No. I've done a lot of time touring. You might say I'm very experienced."

"I've never done any touring proper," Owen said. "I've spent most of my time on research."

"So you never met that woman I just saw you with before?"

"Why do you ask?"

"Because I did. In the eighteenth century, she swindled me."

"You're mistaken."

"What does she call herself—Gabrielle Tourtereau? She's a con artist. She and her partner, an older guy, gray hair, looks to be in his fifties. And as soon as she comes back, I'm going to turn the bitch in."

Owen sat up straighter. "Sir, I don't know who you are, but you had better watch your mouth. This woman is my fiancée. I traveled with her myself, from the future."

"Then you must be her accomplice."

"My name is Owen Beresford Vannice. I have a private fortune of six trillion dollars. I don't hang around with confidence men. And if you keep this up I'll have the management throw you out of this place."

"Well, don't get huffy. It's your funeral, if you want to play games with that little trollop. But when she takes you and your six trillion for a ride, don't say I didn't warn you." The man took out his wallet, pulled a card from inside and tossed it toward Owen. Owen caught it, awkwardly.

"When you get tired of being taken, read that." He crumpled his linen napkin onto his plate, and left.

The card was a electronic file. The label read SALTIMBANQUE TEMPORAL SECURITY.

=Do you want me to say anything?= Bill whispered.

"No."

A con artist. She couldn't be. But then Owen thought some more, and the scaffolding of euphoria he'd been climbing for the last few days began to feel shaky. *Learn to pretend*, she'd told him! But the dancing, the trip to the club, the brush of her hair on his cheek?

Just remember, she'd said, *I'm smarter than you are.*

He ejected the newscard from his paper and inserted the electronic file. He paged past the intro to the first image. It was a photo of Genevieve and August, seated on a sunny plaza overlooking a beach. Beneath it:

August Alexander Faison, aka Colonel Alexander Harrington, aka Sir Alfred McGlennan-Keith, aka Arthur

Greenbaum, age fifty-three, and his daughter Genevieve Faison, aka Jean Harrington, aka Eve Sedgwick, aka Gabrielle Tourtereau, age twenty-eight, on the esplanade in 1926 Cannes. Bunko, short and long confidence games, fraud, theft . . .

Owen turned it off; the card slid out.

The waiter returned and set out their breakfast: eggs, sausage, melon slices, croissants and two perfect glasses of Galilean orange juice. Owen pushed the juice away. "Get me a vodka. A double."

The waiter left.

How coolly she had drawn him in. Why not? He was easy pickings. All the time teasing him along, setting him up. That comedy of errors with Wilma, aborted by the terrorist raid. And he had risked his life for her.

He was going to ask her to marry him.

Images of the last three days flooded back to him, and he began to feel ill. His lectures on dinosaurs, his theories, his plans. Genevieve must have been torn between tedium and laughter. He was just a mark, a fool to be mocked and used. And last night? He stared at the table, blinking back tears.

The waiter brought back the vodka, and he drank a couple of gulps. It burned going down. He was a bumbling clown, a man with dinosaur dung on his boots, a clumsy oaf who stepped on small animals. How could he have imagined that a woman like her would really be attracted to him? It was a bitter joke.

"Mighty early for strong spirits, Professor. What will your dancing instructor say?"

He looked up and there she was, impossibly beautiful. White dress swirling around her legs, the broad white hat pulled low over one eye. He looked away. "I felt like a drink."

His head spun, swept by a mix of emotions so strong he felt

the corners of his eyes burn. He saw her lying in his bed. How she must have laughed with August when she'd gotten back to her room. How sure she must have been that she'd had him on the hook. What a fool he'd been. He belonged back in the Cretaceous, waiting for the asteroid to blow him to bits.

She touched his arm. He did not look at her.

"It's a beautiful day," she said. "After breakfast, let's go for a walk. I have something I want to tell you."

"I'd love to hear what you have to tell me," Owen said.

Gen put her hat on the table. "What's wrong, Owen?"

"Absolutely nothing. Everything is perfect. It's a beautiful morning in 40 A.D." He played with the card in his hand.

"What's that?"

"This? It's just evidence of—of a historical discovery."

"A discovery?"

"That's right. We've discovered something about the women of the past that we did not know."

Genevieve looked sober. "You can't always trust initial findings. What they mean depends on your point of view."

"The researcher who gave me this says I can trust his point of view. He's not suffering under any illusions. Shall we run it through the newsreader?"

She saw the label on the card. The silence stretched, and Owen waited, hoping for Gen to deny it, to say she could not imagine what he was talking about. Instead she gave the tiniest of sighs. "Oh," she said.

"It's full of interesting material," Owen said. "Very revealing."

"When did you get this?"

He turned to her. She was achingly beautiful. Her eyes glistened. "Two days ago. Before the dance."

"Before the dance? Why didn't you say anything?"

"I wanted to see just how far you would go. It gave me the advantage. That's what it's all about, isn't it?"

"I can't believe last night was just an act."

"You can't? You're the one who told me to try pretending. I've been pretending."

For a moment she didn't say anything.

"Owen, I know you're hurt." Gen's voice was husky. "I'm sorry. Maybe in the beginning I was pretending, too—but not now. Not last night."

"I'm not stupid, Ms. Faison—if that's your real name. You're not the first woman after my family's money."

"Don't say anything you know isn't true, Owen. I came here this morning to tell you."

"Don't bother. I've already gotten what I wanted from you."

He stopped, pulled out his wallet, stuck in a blank e-cash chip and typed in some code. He pulled out the chip and slipped it into her purse. "Here's thirty thousand dollars. It's not too much to pay for the services you rendered. The dog must not have come cheap."

She stood up, picked up her hat. He tried not to notice the tears in her eyes. But her voice was cold. "Does it give you pleasure to pretend that you tricked me?" He would not meet her look. She tried to make him face her, but he just turned his shoulder.

"You must be quite a child to want to hurt me so bad," Genevieve said. "Maybe you did trick me after all."

She clutched her purse and walked back through the colonnade into the lobby. He sat watching through the palms long after she was gone. He finished the vodka. Their breakfast went cold on the table. While he watched, some soldiers led the captive Zealots past the entrance, trailing a cloud of video midges and a horde of reporters. One of the reporters spotted Owen and made a beeline for the table.

Chapter 14

Nothing Sacred

He was small dark man with a patchy beard. Blood streamed down his naked back. A dog nipped at his heels as he dragged the wooden beam over the cobbles, prodded by a stony-faced centurion. Some Sadducees and Pharisees walked behind, imperial and sober. Afterward came a couple more soldiers and a gaggle of hecklers. An adolescent girl stood to the side, hands at her sides, silently weeping. Far off, Owen heard the barking of yet another dog. Their tour guide was paying more attention to keeping his charges out of the way than to the spectacle. In a minute the procession had passed. Beside Owen a matron with hennaed hair stood openmouthed. She played with her wristward, disguised as a gold bracelet, turning it over and over. "He's so *short*," she said to her husband.

"So?"

"Can't we do anything?"

"This is just history, Margaret," her husband said. "Get hold of yourself."

The tour was a mixed bag of the overeducated and skeptical, the unconventionally mystical and the plain loony. Since the first visitors to the crucifixion had discovered that Jesus did not rise from the dead, that in fact the Gospels, though in some ways remarkably accurate accounts of the life of a great spiritual teacher, were not the biography of a superhuman god-being in human form, few believers desired to witness this brutal execution. They were happier with the Christ of two thousand years of after-the-fact fabrications. For surprisingly many, the discovery of the facts behind the Gospels had had no effect whatsoever on their faith. Time travel, they said, was a delusion, and this Jesus who suffered and died in other moment universes bore no connection to the true Son of God.

What that meant was that the ones who went to see Jesus were not the conventionally religious. Instead you got historians, amateur and otherwise, a mixed bag of Unitarians and liberal Protestants, a few Zen Buddhists and postmillennial philosophers. Jesus: the attraction for secular humanists.

And for brokenhearted paleontologists, waiting to go home, dodging reporters and seeking to swamp their humiliation in some greater tragedy. The Zealot Simon had spoken of the crucifixion as something that might give him peace. For Owen it wasn't working. The tour guide led them to Golgotha by a back way. This Jerusalem had no electric lights, no amusement parks, no soldiers with automatic rifles, no hovercraft. Noon had been warm and dusty, but as the day wore on a storm front came through and dropped the temperature fifteen degrees, bringing with it blustery winds, clouds, the threat of rain.

On Golgotha stood four crosses. There was no colloquy between the dying prisoners, no lightning in the skies. When the soldiers came by to break the legs of the crucified men so that they might die before the Passover evening, they discovered that Yeshu was already gone. He'd died silently, without protest or consolation.

The guide led them back to the gathering point. When they had all assembled, he used the portable travel unit to translate them back to the time-colonized Jerusalem.

In the midst of this, all Owen could think about was Gen.

As they left the transfer room they passed the main time-travel stage. It bustled with activity, at last up and running for hotel guests to return to the future. And there stood August and Gen, with their luggage, waiting at the customs desk to be shot forward in time. It was time for Owen to pack up Wilma and go back himself. He ducked his head and hoped they did not see him.

Kyle Johnston had been the first boy she had ever loved. August and Genevieve had been living in Frankfurt, where August was involved in an import-export business that pushed the fringes of legality. For one of the few times in her life Gen was able to attend a regular school.

Kyle was the son of an American business couple from Minneapolis. He had the most beautiful brown hair, parted in the middle and hanging to his shoulders, and pale flawless skin. He was the handsomest boy Gen had ever seen, and she had fallen in love with him from a distance. When eventually she worked up the nerve to speak to him, she was overwhelmed to find that he liked her. They would spend nights in the park by the river, or hanging out in the maglev station playing tricks on the tourists. Gen taught him the gypsy switch. Kyle's American good looks let him get away with murder, even brought people to him as if they were looking to get taken.

The moment they got caught, Kyle abandoned her. He told his parents that it had all been Gen's idea. She remembered how, while she'd hung her head in shame, he'd coolly sat there and lied to the authorities. It was all August could do to talk them out of sending her to a social treatment center, and as a result they'd had to leave town.

She'd cried for what seemed like hours on the train to Switzerland, August holding her hand, brushing her hair. "He doesn't know you," August kept repeating. "He knows nothing about you. You're worth ten of his sort." Eventually she'd fallen asleep. After a month she never thought of him anymore.

Until now. Genevieve and August stood waiting at the customs desk for their turn at the transit stage. While they waited, a crucifixion tour group returned from one of the unburned Jerusalems. Among them was Owen. Gen spotted him immediately, but he ducked his head to avoid her gaze. She let him pass without a word.

"When I think of the way that jerk treated me . . ." Gen said.

August put his arm around her shoulders. "A completely heartless act takes a lifetime of preparation."

The customs officer passed them through, and the steward carried their bags to the stage. "Oh, Father," Gen whispered, "I'm such a mess."

"We are all messes, more or less. I would say that that young man is on his way to becoming a particularly pathetic sort of bad man. But no less infuriating for his pathos."

"The worst thing is that he doesn't know it. He thinks he's the abused party."

"That's almost the definition of a bad man."

"When I think of the way he looked at me as he handed me that cash. . . ."

August turned her away from the technicians inside the booth, made her look him in the eyes. "We must spend it on something that he would not approve."

"Someday I'm going to hurt him. You wait."

"Someday. For now, trust me, it's better to let it go," August said. "And if you can't trust a grifter, who can you trust?"

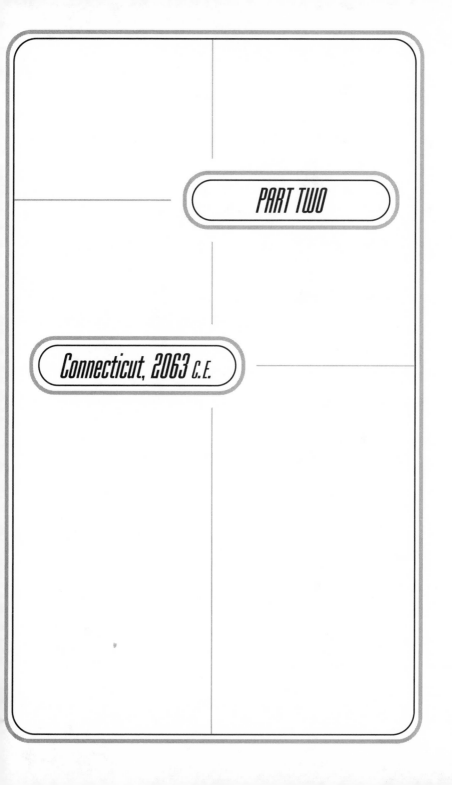

PART TWO

Connecticut, 2063 c.e.

Chapter 1

Easy Living

Owen crept down the back stairs and out through the kitchen, trying to avoid his parents. The staff was already up, preparing breakfast, but they knew enough not to pay attention. He slipped out the kitchen door and down the exterior staircase to the grounds.

Built early in the twentieth century so the rich might flee pre-air-conditioned New York for a month in rural Connecticut, Thornberry, the Vannice summer home, had once been a resort. The big Frank Lloyd Wright–ish house offered sixteen bedrooms, an open family room with a huge fieldstone fireplace and a cantilevered verandah that ran along the entire rear of the house. Century-old oaks and pines lined the estate's shady lanes, and a golf course's worth of lawn rolled down to the shore of the sound. About the grounds of the estate nestled three guest houses and a dozen cabins, a dock and boathouse. And the greenhouse, which Owen had expanded and turned into Wilma's quarters: although global warming had pushed the shoreline fifty yards closer to the house, winter nights could still get chilly.

Owen walked down the paved road toward the greenhouse. It was a cool morning, and a mist rose from the water. Most mornings he liked to give Wilma a break from confinement to roam the estate, but that had not worked out too well for the landscaping. Wilma had stripped most of the conifers up to twenty feet, with the higher reaches of foliage in imminent peril. The lilac bushes that had once lined the north border of the estate were memory. Her right front footprint was permanently indented into the service line of the tennis court, and the next time she got into the swimming pool they'd not only have to drain it, but replace half the tiles.

Owen's parents were after him to move Wilma elsewhere. Twice she had poked her head into second-story windows of the big house, terrifying guests. Uncle Suede claimed he would never sleep another quiet night. It wasn't the money, Owen's father insisted. It was the psychological upkeep.

As soon as Owen entered the new end of the greenhouse— a large stresslar frame over which a single-molecule plastic sheath had been grown—Wilma came crashing toward him through the palms.

=Here we go again,= Bill muttered.

Owen unfolded the quilt that one of Wilma's fans had sent, decorated with a huge blue WILMA. He gathered it together and tried to throw it over her, but the dinosaur kept turning to face him and the quilt kept sliding off.

"Stay still!" Owen shouted. "We'll play later."

Wilma was two meters tall at the shoulder, and coming up on three metric tons. When she stood up on her hind legs and stretched out her neck, her head shattered panes in the old greenhouse roof. Owen was beginning to worry that his theory about the dependence of altricial growth rates on degree of nurturing was not going to be borne out by experiment. Or perhaps he was not taking enough care of her—though he did not see how he could do better without getting himself stepped on.

As if thought were mother to action, Wilma lurched sideways, threatening to smash Owen against the climate-control unit. Bill took over, and Owen dove between her legs, did a quick roll and came to his feet on her opposite side. =Try not to get us killed, boss.=

"That's your job," Owen muttered. Owen hated to admit he was glad he had not had Bill removed. He could not get past the fact that, although Bill's martial-arts frenzy back in Jerusalem might have gotten Owen killed, his alerting the hotel security system the previous night had saved Owen's life. So Owen merely complained to his father about Bill's growing eccentricities, and Ralph Vannice ordered a little corrective programming that, for the moment at least, had gotten rid of Bill's sex and God obsession.

While Wilma was trying to locate Owen on her wrong side, he flipped the quilt over her back and cinched it around her neck and tail. He led her down to the big doors at the other end of the greenhouse and out into the paddock. A gaggle of genetically altered lawn geese scattered at the sight of her, but soon resettled into new programs as they tracked over the estate, keeping the grass eaten down to a half-inch. Unlike Wilma, they would only defecate in designated offal areas.

Owen scanned the skies for helicopters. If there was a pix boat on the sound, it was out of sight. The media barrage had died down, but he could never tell when some infotainment special might want to do an update on the world's only live dinosaur. He did not want to advertise the disruption of the past he'd caused by bringing Wilma forward in time. It was not a consideration he would have had before his return. For the nine-hundredth time he thought about Genevieve.

The past year had been difficult. He hated being back home. To parents you never aged past seventeen; it was a struggle to maintain any control over your life. The worst of it was that you started to *act* as if you were still seventeen, answering questions in monosyllables, spending hours in your room with the door closed, sneaking down the back stairs like a secret agent.

His hopes of returning quietly to the university had been dashed when during his first paleontology lecture a protester had doused him with smart paint that spelled out *time exploiter* on his chest. It had been unrealistic for him to expect no fallout in the aftermath of the Jerusalem raid and the notoriety Wilma had brought. He'd tried to continue his experiment at Thornberry, but there he had to contend with his parents' expectations. His father reminded him constantly how much money had been spent on the Cretaceous research station, with veiled threats to cut off its funds if no way to make it pay off could be found.

His mother was almost as bad. Her intentions for him combined romantic entanglements with media extravaganzas, so that Owen was not sure whether she was more interested in getting him married off, or in broadcasting the wedding, complete with footage of Wilma towing a wedding carriage, to a billion subscribers of ATD Pix.

From the walk-in cooler Owen got a wheelbarrow-load of orchids and dumped them into the stainless-steel washtub that Wilma used for a food dish. The sweet smell of vanilla perfumed the air. Though the dinosaur came from a period before the advent of flowering plants, Owen had discovered that she required a variety of nectar unavailable in the twenty-first century except from the *Orchidaceae*, in particular the *Vanilla fragrans*. Wilma would not settle for vanilla extract, so at six hundred dollars a day, orchids were the cheapest supply. Owen hauled a sack onto his shoulder, pulled the drawstring and poured oats in with the orchids, then mixed them with a spade.

The apatosaur fell to her breakfast. Oats dribbled out of the corners of her mouth as she ground them between her pencil-like teeth. Owen liked to watch the contemplative expression on her face as she chewed her food. She ran through the tub in a few minutes, then snuffled at its bottom, blowing air through her high nostrils and sucking up the dregs. "All gone, girl," Owen said, and opened the gate at the end of the paddock to let Wilma out onto the grounds.

The dinosaur trotted out, whipping her slender tail a meter off the ground. Owen tried to lead her up the slope, but Wilma headed for the sound. The air was warming: the mist had already burned off the water. He followed Wilma down the edge of the road toward the shore. She did not like to walk on the road, and had given the gardener fits trying to maintain the perennials that lined it.

When they were halfway down, passing the guest cottages, a voice called out to him. "Dr. Vannice!"

Jeeves, the household robot, jogged down toward Owen from the house. He had developed a limp. Jeeves was one of his parents' expensive playthings: humanoid robots were totally impractical.

Jeeves stumbled to a stop. Ornamental lights winked on his brushed silver chest. "Dr. Vannice," the robot said. "Your mother wishes to speak with you."

"I'm not coming to her party."

"Yes, sir. She asked me to inform you this is not about your inadequate social life," Jeeves said calmly.

Owen wished his mother wouldn't insult him in front of the help. Hearing Jeeves's voice, Wilma came to a dead stop in the last of the American Beauty roses. She was fascinated by Jeeves. Though Jeeves was wary of her, he was not nimble enough to protect himself. She whipped her tail around. Owen hopped over it, but it caught the robot at the ankles and toppled him flat on the lawn.

"Wilma, no!" Owen shouted.

Jeeves labored to stand, then backed off a few steps. "Very good, sir. Shall I report that you are coming?" A piece of sod was stuck to his grille.

"I'll come in a minute," Owen said.

"Your mother will be pleased, sir. She awaits in the north parlor."

There wasn't much point in dragging it out. An hour alone wouldn't hurt Wilma. He followed the butler back up the hill toward the house. Above the verandah the windows gleamed in the morning sun.

Owen came in through the basement level entrance and went up to the north parlor. To his dismay, both of his parents were there. His father sat in his tall leather wing-backed chair, wearing a mid-twentieth-century business suit, with vest. A white cat slept on his lap, sniffing at the plate of breakfast steaks beside him. More of his father's protein obsession.

Ralph Siddhartha Vannice looked twenty years older than he had the day before, gray hair slicked back from a high forehead. His skin was darker. "Owen, my son," he said, "what have we done to make you treat us with such disrespect?" He scratched the cat behind the ears.

"Excuse me, Dad? Disrespect?" Clearly Ralph had been sampling some new Vannicom personality template. His voice was all raspy.

"Your mother and I call you on serious business, and we expect you to come. You keep us waiting."

"But I came right away!"

"If you paid more attention to the family business, you would know we need to speak with you, and would have been here already."

"Business? What business?"

A look of injured dignity crossed his father's face. He turned to Owen's mother. "Rose, what are we going to do with this boy?"

"Enough of the simulation, Ralph. It's very good, though." Rosethrush Rigsby Vannice wore her Academy of Motion Picture Arts and Sciences Eisenhower jacket, riding skirt and calf-length boots. She leaned against the mantel, rested a foot on one of the massive logs beside the fireplace, and tapped her riding crop against the top of the fire screen. In an age where the wives and daughters of the wealthy had widely reassumed the retiring habits of the Victorian era, Owen's mother was a stunning exception.

"Owen," she said. "Your father and I have a couple of propositions we'd like to discuss with you."

Owen sat on the Civil War–era horsehair sofa, the most uncomfortable piece of furniture in the house.

"We're on the verge of getting the exclusive rights to the Zealot trials," his mother said. "We're hoping to foster the biggest legal extravaganza since the Pope tried to sell Saint Peter's. And you can help us. You and Wilma are the poster children of time exploitation."

"I'm not an exploiter."

"Yes, dear, we know that. But the public at large has a different impression."

Owen looked at his mood boots. They were a melancholy violet. "When does this start?"

"We expect the contract between Saltimbanque and LEX to be signed by next month."

"I don't see why you can't keep us out of the press, Mother. You know I hate it."

"If you truly cared about our feelings, Owen, you'd at least do an interview on *Hour of Carnage*."

Owen cast his glance about the room, trying to avoid his mother's gaze. This was a mistake. Beside him on the end table was a frozen head. His mother had bought up the stock when the cryonics companies had gone belly-up in the wave of post-war bankruptcies, and had turned them to a profit by leasing the frozen dead as *objets d'art*. There was not a trendy apartment in Manhattan that did not have a corpsicle as a conversation piece. His mother had them fitted with microsystems to maintain the hard freeze within their transparent cases, and an AI in each base programmed with the biographical information the cryoclients had carefully preserved at the time of their deaths. You could turn them on and hold a conversation with the deceased.

Theirs was named Morgan. As a boy Owen had been so scared of Morgan he had avoided going into the living room by himself, and even now he felt uneasy sitting next to it. But the torture his parents put him through made him want to annoy them back. Owen thumbed the switch and a snotty British voice came out of the speaker. "Hello. My name is Morgan. I was a writer and controversialist. I will be alive after you are dead, you pathetic loser."

"You are already dead," Ralph Vannice said.

"Check back in three hundred years."

Ralph Vannice was amused by the head's pluck. "Morgan, you are my favorite piece of furniture."

"Maybe you'd like it better if I had Morgan's personality," Owen said.

"This is what I mean by disrespect," his father rasped. "Son, no one cares about your personality. You may have no interest in the family business, but even you might have noticed that body-shaping has become a major profit center." Ralph Vannice set down the cat, brushed the knee of his suit. He was visibly shifting out of character. "SomatoDream nets eight billion a quarter twanking the ugly into the beautiful. But the next phase is going to be radical gene-shaping. Already some people aren't content to make themselves into Cary Grant. They want to be an eagle, an angel, a six hundred-pound gorilla."

"What has this got to do with me?"

"Imagine it, Owen," his father said. "We don't just give them a chance to be a celebrity, we give them the opportunity to become a *dinosaur*. There's not a high school boy in Connecticut who wouldn't give his eyeteeth to be a velociraptor. It would have helped if you'd brought back a meat eater, but this brontosaurus is a start. We clip a few genes and give the public the thrill of knowing what it's like to be a genuine thunder lizard! It can't miss."

"But Dad, you know that I'm against messing with Wilma's genes. That's why we haven't cloned her."

His mother joined in. "You steal her out of her era, but you won't take a few *cells* from her." She rested the riding crop against the rack of fireplace tools. "This trial raises important legal issues. The chronoprotection people want to get real restrictions on exploiting the past. If they get their way they won't let you study dinosaurs in their natural era, let alone bring them into the present."

"Maybe I agree with them."

"The people who drove you out of your university?" his mother said. "If you don't let us strike back, we're going to lose this fight, and you'll lose Wilma with it."

"I'll think about it," Owen said.

"You should do more than think." Ralph Vannice ran a hand through his hair, and sighed. His mother exchanged a look with him, then, like a tag-team wrestler, resumed the assault.

"Owen, when was the last time that you had a date?"

"*Mother—*"

"I want you to get out of the house. It's unnatural for a man of your age to spend his time with a dinosaur."

"You're our only child, Owen," his father said. "We don't want our genetic information withering on the vine." He held the plate of breakfast steaks out to Owen. "Are you getting enough *protein*, son?"

Owen was going to have to put up a fight or he would be reduced to a heap of pencil shavings on the fine oak floor. "My vine is not withering, Dad, thank you. Given how hard it is to get a divorce these days, you ought to be glad I'm being careful who I marry."

"Can't you just get some girl pregnant?" Ralph said.

"Mother, how can you let him say that? It goes against everything you've taught me."

"We should never have sent him to that finishing school, Rose. I think they finished him."

"I really can't see why this is any of your business," Owen said. "You could just as easily generate a new child yourselves. Pick out just the traits you want, engineer him to be dutiful and stupid."

"Now he's angry," Rosethrush said. "Come here, son."

"Mom, please."

"Is Dr. Nice going to throw a tantrum?"

Reluctantly, Owen went to her. She pulled his head down, hugged him to her chest. The battle ribbons she'd won chairing the Academy's ratings board were rough against his cheek. "You know we love you, Owen. We have only your best interests—plus those of several multitrillion-dollar commercial enterprises—at heart. So I want—"

Jeeves limped to the door. "I beg your pardon, madam. A phone call for Dr. Vannice."

Owen thanked the gods. "I'd better get that," he said.

"Can't you have your simulant take it?" his mother asked.

Learn to pretend. "Dr. Pemberton at the college is supposed to call me about setting up a habitat for Wilma. You want her out of here, don't you?"

His mother looked disappointed. "Take it on the screen in my study," she said.

As he passed the verandah he could see Wilma down by the waterside ripping shingles off the boathouse. He headed for the phone in his mother's office. "Yes?" he said, hitting the display key.

A woman appeared on the screen. It was Genevieve Faison. Owen swallowed hard and sat down. "Genevieve!"

"Pardon me?"

"Genevieve, don't pretend you don't remember."

"My name is not Genevieve, it is Emma Zume. I represent the Committee to Protect the Past. Are you Dr. Owen Vannice?"

"The Committee to Protect the Past?"

=Don't believe her, boss.=

"I am calling to urge you to meet with our organization regarding your removal of a dinosaur from its natural habitat for commercial exploitation."

=Make her prove who she is.=

"I'll find out who she is," Owen subvocalized. To the woman on the screen he said, "I'll need some proof that you are who you say you are."

"If you'll check your mail, you'll find my bona fides, certified by Electronic Vouchers Limited."

Owen called up his mailbox on a window, and sure enough, the top item was a bonded identification file for Emma Amelia Zume.

"Ms. Zume, I've never heard of your committee. But you are about the fiftieth chronological protection activist to pester me about what is a scientific experiment, not an attempt to exploit the past. Personally, I am all for a 'Hands Off the Past' policy. If you'll give me your address I'll even send you a contribution. Other than that we have nothing to talk about."

A flush crossed the woman's cheeks. It was a beautiful face, and the resemblance to Genevieve Faison was uncanny. There was something more formal about her manner, however. Her hair was much longer than Gen's, piled up on the top of her head in a fractal snarl. And her eyes seemed different. But if his father had customers twanking themselves into gorillas, Owen was not going to be taken in by some elementary ruse.

"I ask you in all simplicity, and with goodwill," Emma Zume said, "to put aside your greed and think about the welfare of this animal. Your fame won't last forever. Consult your conscience."

=This is ripe, boss, her telling *you* to consult your conscience. Hang up.=

It was good advice. "I'm not interested in money," Owen said. "And I'd rather be dead than famous."

"If you're not interested in money, then why is this creature's image all over ATD's tabloid pix shows? Why does every gang have a flag replaying your assault on the Zealots? Why does *Hemisphere Confidential Report* call you 'Professor Extinction'? 'The Paleontologist Plutocrat'? 'Feet of Death'?"

"Jerusalem led to a lot of publicity that, believe me, I did not want."

"Even though ATD Pix bankrolled your 'experimental' research station in the Cretaceous to the tune of fifty billion dollars?"

"That money was a personal gift from my mother. There were no quid pro quos. ATD did not even know my intention to retrieve this specimen from the past."

=You're arguing on her ground, Owen. Don't rise to her bait.=

Emma Zume's eyes misted up. "Taking this creature from the Cretaceous violates the natural temporal order. How can you expect anyone who has a respect for the Tao to be other than deeply skeptical of your motives?"

"I certainly understand your point of view, Ms. Zume. I'm only interested in understanding that natural order, not exploiting it."

"If that's so, are you willing to let a team from our organization inspect the conditions under which you're keeping this dinosaur? Are you willing to certify that you will not use her for commercial purposes? Are you willing, at the end of this so-called experiment, to return this specimen to its own era?"

She was pushing too hard. Bill was right. Why should Owen argue with her on her premises? "Let's forget this charade," he said. "You know that we've met before."

That stopped her.

=At last,= whispered Bill.

"Possibly," the woman finally said. "Were you at the Historicals for the Future rally in Rio last year? Or the Gaian Planet Bake-off at Mount Shasta?"

"No. I was thinking Jerusalem, first century."

"I do not time-travel. It's a matter of principle with me."

Owen calculated furiously. "Listen, I might be willing to allow your committee to inspect Wilma's surroundings—if it's represented by you."

=What, are you crazy? Hang up.=

Owen needed to shut Bill up. "Be quiet and listen," he subvocalized. "Pay attention to her every move. I have a plan."

Emma Zume looked wary. "It's much more likely we will send our Mr. Thrillkiller."

"No deal, then. It has to be you."

"Why?"

"Let's just say I want to get to know you better."

Emma Zume smiled an unhumorous smile. "Don't think you're going to get anywhere with me. This is strictly a matter of principle, not a social visit."

"I wouldn't think of it, Ms. Zume."

"I'll tell you right now, I'm an active supporter of the sexual deliberation movement."

"I respect that decision. I think it's a wise one."

She paused. "When can we arrange for our visit?"

Owen called up his calendar. "How about Wednesday at three?"

"We'll be there."

"I'll look forward to meeting you," Owen said.

"Dr. Vannice, if you are as good as your word, you will receive my personal apology," Emma Zume said, and rang off.

Owen pushed back from the phone screen, got up and went to the window. Wilma had come back up the hill, broken through the hedge, and was wallowing in the swimming pool. A half-hour ago Owen would have been dismayed, but now his mind was elsewhere. Emma Zume—whoever she was—had turned the day around.

=Positively the same dame,= Bill said.

"You think so?" Owen said. "Well, we're going to find out. Help me come up with a disguise."

Chapter 2

Two-faced Woman

A windowboard in Times Square flashed a big head-and-shoulders of Jesus hugging an adorable fluorescent-orange puppy. The copy followed:

> Miracle Dog!
> HIS Favorite—Why Not Yours?

This was the twenty-three-year-old Jesus, riding his charisma for all it was worth, oblivious to the advice of his older avatars. The ad reminded Genevieve of Max, the apartment in Toronto and her mother. She wondered if her mother was still alive.

Gen passed a man dressed in a tattered ruff and codpiece, playing a harmonica, an upturned hat in front of him. Times Square was full of displaced historicals. This would never be allowed in the privately run areas of Manhattan. The city government was looking for some corporation to sponsor midtown, but so far nobody had bitten.

She took the escalator down to the Times Square station, ran her ward over the turnstile sensor and stepped onto the platform. RECLAIM THE FUTURE! blared a poster pushing the upcoming metric conversion. But the poster crawled with smart paint spelling out anti-metric slogans. As she watched it switched from LITERS ARE LAME! to CENTIMETERS SUCK!

A couple of businessmen with discreet corporate logos embroidered on the shoulders of their dark suits made way for her. Gen had pulled her broad-brimmed hat below one eye, but her spotless white gloves and ankle-length dress of watered silk proved she was a lady. She had let her hair grow long, reddened it slightly; today it was pinned up, a few wisps curling past her ears.

The uptown train arrived. A man in a four-button suit stood to offer her his seat. Across from her sat a teenaged girl wearing a video shirt that replayed the famous sequence from the Jerusalem hostage crisis. Owen, in a martial-arts frenzy, snapped Jephthah's knee, then, hair flying, whirled toward the camera.

Above the kid a sign read, *Hard Times? Pick a New One! Contact NAFTA Directory of Colonization, 001-NEWCHANCE.*

The man who had sacrificed his seat noticed her gaze. "A lovely young woman like yourself doesn't need to think about emigrating," he said. Red carnation in his buttonhole, he stood, legs spread apart to balance in the swaying train, one hand resting on the knob of his black-lacquered cane.

Gen looked him in the eye. "I'm not thinking about emigration."

"You're fortunate. Because if you were short of cash, or in danger of losing your job—"

"—you could help me out. You're a public-minded man."

"Once you get to know me, you'll be impressed by the size of my . . . mind." As the train swayed through a bend, the man's hip brushed her shoulder.

Gen leaned forward. "Let me show you something."

The man lowered his head. She pulled the phony badge from her purse. "Delta Uberrasch, NYPD undercover," she said in a low voice. "Thanks for your offer of assistance. You see that man over there?" She indicated a big, square-shouldered man wearing an eyepatch. "He's a slave dealer. You can help me bring him in."

"But I—"

"When we pull into the next station, I want you to obstruct his path off the train. I'll come up behind. I don't think he's carrying a weapon. Even if he is, I doubt he'd kill you in public."

"Uh—I think this is a mistake."

"No, that's him all right, Jerry the Nipper."

The train slowed. "Broadway and Seventy-fifth. Llannely Ward," the train's speaker announced. Gen stood up. "Get ready now."

The man scuttled toward the doors, looking over his shoulder at the big fellow, who got up and approached behind him as the train glided to a stop. Mr. Carnation was trembling visibly. When the doors opened, he bolted from the train and dashed up the stairs.

The man with the eyepatch stood aside to let Gen off the train. "Thank you," she said.

"You're very welcome," the man said.

At street level she crossed over into Llannely Ward. The security station examined her ID and checked her for concealed weapons, then passed her through to the sunny street. Corporation Llannely ran the blocks north of 72nd and south of 79th, west to the Hudson River dikes. The streets, shops and restaurants were full of employees with Llannely patches on their shoulders.

The trees lining the immaculate sidewalks were green, and a fresh breeze from the river wafted the smell of lilacs. In a playground a knot of teenagers—one of them wearing the Owen Zealot assault shirt—were dancing to a music box. "Number one for the third week in a row," the DJ stuttered over a song intro, " 'Desert Slide' by Ben Simeon!" Eerie pipes and a blues vocal over hypnotic drums.

A shop windowscreen hyped the upcoming Madison Square Garden bout between Muhammad Ali and Jack Dempsey. A few buildings farther along the smiling face of Voltaire, a respirator loose around his neck, beamed out of a flotilla of promos for his top-rated gab-show. Behind him stretched a rusty landscape. "—This week, live from Mars!" Switch to a clip of Voltaire's sidekick William Jennings Bryan, the butt of the cynical megastar's jokes, ogling a statuesque settler in a form-fitting surface suit. "Cultivate your garden, Billy!"

The Acropolis Center smothered the old West Side Expressway like some art deco monstrosity from *Things to Come*. Gen rode the pedestrian mover to the Riverside Esplanade, and took an elevator up ninety-two floors. Among the offices of lawyers, commodities brokers, genetics counselors and time exporters, Lance Thrillkiller rented a suite for his Committee to Protect the Past.

"May I help you?" asked Lance's receptionist, a pudgy man with thinning brown hair, blue eyes shrunken behind archaic glasses that were not just an affectation.

The receptionist was an aging version of James Dean. There were a number of hopeless James Deans around; it had taken the time recruiters numerous tries before they realized his personality was so fragile they couldn't get decent work out of him for any length of time before a breakdown or a suicide. Besides, he lost most of his hair by the time he was forty, and in every version had a tendency to put on weight. This one was fairly nice, but bemused.

"I've been here before," Gen said. "Ms. Emma Zume?"

The receptionist tried hard to focus. "Oh, yes."

"Is Mr. Thrillkiller in?"

"He's out right now. He'll be back soon, though."

"He usually lets me wait in his office."

"Suit yourself."

Gen went on back.

Lance employed a lot of used historicals. It was good PR. Overeager speculators had retrieved numerous celebrities hoping to make a killing representing their services. But for every Voltaire or Truman Capote, there were a dozen who put future audiences to sleep or cracked under the strain of an alien world. Who wanted to see new plays by Eugene O'Neill?— who was, let's face it, a downer in his first incarnation anyway, and a hopelessly addictive personality besides. After the John Keats fad waned, who cared about John Keats, especially when most of them were so susceptible to modern tuberculosis strains that the medical upkeep was prohibitive?

Lance's office boasted a spectacular view. From the edge of the dike fishermen cast their rods into the Hudson. Brightly colored sailboats were tacked by their AIs down the river while passengers took the breeze on the spring day. Across the river the white stucco-and-glass outcroppings of apartments clustered like grapes on the gardenlike Jersey bluffs.

Gen settled down on the divan. A crumpled TV lay on the side table; she picked it up, shook it out, lay it across her lap. She flicked idly through the stations, then switched to information services. She called up SEARCH, typed in the name VANNICE and set it to scan news reports over the last week.

She found two stories. Esmerelda Vannice, twenty-two, of Scranton, Pennsylvania, had won 680 million dollars in the Northern Hemisphere Lottery. Vannice had been putting in her time as a diaper processor at a Pennsylvania landfill being reclaimed by the Sri Lankan conglomerate Enterprise Trincomalee. Asked how she planned to spend her windfall, Vannice said she was going to get her body refurbished. "I already sold one ear, one eye, a parathyroid gland and a kidney. We was ready to emigrate. And then this happens. Whooee, am I relieved!"

The second story was a business report announcing that ATD Pix, a wholly owned subsidiary of Vannicom Limited, had secured exclusive rights to cover the trial of the Jerusalem Zealots. A spokesperson for CEO Rosethrush Vannice said that the trial, scheduled to begin in a month, would be broadcast live on Legalwire One.

There was no mention of Owen: his notoriety was dying down.

After Jerusalem, Gen and August had spent a couple of months in Japan. Then Paris in the 1920s, to run a version of the Wire on a Bourse bullion trader. Three months playing bridge in the ninth-century Maya resort at Palenque, then back to contemporary New York, where they had run into Lance at a Knicks game.

During all this time, much as Genevieve had sought to put Owen behind her, she couldn't.

August tried to explain Owen to her. "We were fooled because he treated everyone the same. Good old egalitarian Dr. Nice. The problem is that he assumes everyone shares his values. His egalitarianism makes him blind to differences.

"The dark side of this is that when it's brought home to him that someone is different, he can't continue treating them as equal. He feels betrayed. He invented a version of you that's unreal, then blames you when you don't fit."

It sounded right. But August ignored the fact that he and Gen were in the business of projecting unreal versions of themselves. So although, whenever she thought of Owen dumping her, she grew murderously angry—still, at some level, for some reason, she feared that Owen *was* better than she was.

It was all she could do to push these thoughts away. At that basketball game August told Lance about his failed plan to liberate Wilma for ComPP. Lance commiserated, and urged them to join him anyway. "Why chase marks from resort to resort when you can settle in one place, set out your bait and they'll *send* you money—and feel good about doing it?"

Before Lance had finished talking Gen had a plan. She didn't have to forget Owen. She could humiliate him.

She plucked a Bliss egg from the dish on Lance's desk, peeled off the foil and let the drug-infused chocolate dissolve on her tongue. She imagined meeting Owen in his native habitat, a dinosaur among his own extinct class. She smiled. She didn't want his money. She wanted his heart, ripped out and steaming on a plate.

Lance entered the office, with August right behind. "—When that happens I always try a Philadelphia opening, or you could double the bird," Lance was saying. "Hello, Gen."

"Call me Emma. Emma Zume."

"Sure, Emma. Nice name."

Lance Thrillkiller was a homely man: no chin, overbite, a big nose, receding hair. *His* thick eyeglasses were an affectation. He looked the way Owen ought to, Gen thought. Such a perfectly ugly man, you told yourself, could not be up to anything tricky. That was why the Killer had twanked himself into a frog from his natural princelike good looks.

"How would you like to take a little trip out to Connecticut this Wednesday?" Gen asked him. "To visit a dinosaur."

"You made the date." Lance did not sound happy. He went over to the wall and opened a bar. "Would you care for a drink?"

"No, thank you."

"Scotch, August?"

"On the rocks." August kissed Gen's cheek and settled into an armchair.

Lance poured August a scotch. "I'm having second thoughts about this, Genevieve."

"Emma."

"Sorry. But I don't need to draw the attention of somebody

like Rosethrush Vannice. After the press this dinosaur's drawn, if she even knows we're coming we won't get past the gate."

"Half of that publicity has come from her own operatives."

"Perhaps. Still, I don't like the idea of putting myself in her crosshairs. At the risk of seeming selfish, my dear, what's in it for me?"

Gen balled up the TV and tossed it into the middle of his desk. "Check out the *Wall Street Journal*. They just announced she's got the exclusive rights to the Zealot trial. How would you like to get a piece of that action?"

"How?"

"She wants as many people as possible to tune in. She doesn't care who wins, or what side they're on. The Zealots are ideal representatives of everything that gets your contributors thrumming against time travel. They've been locked up for most of a year, in a time two thousand years removed from their own."

"My heart bleeds for them."

"I'm sure Rosethrush's heart does too. So while I talk to Junior, you unleash that fabled charm of yours on Mom. Get her to lean on the court to release one of the Zealots under your supervision. Originally August was going to get you a dinosaur; I'd say a persecuted historical will stand in perfectly well, maybe even better. You'll double your contributions in a week."

Lance's eyes lit up. "I knew there was a reason why I loved you."

"Have you decided which of the Zealots Lance should ask for?" August asked.

"How about the leader?" Lance said. "What's his name, Jephthah?"

"A rather bloodthirsty character," August said.

"He's not a guy you're going to be able to control," Gen said. "They'd have to chain him to his chair."

"That could be good."

"He's a hater. No, go for Simon. He's more sympathetic. He was an apostle. That's a hot angle."

"August? What do you think?"

"I think this is a perfect reason for you to visit the Vannice estate. But I don't want Genevieve with you." August put down his glass and plucked an egg from the desk. "Is this such a good idea, Genevieve? What's to be gained by crossing paths with Dr. Nice again?"

"Sweet revenge."

"Revenge is a bad motivation for a grifter. Did I ever tell you about Arky Birnbaum and the college chancellor?"

"When I was twelve. And fourteen. And seventeen. And twenty-two."

"How old are you now?"

"Dad, I'm not Arky Birnbaum."

"You're putting yourself at risk. How can you hope that Vannice will believe you're not who you are?"

"He'll believe, all right. I'm not Genevieve Faison, I'm Emma Zume. Emma Zume is an idealistic innocent. She needs protection. To her, Owen Vannice is a man of the world."

"She must be cerebrally challenged if she thinks he's a man of the world."

"On the contrary, Emma is highly intelligent. Only she's got a very stiff backbone."

Lance took two of the chocolates. "Given this Zealot plot, August, I think I'd *like* Gen to come along. She can distract Vannice."

"That's what I'm afraid of," August said. "Let's turn this reasoning around. If Simon will stand in perfectly well for the dinosaur, then raising the issue of the dinosaur is not necessary, Gen. Rosethrush Vannice is not someone to be taken lightly. And the father is an eccentric buzzsaw."

Gen knew he was right, but she wasn't going to let it go.

"August, if this plan of mine works out, I'll have both his parents urging me to complete this scam."

"But you won't even tell me what it is!"

"What it is will become evident soon enough, if it's going to work at all."

August folded his hands over his slight paunch. "I guess what really bothers me is that I won't be there to watch out for you."

"You can't be, Dad. I can put one past him, but the two of us together would be too much."

"I could change my appearance."

"Now who's talking about things that aren't necessary? Lance will be my chaperone, and it will run smooth as a Massachusetts workhouse."

"We'll be prepared," Lance said. "We're a well-established public-interest organization. We're just there to examine his dinosaur. If they question our credentials, they'll find out everything we're saying is the truth."

"And if it comes down to it, Dad, I'll tell him the *true* truth."

"Which is precisely my point," August said. "Once you start telling the truth, sooner or later it gets out of hand."

Chapter 3

Trouble in Paradise

The compressor on the disinfectant blaster made it hard to hear anything anyway, so Owen had Bill play Schubert's *Unfinished Symphony* to cover the noise. He hummed along happily.

Wilma's most recent bath had wrecked the swimming pool again. Owen, pretending to be one of the Thornberry custodial staff, wore hooded coveralls, plastic gloves, a respirator and goggles as he cleaned the tiles. He'd asked the workmen to treat him like one of them. Under the coveralls, padding made him look thirty pounds heavier. To top it off he had incorporated a voder in the mask that lowered his voice half an octave.

The Schubert had reached a passage that always, to Owen, sounded like a threat of dire events to come. Bill lowered the volume and said, =This isn't going to work.=

"What? In this getup even Mother wouldn't recognize me."

=She's not your mother. The voder isn't going to disguise your accent.=

"I'll change my accent."

=You're a master of deception. But the whole plan is hinky. What do you expect to accomplish?=

"I expect to spy on her without her knowing it's me."

=Why waste the time? It's the same woman, I tell you.=

"Right. Just like you thought that Girl Scout was dealing designer drugs."

Bill was silent for a moment, his version of disgruntlement. =I still say I never saw any cookies like that before.=

Owen turned off the disinfectant blaster and ran his hand over the tiles. "What about her name? Emma Zume? Is that a Hopi name?"

=Hopi. Spelled H-O-K-E-Y.=

"You read the Saltimbanque file. All Genevieve Faison's aliases are upper-crust; most of them are French. Once con artists establish a modus operandi they seldom vary."

=Suddenly you're the expert on con artists.=

"Turn the Schubert back up." He fired up the blaster again.

During the last months Owen had compulsively replayed every minute he'd spent with Genevieve. Was *any* of what she had said to him genuine? When he considered that Gen's attraction for him might have been real, his final minutes with her came back to torment him. He remembered her eyes brimming with tears. How cold he must have seemed. Sometimes late at night, waking from a dream, he would catch himself speaking aloud, "I'm sorry. I'm sorry. I'm sorry."

Bill would ask him what he was muttering about, and Owen would roll over and try to sleep.

The credentials that Emma Zume had sent to him, under the electronic certification cyphers of the City of New York Identity Authority, described an entirely different woman. Born in Glenwood Springs, Colorado, in 2036, a 2058 graduate of Berkeley in Public Pleading, living in Manhattan, private identity number, medical clearances.

Still he was wary. Hence the disguise. He told Jeeves to greet the Committee to Protect the Past visitors, tell them that Dr. Vannice was delayed on business, lead them down to the south lawn and leave them unsupervised. He looked at his wristward. It was 3:10. He peeked over the edge of the pool.

Jeeves appeared at the rear ground-level entrance, leading two people out of the house. The robot pointed toward the greenhouse, then retreated.

One of the visitors was a homely man in a checked jacket. Beside him walked a young woman wearing a dark blue shirt open at the collar, a khaki skirt—culottes, actually—cut at mid-calf, fitted at the hips but loose below, white rolled stockings and flat-heeled sturdy shoes. Her long hair was pinned up. She carried an electronic notebook.

The man went down toward the greenhouse, but once they were in the shadow of the oaks the woman turned abruptly left and began poking around the grounds. She squinted up at the house, then followed some of Wilma's footprints in the turf to a clump of holly bushes. She reached for a branch of the holly, pricked her fingers and drew back, then leaned forward to examine the leaves. When she turned from the bush, she caught her skirt in the holly, took a step and stumbled. Her notebook slipped out of her hands, and she sprawled on her hands and knees.

Owen came down from the pool. "You all right, ma'am?" he asked.

The woman stood up, brushing off her skirt. There could be no mistake—it was Genevieve Faison. "Oh—hello," she said.

Owen worked up a New England accent. "May I help you?"

"I'm here to meet Dr. Vannice."

"We were told he'd meet you at the greenhouse."

She blushed. "I was doing some snooping. Please don't turn me in. I'm Emma Zume, from the Committee to Protect the Past."

"Hello."

"Gosh, that mask looks hot."

"Can't take it off. Fumes."

"Oh, certainly—I understand." She clutched her notebook. Her eyes—startling violet—flicked from Owen's to the ground.

"What are you trying to find out? Maybe I can help."

"We're here to inspect his dinosaur. Maybe you could tell me—if you don't think it would be a betrayal. How does he treat her?"

"Dr. Vannice? He's completely responsible."

"You're not just saying that because you work here?"

"He couldn't pay me enough to lie."

"I'm glad to hear that. I hope he doesn't lie to you."

"He's actually quite a good employer."

"How long have you been working for him?"

"A long time. I'm like one of the family. Haven't you met him yet?"

"No. I'm not eager to."

"But you must have seen pix of him. He's become so famous."

"I spoke to him over the phone. He was very tricky. I couldn't get a straight answer out of him, and"—she blushed again—"he was so interested in meeting me in person that I got suspicious. Is he—" she looked down at the notebook "—some sort of libertine?"

"Oh, no! He's not like that."

"Excuse me for saying this—how would you know? You're just his employee."

"Employees know things. I see him every day."

Emma Zume held the notebook in her crossed arms, over her chest. "I don't know you, Mr. . . . ."

"Oakley. Bill Oakley."

"Mr. Oakley. But Dr. Vannice strikes me as an opportunist. Look at the notoriety this dinosaur's gotten him."

"No, no. He's very much against time exploitation."

"Right. He just happens to collect dinosaurs."

"I don't think he's very proud of the contradiction."

"Then he shouldn't base his scientific career on it. He's just an amateur anyway. Most real scientists are deeply skeptical about him."

=Want me to deck her, boss?=

Owen pulled off the mask and hood. "Good afternoon, Ms. Zume."

Her face went pale. "Dr. Vannice! Oh—excuse me. I didn't mean—I mean I didn't know—"

"No, you didn't."

"Oh, dear. I knew I should never have gone about the grounds without permission. I guess I'd better leave now." She started to go, then stopped. She turned back to him. "Hey! That was a dirty trick!"

"You were the one snooping around the grounds."

"Maybe I need to snoop, if you're such a devious character as to spy on us!" Clutching her notebook with white knuckles, she stepped toward him, into one of Wilma's footprints, and fell forward. The notebook went flying. Owen caught her.

She struggled out of his grasp.

"Are you okay?" Owen asked.

She picked up the notebook and checked to see that it was still working. "I suppose so." She looked back up at him. "Can we start this whole thing over again?"

Owen was surprised by her forthrightness. He tried to stay mad, but she was so clumsy. "Okay. I won't trick you again."

"And I'm sorry I overstepped the bounds of your invitation. I hope I haven't ruined everything. Can we still see your dinosaur?"

"Let's go."

They walked toward the greenhouse, Owen stripping off his gloves, pulling the padding from out of the coveralls.

=Well, what did that accomplish?=

"She isn't acting much like Genevieve," Owen subvocalized.

=She isn't? Women after money do God's own bicycle repair.=

Owen kept quiet until they reached the greenhouse, where the homely man was peering through the glass. "That's Lance—Mr. Thrillkiller," Emma said. The man turned, and Emma introduced them.

"Do you have any equipment?" Owen asked.

Thrillkiller held up a camera. "At present it will be enough just to inspect Wilma and her accommodations," he said. "The reports we've had are unclear as to the nature of the experiment you are running."

"It's no wonder, with the lies that have been broadcast. You'd think I intended to cut Wilma into steaks and barbecue her."

"Could you tell us something about it in your own terms?" Thrillkiller asked.

While Emma Zume took notes, Owen told them about his theory of altricial versus precocial growth rates in sauropods. He was warming to his topic when Thrillkiller interrupted.

"But aren't these sauropods social animals?"

"Yes. They brood in nesting areas together, and migrate in herds. Back in the Cretaceous, Dr. Dunkenfield is plotting seasonal movements. The adolescents, actually, spend more time with the infants than—"

"There are no other sauropods here. How do you expect her to develop in their absence? Leaving aside the emotional considerations—animals, like people, are remarkably sensitive to emotional factors—strictly from a scientific point of view, doesn't this mean your experiment is impossible to control? What validity are any results you arrive at going to have?"

=Don't let him throw you.=

"Uh—that's a good question. I conceive of this as a first-order series. Later I intend to run other experiments—"

Emma Zume interrupted. "You intend to steal *more* of these creatures from their natural environment?"

"Ms. Zume, don't misunderstand. Wilma does not lack attention. I spend a great deal of time with her. The whole premise of this experiment was deliberately to alter the circumstances of her childhood, to see what the results would be."

"And you don't care about how she feels," said Thrillkiller.

"That's not a scientific way of looking at it."

"The myth of scientific objectivity was exploded sixty years ago, Dr. Vannice."

Owen looked to Emma for help, but met only a furrowed brow. "I don't deny subjective factors," Owen said. "And I love Wilma as if she were my own pet."

"I see," Emma said quietly, making a note. "Your pet."

Owen gestured toward the greenhouse door. "Look, let me just show you the measures I've taken to care for Wilma." He punched the security code and placed his hand against the telltale. The lock snapped open. "I had to get special permission from the state police even to move Wilma over the public roads. In order to expand the greenhouse, I had to get a zoning variance. The zoning laws in this county are very strict."

"That didn't seem to keep your neighbor from constructing that Statue of Liberty," Thrillkiller said.

"That's a special case. We don't associate with them."

There was no immediate sign of Wilma inside, but a bed of ferns had been trampled. The air seemed to be cooler than normal. From the other end of the greenhouse came a sharp thump, a crash of foliage, then another thump. Owen forgot Ms. Zume and Thrillkiller and rushed through the interior.

At the other end, in the modern addition, Wilma was beating her head against the double doors to the paddock. "Wilma!"

"What's wrong with her?" Thrillkiller asked.

"I don't know." Owen tried to figure out how he was going to approach the dinosaur without getting hurt.

"Maybe we can distract her?" Emma asked.

"I'll do it," Owen said. "She's usually distracted by bright colors."

Owen ran to the supply room and grabbed a red blanket from a shelf. He raced back and began waving it. Wilma turned. Her eyes were wild. She panted like a steam engine.

=Don't get yourself between her and the door. I want room to operate if I have to.=

Thrillkiller kept well back, but Emma stepped forward, cooing to the dinosaur.

Wilma moved toward Owen's blanket, away from the door. She swayed, a little unsteady on her feet. She took a couple of steps toward Owen, and he backed off, still waving the blanket. She was slowing down now. She dropped to her front knees, then sat down. Her wedge-shaped head swayed on her long neck. She chuffed out a great belch and lay down.

Owen put aside the blanket. He reached out his hand, stroked the deep green markings on the top of Wilma's head. She blinked.

"What can I do?" Emma asked.

"There's a veterinary kit on the table in the office." Owen ran his hand down the front of Wilma's snout. Emma went off and came back in a minute with the kit. "Thanks."

Thillkiller was wary, but Emma crouched on the other side and laid her hand on Wilma's neck. Owen examined the apatosaur's eyes. He took some tests. Her body temperature was normal, her blood count was fine. The arterial bood was bright red, highly oxygenated. He gave Wilma an injection of sedative. "Stay with her while I check the climate control," he told Emma and Thrillkiller.

Owen opened the panel and checked the controls. The oxygen level in the greenhouse was a little high, but that shouldn't have caused such a reaction. Keeping Wilma confined so much probably wasn't helping her disposition.

As he reset the system, Bill began a running commentary. =This is the same woman.=

"Bill, shut up. I've got more important problems right now."

=If you're worried about sabotage, this is the one who'd do it.=

"If she's Gen, why would she look the same when she could just as easily twank herself into looking completely different? It doesn't make sense."

=Twanking would be too obvious. This is more subtle.=

"She sure doesn't act like Gen. She works for a nonprofit organization, for god's sake!"

=A nonprofit organization that's after your dinosaur, just like that Faison woman. And what about this fiasco? It doesn't make you look very good. Something fishy is going on.=

"Did you see any signs of trespass on the way in?"

=My field of vision was restricted. You kept looking at this woman's legs.=

"There isn't much to see, the way she's dressed. Which is another reason I don't think this is Genevieve Faison."

=Reverse psychology. The oldest trick in the book.=

"Bill, give it a rest."

Thrillkiller came back to see Owen. "We're going to video the dinosaur," Thrillkiller said. "I'm sure you'll understand why we need to do this."

"I guess. How long have you known Ms. Zume?" Owen asked.

"Emma? She's been my assistant for three years."

"Has she ever been on a vacation—say about a year ago—to the past? Ancient Jerusalem?"

"Jerusalem?" He laughed. "It's all I can do to get her to take an afternoon off."

Owen closed the panel on the climate control. "I don't see

how it could be; she looks so *exactly* like—"

Thrillkiller put his hand on Owen's arm. "You met a woman who looks like her."

"How did you know?"

The chronoprotectionist glanced back toward the end of the greenhouse, drew Owen aside, lowered his voice. "I know all about this. This woman you met, did she go by the name of Celeste Parmenter?"

"No."

"Jean Harrington? Genevieve Faison?"

"Yes, that's her!"

"Traveling with an older man, her husband, or maybe her father?"

"That's them! And this is her!"

"Not by the remotest of chances. No, what you've run into is one of the vilest scams you could possibly encounter. Celeste Parmenter and her brother Alex are con artists."

"But Ms. Zume looks exactly like her!"

"You might better say that Celeste looks exactly like Emma. This Parmenter woman, or whatever her name is, has had herself twanked to look like Emma. She and her brother have been running scams on idealistic time travelers associated with the Protect the Past movement. It threatens to discredit our whole enterprise. Emma has been near despair trying to dissociate herself from their actions."

"But the woman I met didn't call herself Emma Zume. And she didn't argue to protect the past—just the opposite, in fact."

"I can't tell you what con game they were running. And I'd rather not know."

"Can't you sue them?"

"They have to be caught to be sued. No, it's just something we have to live with. I hope you won't burden Emma with it. Can you imagine what it's like to have a criminal assume your identity?"

"I know it happens. But Genevieve Faison wasn't a criminal, really. She just—"

"Not a criminal? She most definitely is."

"But she didn't do anything illegal."

"You must not have known her very long."

Owen clutched Thrillkiller's arm. "Thanks for telling me this. It explains a lot."

"Don't mention it." Thrillkiller's sincerity, his concern for his coworker's feelings, was touching.

Emma came back, pushing her way between two cycadellas. "Dr. Vannice, you'd better come back," she said. "She's gotten to her feet again."

Owen hurried with Emma back to Wilma, who was placidly drinking from the little pond at the end of the greenhouse. He was relieved. "I think we're okay now."

"What was wrong with her?"

"I'm not sure. It could be some long-term effect of oxygen overload. The Cretaceous oxygen level was lower than today's. But I want to go down to the boathouse to look at some shingles that Wilma ate. They may contain some substance that's affecting her behavior."

"I'm sure that keeping her cooped up in here is not good for her," Thrillkiller said. "I want to video the rest of these facilities."

Owen hated to admit that he might be right. "As you please," he said.

"I'll go with Dr. Vannice," Emma said. She and Owen left the greenhouse and headed down the slope. The sun was in the west now, casting the shadows of pines sideways across the road. They stopped several times while Emma examined Wilma's tracks in the topsoil, her bite marks on the tree limbs.

"Have you ever had a qualified veterinarian examine Wilma?" Emma asked.

"There's nobody more qualified to care for Wilma than I

am," Owen said. "What vet in this century has any experience of dinosaurs?"

Emma crouched beside the road to examine a footprint, with a childlike awkwardness that made Owen want to help her.

=Keep your eyes on the road, boss.=

Embarrassed, Owen directed his gaze to the boathouse.

=Never a free bed in the land of funny money.=

He was beginning to wish he hadn't started by playing a trick on Emma. Here was a woman who looked like Genevieve, but with a completely legitimate career. Practical, direct, intelligent, not at all flirtatious. And all she thought of him was how irresponsible he was. "I appreciate your helping me in there with Wilma," he said. "You think quickly, and obviously are concerned."

"We don't agree with your bringing Wilma here, Dr. Vannice," Emma said. "Tampering with time is dangerous."

"I agree with that."

"If that's so, Wilma is a pretty big demonstration that you're a hypocrite."

"It's hard to live up to one's principles. Sometimes two ideas come into conflict, and one loses."

"In such cases, you can tell a lot about a person by which one he chooses to abandon. A brontosaurus has no place in this era. But as long as Wilma's here, we want to make sure she's used for serious purposes. Not for some frivolous media sideshow."

"So do I."

"I don't know you well enough to judge your motives. In the light of the attention you've already gained through this creature, I hope you'll understand if we assumed the worst."

"Certainly, Ms. Zume. I don't expect, from the media, you could assume otherwise."

They came down to the boathouse. "You certainly don't act like a Heinleinian," Emma said.

"I beg your pardon?"

"Come, come. We've heard the reports you make a game of sleeping with your ancestors."

"Ms. Zume! I don't even like people."

"I see."

"By people, I mean my family. I don't like my family. Especially my ancestors, none of whom I've ever met. So I haven't slept with them. I've hardly slept with anyone, actually."

=You're babbling.=

"Thanks," Owen muttered. "I know that."

"Excuse me?"

"No slats," he said, waving his arm at the building. "There are *no slats* in the shutters on this side of the boathouse, you see?"

She looked at him. "You're sure it wasn't you who ate these shingles?"

"No. I mean, yes. I mean, no, I never eat shingles."

He circled around the boathouse and out onto the dock. His parents' forty-foot sailboat *Recapture* rested on one side, and the ancient spruce motorboat on the other. Avoiding Emma's gaze, he made a show of checking the sailboat's moorings. When he turned, squinting into the sun, Emma had come down onto the dock.

"My parents are having a fund-raising ball at my father's College of Advanced Thought this Saturday," he said. "Do you think that you could come?"

"Why, whatever for?"

"So I might see you again. I could explain further about my research. I think you've gotten the wrong impression about me."

"I don't know if that would be proper."

"Don't say no yet. Think about it."

Up at the house, he could see figures on the verandah. Owen realized they'd been watched all the time they were together. He selected a piece of shingle for analysis and they headed back up the slope. They stopped at the greenhouse. Wilma was fine now, but Thrillkiller was not there.

When they got back to the house, they found Lance Thrillkiller sitting on the verandah with Owen's mother. A pitcher of lemonade stood on the table between them, and they were having an intense conversation. Owen had never seen anyone ingratiate himself to his mother so quickly.

Rosethrush waved them over. "We were watching you," she said. "Owen, you acted the perfect gentleman. I expected you at least to knock her off the dock, then rescue her. What's wrong with this younger generation, Mr. Thrillkiller? No initiative."

"Our Ms. Zume is full of initiative," Thrillkiller said.

"You seem to have hit it off mighty well," Owen said. "I hope you haven't sold Wilma out from under me, Mother."

"Wilma is the obsession of the male portion of this family, Owen."

"We were discussing the upcoming trial of the Zealot conspirators," Thrillkiller said. "Ms. Vannice did not realize that the ComPP is part of the consortium paying for the defense of the historicals—though I was well aware that ATD Pix will be broadcasting the proceedings."

"Which doesn't mean that I'm prejudiced against the defendants," Rosethrush added hastily. "The defendants must have first-class representation. We just want to be certain that justice is served."

"And if the trial goes on for six months, so much the better for ratings," Owen said.

Rosethrush leaned toward Thrillkiller. "For a well-bred young man, my son is a considerable cynic."

Thrillkiller nodded. "Of course, it's an injustice that the Zealots have been locked up two thousand years from their families, their homes, their culture and their era. They don't have the rights of citizens, yet we presume to try them as if they were."

"That's unfortunate, true. What would you have done differently?"

"ComPP has been trying to get Simon released into our custody. It would help if someone with influence stepped in on his behalf."

"Why would such an influential person do such a thing?"

"Justice. Oh, and I suppose the exclusive story of Simon the Zealot might be worth some money. Some public appearances could generate interest in the trial."

Rosethrush sipped her lemonade. "I think I might know someone who could help you out."

Lance handed her his card. "Call me."

"My husband has been planning a little get-together this weekend," Rosethrush said, rising. "A fund-raising dance at his College of Advanced Thought. We'd be honored if you and Ms. Zume could attend. We can speak further about these arrangements at that time. And you can tell Owen the results of your report on his dinosaur."

"I'd love to come," Emma said. "Thank you."

"What a charming girl you are." Rosethrush took Emma's arm and, folding it over hers, led them to the front door. "Next time, you have my permission to push Owen off the dock."

Chapter 4

The Good Fairy

The books were full of the history of time travel. Simon was not able to understand much of it at first, but he had little else to do.

The rationalization of Gödel's theories of closed timelike curves with a self-consistent quantum theory of time was accomplished by Alexander Davidovich Berman in his elegant paper of 2016. For twelve years time displacement remained no more than a theoretical possibility, until researchers at Nomaclade Technologies' lunar facility under the direction of the brilliant theoretical physicist Angela Patel created the first artificial singularity in 2028. The possibilities for space and time travel inherent in Patel's discovery were recognized immediately and intensively pursued. Research and development sparked by Food War I confirmed Berman's moment universe model and, after the close of hostilities, the first successful time displacement experiments occurred in 2035. Once-only time travel to past moment universes began in 2037, and found immediate commercial uses. For a decade or more time travel was confined to unburned moment universes, but in 2048 Tempenautics perfected the ability to revisit the same moment universe (with the side benefit of the application of Berman physics to space travel), and rapidly the settlement of specified moment universes, and the widespread commercial exploitation of the past, followed.

Simon's cell was a white room three meters square. The hard plastic walls were graffiti-proof. A bed folded down from one wall. Beside it stood a toilet and small sink.

Simon sat at a table opposite the bed and listened to a blues song on headphones. One of the few advantages of being jailed in the future was almost unlimited access to music. In front of him, below the photograph of Alma that he had taped to the wall, lay an electronic book running the text of *Berman Physics for Blockheads,* beside a scattering of chips for *Pop Goes the Twenty-first Century, Understanding Fractal Economics, A New Outline of History* and a dozen others, plus a notebook full of handwriting in Hebrew. But Simon had put down his pen. He hunched over the table, rocking back and forth to the wail of Robert Johnson singing "If I Had Possession Over Judgment Day."

He did not hear the unlocking of the door, but the change in the shadows of the room as it swung open drew his attention. He stopped the music, turned, then slowly removed the headphones. It was the guard named Brody, Warden Sikora and a stranger in a sleek gray suit.

"Simon," the warden said, "this is your lucky day. This here is your good fairy, Mr. Detlev Gruber, who represents ATD Pix. You're getting out."

"Pardon me?"

"We've arranged for you to be released on bond, Simon," Gruber said. Detlev Gruber was a handsome man, taller than Simon but average for these people, with light brown hair, an open face, green eyes. He sat down on the bed. "You'll have to wear a monitor, but you'll be out of prison."

"This godforsaken age is a prison."

"Yes, but the air is better outside. The Committee to Protect the Past is going to pay for your defense. Mr. Lance Thrillkiller will take care of you until your trial."

"What about the others?"

"They're not part of this deal. Since the court has decided to try you separately, and you're first, the committee is starting with you. We'll do what we can for the others as their time comes. The important thing is, if you're acquitted, your friends stand a better chance of being acquitted, too. So it's up to you to make a good impression." Gruber looked at Sikora, then stood. "Come on now, we need to go."

"What about my things?"

"They will be sent along later."

"I won't leave unless I can take some things with me."

Gruber hesitated, looked at Sikora. Sikora shrugged. "Of course," Gruber said.

Simon opened his carved olivewood box and put the photo of Alma and the Robert Johnson bead in, with a handful of other music and books. He closed the box, picked it up and turned to them.

"That's all?" Sikora asked.

"That's all."

They led him down the hall in the direction opposite to the exercise yard, through a barred door to another corridor and eventually to another room. In the room they made him change out of the orange prison coverall and into contemporary trousers and a shirt. They attached a skintight ward to his wrist. While the technician worked, the warden and Gruber talked about Simon as if he were not there.

"This one's handled incarceration better than the rest of these terrorists," Sikora said.

"If that's the case, they should have let him loose long before now."

"It's for his own good," said the warden. "These towelheads don't know slime about the present day. They'd either be victims of somebody looking to make a political point, or ripe bait for some shark."

Gruber leaned over to slip a finger under the wristward. "Not too tight, is it, Simon?" He turned back to Sikora. "That's why Mrs. Vannice has assigned me to take care of him. We'll see that nothing happens."

The warden didn't say anything.

They walked Simon down another corridor, through another barred door, past another checkpoint and, by way of a door Simon had never been through before, into the yard. The sky was overcast. The warden walked Simon and Gruber to the gate. They opened the door within the gate, Gruber stepped outside and Simon followed—and that was it, he was out. In a parking lot on a hill. The lot had a good view of the Hudson, which Simon had never seen, since they had brought him here in the middle of the night. They stood beneath the trees at the edge of the lot, and he breathed deeply of the cool air. He could feel his pulse throb against the wristward. "Thank you for getting me out of there," he said.

Gruber opened the door of his car and Simon got in. Simon held his box on his lap. When Gruber started the car the compartment filled with music, the middle of a song. Over a hypnotic drumbeat floated the slow sound of a pipe, and a young man's voice.

> "My fault, wrong time
> I thought you wouldn't be taken
> A sound that rattles all your bones
> A loss that can't be shaken."

Simon recognized that mournful voice. How could such a sad voice fill him with such hope?

Gruber drove them down the hill to the highway that ran

south along the river. He set the car on autopilot. He touched a control, the music stopped and he swiveled his seat to face Simon. "You don't know about this," he said, "but I met a version of you before. I started out as a talent scout for the studios. It was twenty years ago, the first time anyone recruited Jesus. We snatched him from the middle of the audience before Pilate. It was poor planning, but we were new at it. Later we got more subtle."

"I don't remember any of this."

"Right. Your Jesus was the second one. This was in a different moment universe from yours."

"What happened to me?"

"Uh—well, I don't think you survived. Sorry. Actually, it was a mess. A lot of shooting, and we had to leave in a hurry. Time travel was a new thing then. Once you visited an M-U, it was burned, and you couldn't go back. But there was an edge to it back then, a charge. Every time you went someplace, you were the first and only time traveler to go there. High risk, no responsibility."

No responsibility. That sounded about right. Months of study had cleared up many things about these people that had seemed mysterious back in Jerusalem. A man like Halam, who had seemed completely without scruples back there, now was comprehensible. Gruber could be Halam's brother.

The future had lost its ability to strike Simon dumb with awe. But its callousness was all too familiar. To the sinful neglect that the rich of his own time had practiced, the rich of the future only added a few new rationalizations. They believed in something called heredity, for instance. The poor were born inferior; why else would they be poor?

This did not keep the futurians from holding directly contrary beliefs. The same people who thought the poor were *born* inferior also believed poverty was a *choice*. The poor were wicked, and poverty a crime. Therefore if a harsh-enough stigma was attached to it, fewer people would choose it. Future prisons, Simon had discovered, were more full of the poor than the prisons of his own time.

Charity bred indigence. The most serious moralists of this time even attacked "employment opportunity centers"—what had in earlier times been called workhouses—as "pauper palaces." What to do with these morally and genetically worthless people? Ship them off into the past, into some rude era where, the rich could tell themselves, the poor could "make something of themselves"—if they were capable of it. Let them displace the Simons of history.

But such thoughts only brought on rage. Simon needed to think, to turn this knowledge against them. He tried to concentrate on the wooded hills as the car sped along the river highway. It began to rain, heavily, and the road ahead disappeared in the downpour.

"I need to make a phone call." Gruber pulled what Simon had assumed was a deep green handkerchief from his breast pocket, tugged it rigid on the drop table between them and punched a number in a keypad in its corner. The handkerchief became a screen. The face of a large pink bird came onto the screen. Its yellow beak ended in a black hook; its eyes were bright green. It took a moment before Simon realized it was another of the artificial images these people liked to project in place of themselves. "May I help you?" it asked.

"Let me talk to Ms. Overdone," Gruber said.

The screen wiped, and a woman came on. "Daphne, you look lovely," Gruber said. "Not a day over twenty-three."

"I'll let that go. You shouldn't call so early in the day."

"Well it's set up," Gruber said. "You'll meet Vannice at the dance, and sweep him off his feet. Once you get the sperm sample the rest will be up to the doctors."

"I want to see the money in my account before I get on the train to Connecticut."

"It's being done as we speak."

Daphne rolled her eyes. "The things I endure for science."

"For love, Daphne, for love. And cash."

Daphne saw Simon out of the corner of her eye. "Who's your handsome friend?"

"No one you need to worry about, darling. What time does your train arrive at the station?"

"Seven-ten."

"I'll pick you up there. Wear white."

"I'll start off wearing white. Can we get together afterward, Det?"

"Anytime, anyplace, anyway, Daphne. See you." Gruber touched a key and the phone turned a dusty lavender. He shook it until it went soft, crumpled it up and stuffed it into his breast pocket, where it made a handsome accessory to his jacket.

"You referred to someone named Vannice," Simon said. "In the prison you also mentioned that name."

"So?"

"Dr. Owen Vannice was one of the hostages in the Herod's Palace Hotel."

"Well, Simon, it's a small world. I work for his mother."

Simon pondered that. "You work for the mother of a man who is going to testify against me. But you're getting me released to the man who is paying for my defense?"

"What was your impression of Owen Vannice? At one time I used to see a lot of his family. I supposed him to be a little slow. Playing with slimy animals, down in the basement creating new creatures with his Expando Gene-Splicing Kit."

"In the hotel, I did not take advantage of my opportunity to murder him."

"You know, Simon, I'm quite impressed by your English," Gruber commented. "You can read English as well?"

"They made certain bio-software available to me. I have had a lot of time to practice."

"You don't object to such modern technology?"

"Necessity has overcome my scruples."

"That's good." Gruber contemplated the highway, as if there were nothing more to say. "It's good to be realistic."

Realistic. "I have been studying, and it has come to me that whenever one of you speaks of the need to be realistic, one may be sure that this is always the prelude to some bloody deed."

"You've caught hold of the true modern temperament there, Simon. But the past is full of bloody deeds, too. You see this scar on my wrist? I got this in Napoleon's tent before the battle of Austerlitz. I rogered the little man's mistress, but he caught me pissing in his bordeaux. 'Be realistic,' I told him. 'It wasn't very good wine to begin with.' He yanked out his pistol and shot me as I was diving out the door. Never liked the French; it's heredity with me."

"I have not forgotten that you haven't answered my question yet."

"Question?"

"About working on both sides of this trial."

"Oh, that. Well, it's simply that one of Rosethrush Vannice's companies bought the rights to the trial."

"Which explains why you need me to create a good impression. The trial is being broadcast."

Gruber looked at him. "You didn't waste your time in jail, did you?"

"This Mr. Thrillkiller of the Committee to Protect the Past. Is he working for Ms. Vannice as well? Is he perhaps going to make sure that I am convicted?"

"No, he's a completely independent agent. His committee is against time exploitation. Nothing would please him better than to see you acquitted."

"Does he expect me to make public appearances?"

"You'll have to talk to him about that. I wouldn't be surprised."

"And he wants me to be sympathetic. Or perhaps simply pathetic?"

Gruber smiled. "Publicity is vital to our modern legal system, Simon. Do you know what a legal AI is?"

"I have some idea."

"Well, the decision will be handed down by LEX, a legal AI. The question of who has jurisdiction over you historicals had been snarling up things, until the Saltimbanque Corporation agreed to submit its claim to LEX.

"LEX is programmed with the legal code. But the reason the old U.S. legal system broke down is that it consistently tried to eliminate public opinion from its workings. You might as well try to breathe without air. So we've incorporated the opinion of subscribers to the legal system into LEX. Twenty percent of LEX's judicial temperament is bound to a scientifically sampled cross-section of subscriber opinion. It's up to you and your lawyers to see that such opinion goes your way."

"I must work to create a favorable impression."

"If you want to maximize your chance of acquittal."

"And Ms. Vannice is willing to help Thrillkiller accomplish this. Despite the fact that her son was almost killed?"

"I think the operative term there is 'almost,' Simon. Why not assume that she's grateful to you for *not* killing her son?"

As long as the publicity is good, Simon thought. He sat in silence as the rain ended and they entered the outskirts of New York City. Simon had taken a virtual trip to New York while in prison, but the reality was impressive. Hundred-year-old glass towers glittered in the sun, verdant gardens spilled over the sides of architectural ramparts, signs flashed and music blared. The wet pavement shone. The car carried them down the West Side Highway, until Gruber took control and drove it to an underground garage beneath a complex of buildings towering above the river.

Gruber led Simon out into a pedestrian mall of stupendous proportions. Swarms of people in colorful clothing, shouting children, more music. The gabble of voices echoed off a skylight far overhead. Bright sunlight filtered down between the branches of trees, was broken into fragments by a fountain noisy as a waterfall. Everywhere were screens and display boards and advertisements talking above the noise of the crowd. Huge faces, smiling. Bright clothes. Yet more insistent music. It was the celebrity world he had seen over the prison television, and he was in it.

They needed a celebrity for this trial. Well, perhaps he could give them one. As he walked along behind Gruber, Simon smiled and waved at the people who passed, just to see how many would wave back at a complete stranger. A surprising number did.

Chapter 5

Dancing in Connecticut

Owen had spent the afternoon running intelligence tests on Wilma. In cleaning up afterwards he found an opened box of surgical gloves in his supply cabinet. Someone was messing with his dinosaur. He looked for further signs of tampering, but found none.

By that time he was late for the ball. But he could not leave Wilma without taking some precautions. He broke open a case of security midges and spent fifteen minutes programming them. "Bill," he said. "I'm going to hook the alarm into your remote."

=Smart idea.=

He turned on the midges, which flitted into the shadowy corners of the greenhouse, then he locked the doors and hurried back to the house. It was already six o'clock. The dance would take place in the college commons ballroom, and the college was in Alcott's Corner, twenty-three miles from Thornberry. His parents had gone on ahead. Owen ate some newfood, stripped off his sweaty coveralls, took a shower, grabbed a white shirt and tuxedo. On the wall a TV tuned to one of his mother's outlets blared away. It was a report on the upcoming Zealot trial. A video of the hotel siege ran through the depressingly familiar security pix of Owen's kickboxing frenzy and culminated with Simon refusing to shoot Owen as the SWAT team broke in. The report switched to a clip of the New York press conference following Simon's release on bail. Simon's handlers had gotten him up in traditional first-century clothes.

They had to be more comfortable than Owen's tux. He cast a longing glance at his mood boots and settled on sadistic genuine leather dress shoes. He hoped his parents appreciated what he was willing to go through for the family.

But why kid himself. Owen would not have gone to the dance had it not been for the chance to see Emma Zume there. He had been able to think of little else since her visit. He only hoped he could get her alone.

He checked his watch. It was after seven. He moussed and combed his still-wet hair, and ran down to his car.

"To the College of Advanced Thought," he told the BMW, and the car glided out of the drive. Owen tried to collect his thoughts. With all the rushing around he was sweating like crazy. He could feel the wet hair lying on his collar. He rolled down the window and let the breeze blow his hair dry.

The two-lane country road was beautiful in the darkening evening. As the sun set, the boles of the trees flitted by in darkness, while the tops were still in bright orange light. On one side a white board fence ran along the road, surrounding a pasture as tidy as a Puritan kitchen. A couple of horses looked up to watch him pass. The traffic was light, and the BMW hummed along with a machine's efficiency.

He supposed the gloves could have been used by Thrillkiller, though Owen had not seen him wearing any. Could ComPP be trying to steal Wilma? But then why would they approach him so openly? It might be a reverse ruse to draw suspicion away from themselves if Wilma disappeared later. But he had to be turning as paranoid as Bill even to come up with such a scheme.

Arriving at the campus, he pulled up in front of the union, got out of the car. "Go charge yourself," he told it. He straightened his tux, took a deep breath and entered.

The College of Advanced Thought had originally been Word of God Ag and Tech, a post-millennium sectarian school that went belly-up after the religious upheavals resulting from time travel. Ralph Vannice bought the physical plant and stocked it with his eccentric collection of historical figures and cast-off celebrities. Most of the buildings were in the old New Millennial architecture of sixty years ago, full of fins and setbacks, private courts and security ziggurats. The redbrick union building was an exception, with genuine ivy and tall, many-paned clerestory windows.

For a number of reasons, the College of Advanced Thought had not made back its investment. The faculty of historicals had a certain novelty attraction, but their academic credentials were not recognized by current institutions. Most of the teachers were out of touch with their disciplines and taking a pharmacopoeia of contemporary drugs just to cope.

But it made great tabloid news. In publicity for the family enterprises Owen supposed the college might be paying off after all.

By the time Owen entered the ballroom the dance had moved past the opening minuet into a waltz. Around the gleaming hardwood whirled women in gowns adorned with feathers, men in formal black jackets and waistcoats, white ties and gloves. Two massive crystal chandeliers hung from the high ceiling. Midges glided throughout the room, recording the glitterati for later PR. At the far end of the ballroom, a Victorian orchestra played "The Beautiful Blue Danube," under the direction of Strauss himself.

Rosethrush Vannice had called in every client on her list. Wearing a gown that showed her bosom to good effect, she stood chatting with Shakespeare, flown in from Hollywood, resplendent in a white tux, hair down over his collar and a ruby stud glinting in his ear. The Bard of Paramount had his arm around a woman in white whose décolletage made Rosethrush's gown look modest. Owen's father was there too, sporting a Ben Franklin personality mod: he wore knee breeches, a fur hat and wire-rimmed bifocals. Which was ironic, as a young Franklin, the real one, was standing not ten feet away dressed in the fatigues of a lunar colonist. Franklin's brown hair stood up in a fright cut.

Owen spotted Emma Zume and Lance Thrillkiller together at the entrance to one of the drawing rooms. Before he had taken two steps his mother's voice rose above the music. "Owen! Come here! You must meet someone."

Owen smiled, pointed at his ear as if he could not hear, and powered toward the drawing room. When he entered there was no sign of Emma.

The room was crowded with the well and oddly dressed. Although Owen could not always tell the faculty from the guests, he did recognize some of the more notorious historicals. A young Einstein and a younger Goethe had cornered Dorothy Parker by the bookshelves, but she seemed to be holding her own. In bizarrely accented English, Gandhi swapped stories with Cortés. Owen wandered through the room, eavesdropping. The economics department had seized the conversation pit, where Marx and Friedman went at it. "If you want to help the indigent seize control of their lives, abolish their civil rights," Friedman was saying. "You can't legislate human nature."

"There is no human nature independent of culture," another man said.

"Help me out," Owen subvocalized. "Who's that?"

=Clifford Geertz,= Bill whispered. =Twentieth-century anthropologist.=

"There is no human nature independent of *coture*," an elegant man observed in French-accented English.

=Hubert de Givenchy.=

"Ah, yes—'Clothes make the man,' " quipped another.

=Either Vladimir Nabokov or Groucho Marx.=

A man Bill could not identify was inhaling scotch and talking space. "Exploration has come along somewhat since your time," he explained to an older one with an impressive beard.

=Santa Claus there is Konstantin Tsiolkovsky.=

"Colonies on the Moon, Mars. Expeditions to Io, Titan. Orbital scientific stations around Venus. Some historicals are involved: Oberth, Korolev."

"Korolev? A Russian?"

"The chief designer of the Soviet program. You know who the Soviets were?"

"It is hard to grasp history that happened after your own death."

"Berman physics has opened wormholes for space travel. You can take a step to Mars. We pipe air and water from old moment universes up there."

"Why not simply send colonists to the Mars of the past, when it had an atmosphere?"

"That old Mars is hard to find. The solar system's moved a long way in the last billion years."

A remarkably beautiful woman that Bill tagged as Sarah Bernhardt: ". . . but if Jesus got involved, that might swing some sympathy to the Zealots."

"Jesus is only twenty-three. He was taken from Galilee long before he was involved with the Zealots," another woman said. "He doesn't even know Simon. He's got his career to think about."

"How about Yeshu?"

"What?—he must be fifty now. No, the defense's only chance is to mount a major publicity campaign. Get Simon to weep on the net . . ."

"... this place will never be accredited," a portly man blared. "Not in science, anyway. In a real university AIs do most of the heavy lifting. Nothing compares with the cool rationality of machine intelligence. The kind of physics these fossils do would be part of the humanities. The history of science is full of intuitive missteps, ideas rejected because of fear, envy and simple inability to change. Look at the Copernican revolution, evolutionary theory, relativity, chaos, the IQ debates. Just go to one of Vannice's faculty meetings and you'll see the errors of the past living on. How could anyone accredit such a farrago?"

Still no sign of Emma. Owen was about to take another chance on the ballroom when he was accosted by a short man with a neatly trimmed beard. He peered at Owen. "Your parents' soirees are indeed a hair-raising experience." He chuckled. "How are you, my boy?"

"I'm fine, Professor Jung."

"And your dinosaur?"

"She's fine. You must come to see her. She's gotten much bigger."

"Not surprising."

A dour, bearded man stood a few feet away, clearly eavesdropping. He did not turn to them, but spoke loud enough so that people's heads swiveled his way all around the room "I would not put much credence in anything Jung tells you, young man."

=I give you three guesses.=

"Dr. Freud? Nice to meet you. Father said you had joined the faculty." Owen could not imagine what psych department meetings must be like with both Freud and Jung on staff.

Freud seemed to be focusing on a point somewhere past Owen's left ear. "So, young man, why the interest in such large, extinct animals? Animals with long, snakelike necks, not so?"

"Let the boy be, Sigmund. He's not interested in your archaic reductionist quackeries."

"Always you are afraid, Carl. You fashion your dreams into collective fantasies rather than face the neuroses they indicate. I am trying to keep this boy from wasting his life, as you have."

"If I've wasted my life, then why am I here? Have you read the papers I wrote after you died?"

"You didn't write them. They brought you forward before you got to them."

"I *would* have written them. And yes, they did bring me here—ten years before they got around to bringing you."

"It took them that long to see through your unscientific mystifications. Ten years they wasted before they figured out they needed to go to the source, not some polluted tributary."

"Excuse me," Owen said. "I think I forgot to wind the grandfather clock on the east landing."

" 'Grandfathers,' he says now." Freud nodded significantly.

"Just a minute, Owen," Jung said. "Tell Herr Freud about that dream of yours—the one with the *Australopithecus* and the garden hose. I challenge him to analyze it."

Owen pointed toward the door. "Isn't that Moses calling me?" He pumped Freud's hand vigorously and fled the lounge.

In the corner of the ballroom behind a jungle of potted plants, Owen located the bar. He ordered a scotch, then scanned the room in search of Emma Zume. Had she left already? The bartender sorted cocktail napkins, watching Owen. Finally he meandered back. "Quite a circus they run here," he ventured.

"Complete with costumes," Owen said.

"I wouldn't mind having some of the cash Vannice Senior spends to stock this gene pool. But I wouldn't waste it on dead people."

Owen looked him over. "It brings jobs to the area. Must

have been pretty quiet around here when the old college closed down."

"There was more drinking at the church school," the bartender said. "I'm thinking of emigrating."

"Where to?"

"Nineteenth-century America. I figure I could even live right in the area here, a couple hundred years ago."

"What would you do?"

"The government gives you a hundred acres, technological support, medical. Sure it's primitive, but hey, at least you got a chance to respect yourself."

"No VR clubs. No twanking salons. No flash parlors."

"Have I got the cash to get twanked? In the past, instead of being behind the curve, I'll be ahead of it. I know a lot of things those historicals don't. I'll be part of the ruling elite instead of third class."

"Why not just go to Mars?"

"I like a place with air. What do you care, Dr. Vannice? You're sitting pretty."

Owen was nonplussed. "Have we met before?"

"No. But if your conscience is bothering you, you can get me into your mother's agency. I've got a degree in drama from Yale, for what it's worth. Which is not much when every job on Broadway goes to people who were dead before I was born."

"I'll see what I can do."

"You ought to. Enjoy the party," The bartender turned his back and adjusted a bottle on the shelf behind him.

Was that some sort of threat? "Bill, is everything all right with Wilma?" Owen subvocalized.

=Copacetic.=

How much credence should he put in the resentments of bartenders? Owen scanned the room. Still no sign of Emma, and he'd also lost track of his parents. People looked at him strangely. Discomfited, Owen left through the French doors at the end of the hall. The limpid sky, the darkest of blues edging toward black, set him to thinking about the sky over Jerusalem. A big magnolia at the corner of the stone balustrade proffered blossoms the size of dinner plates, and its sweet scent wafted across the lawns. A number of guests, elegant in evening wear, were strolling down to the lake at the heart of the campus. Owen found a quiet place at the end of the verandah and tried to collect his thoughts.

A few moments had passed when a woman in a white ballgown glided outside. She came directly over to him. "Hello, Dr. Vannice."

It was the improbably beautiful blonde who had been with Shakespeare. "Are you sure you've got the right Dr. Vannice?" Her forwardness indicated that she was not familiar with the protocols of a formal dance. She must be a historical from a non-Victorian era.

She took his hand. Hers was quite warm and, to Owen's surprise, a trifle moist. "You're the right man."

"I don't believe I've had the pleasure."

"It's early yet." She moved closer. "My name is Daphne Overdone."

The name was vaguely familiar, but he couldn't place it.

"I saw you with my mother earlier."

"Yes. She was hoping to introduce us. I'm on the paleontology faculty here."

"Really?" Owen was embarrassed that he didn't recognize her. Assuming she *was* a historical. "I'm afraid I'm not familiar with your work. *When* did you work?"

"I was involved in some of the Hell Creek Formation discoveries in the 1980s." She took his hand, pulled him over to sit on the balustrade, secluded from the rest of the verandah by the shield of the magnolia. She put her hand on his chest.

Owen slid away from her. "Did you work with Horner or Rigby?"

"Bakker was my man. I like to take risks." Daphne slid still closer, and when he tried to retreat he found he had run out of railing. "I was particularly interested in the concentrations of baby teeth in sedimentary levels near the K/T boundary," she whispered, tugging at his tie. "It seemed to indicate that immature hadrosaurs would gather in particular areas to drink."

=Boss, do you think this is the way to spend your evening?=

Owen's body was reacting to pheromones, not dinosaur paleontology. "Makes some sense," he gasped.

"I thought you might be able to give me firsthand confirmation." She had unbuttoned his shirt and was reaching for his belt.

"Ms.—uh—Dr?—Dr. Overdone, I don't think—"

"Call me Daphne."

"Daphne, this sort of thing might have been common in your own time, but ours is . . ." Her perfume was quite intoxicating. Her lips were inches from his, her eyes half-lidded in the darkness.

=Want some help, boss?=

Owen grabbed her by the waist to swivel her away from him. He looked past her shoulder to find Emma Zume watching, a few feet away, with a curious expression on her face.

"Ms. Zume!"

"*Daphne,*" Daphne whispered.

Emma turned and rushed back into the hall. Frantically tucking his shirt into his trousers, Owen ran after her. "Emma!"

He caught up to her at the doorway from the lounge to the ballroom. He grabbed her arm, turned her to face him. She looked at his hand icily, and he drew it away. "I don't believe we have reached the stage of intimacy where you are free to call me by my first name."

"Please. I don't even know that woman."

"You were simply showing her your tattoo."

Owen buttoned his shirt. "I don't have a tattoo."

"I hope she wasn't disappointed."

"She was just telling me about her work at Hell Creek."

"The road to which, I am told, is paved with good intentions."

"No, that's a paleontological dig."

"Dr. Vannice, you don't need to justify your behavior. In fact, you merely confirm what I already knew about you and your class."

"Please, Ms. Zume. That wasn't what it appeared to be."

"Thank you for admitting that it appeared to be *something.*"

He drew her away from staring people. "I've been looking for you all evening. I so much wanted to talk to you."

"And since you could not find me, you had to occupy yourself somehow."

The master of ceremonies announced the next dance, a gallop. Owen remembered Jerusalem. "Please. May I have this dance?"

She looked at him pityingly. Her eyes were so remarkably like Genevieve's. "All right," she said at last.

Thrilled, he drew her onto the floor. The orchestra began, in lively 2/4 time. Owen threw himself into it.

But it did not go as well as Jerusalem had. Emma did not follow his lead as well as Genevieve. In fact, they moved at cross purposes, fighting for the lead in a way that turned the dance into a subtle wrestling match. As they circled with the other couples he tried to explain.

"It's a classic paleontological site—Hell Creek."

"And there you were, without a paddle."

"She's not accustomed to our society, she's a historical."

"Which means anything goes?"

Flustered, he missed a step and jerked her sideways. "No, it's just that she was telling me about her initial research."

"And conducting some at the same time." Emma pushed herself away, and executed a furious pirouette. She moved as if she were angry, and he supposed he couldn't blame her. Owen noticed that people around them on the dance floor shot them occasional stares and double takes. His tie had come loose, and one of his gloves was unbuttoned. Emma came back into his arms. He wondered if his fly was undone, but when he glanced down to take a peek, it seemed as if he was looking down Emma's dress. Her eyes locked on his. He missed another step, stumbled, stepped on her foot.

"Ouch," she said quietly.

Self-consciously, he held her farther away.

"Sorry," he said.

"That's one way to describe it."

He felt beads of sweat running down both his armpits, and his collar choked him like a noose. In an effort to steer her to the side of the dance floor, where at least they would not be so conspicuous, he ran her across the feet of another couple. Emma tripped, and he fell forward in his attempt to catch her. She tried to get her feet under herself, backpedaling. Owen held on, yanked along, twisting to break her fall. They collapsed into a divan at the side of the floor with such force that a potted palm fell on top of them, just as with a flourish, the music ended.

The dancers applauded.

Owen pushed palm fronds away from his face. Emma pulled herself off him.

An older woman rushed over, limping. "Owen, that was wonderful! But how did you find the time to learn stumble-dancing back in the Cretaceous?"

Owen did not recognize her at first. Then he did. "Ms. Talikovna! How nice to see you again. How is your leg?"

"Only hurts when it's going to rain. I hope you brought your umbrella tonight. Who's your partner?"

"This is Emma Zume, from the Committee to Protect the Past. Emma, this is Ms. Talikovna. She used to be my dancing teacher."

Emma smoothed her dress. "Charmed. What was he like *before* the lessons?"

"His kinesthetic IQ was in the forties. But he seems to have learned a lot since then."

"There are schools of thought."

Owen was brushing potting soil off his tux when Bill broke in. =Love is money, trust naked poetry for details! I hate to interrupt, but Wilma is acting strangely.=

"How, strangely?"

=Beating her head against the walls of the greenhouse. I eat your bleeding dysfunctional god for breakfast!=

"Excuse me," Owen said to Emma. "I need to get home."

"It wasn't that bad, Dr. Vannice. I'm partially responsible."

"No. Something's wrong with Wilma."

Immediately Emma was all business. "I want to come with you."

Although participation by the ComPP could lead to trouble, Owen was glad she'd be there. "Let's go."

He hurried out of the building and summoned his car. While they waited, Emma asked him, "Do you always wear your hair like that?"

"Like what?"

"That sideways look."

The car glided up in front of them. Owen caught his reflection in the dark window. The hair on the left side of his head was standing straight out to the side. It must have dried that way when he was driving to the dance with the window open.

"Yes," he told Emma. "It was completely intentional."

Chapter 6

Adventures in Moving

Either Owen had forgotten a lot about dancing in the last year, or else Jerusalem had been an aberration. Genevieve got into Owen's BMW and they headed off to the Vannice estate. As he drove she watched him. He kept trying to plaster the wild hair against the side of his head with his hand.

Gen didn't know what the wrestling match with the blonde was about, but she did not find Owen's fecklessness as amusing as she had the first time. Yet he drove with a dogged intensity that told her his mind was entirely with Wilma. It was hard to dislike him when he was so outside of himself. It was a kind of selflessness. A devotion to something besides money, or career, or sex.

"What's wrong with Wilma?"

"I'm not sure. But I'm convinced that someone has been tampering with her. What I can't figure out is how. The only person who ought to be able to enter the greenhouse is me."

It did not take them long to reach Thornberry. Owen passed through gate security and drove directly to the greenhouse. The doors were unlocked. Owen rushed inside. The greenhouse was completely silent. "Wilma?" Owen called. Before they had passed halfway through the old portion of the enclosure, they found a huge hole broken in the glass wall. They pushed through to the outside. Owen turned on the exterior floodlights, which revealed dinosaur footprints leading off across the lawn. They ran along after them.

"Could she have just gotten restless?" Gen asked.

"Restlessness doesn't account for the unlocked door. Someone spooked her. We've got to get her back."

Gen gestured behind them at the ten-foot hole in the wall. "You're not going to be able to keep her here."

Owen looked over his shoulder. "There's a vacant vet school at my father's college. They have all the facilities necessary; I was going to move Wilma there eventually and let my parents restore the grounds here."

They followed the footprints to the tennis courts, where they found a new depression just beyond the service line. Wilma had scratched the green plywood backboard to flinders. Her footprints led through the burst chain-link fence to the pool. Water was splashed over the deck, and wet prints and tilted flagstones led to the hedge marking the border of the estate. Wilma had eaten part of the hedge, then broken through the perimeter fence.

"I hope she stays out of town," Owen muttered.

"If you find her, maybe we should take her directly to the college."

"We'll need a truck. There's a rental place in Bridgeport." They ran back to the house and Owen called the rental office from a phone in the basement. After he hung up he told Gen, "They don't send them out under programming at night. We'll have to go pick it up."

They drove to the Bridgeport Redi-Haul. Owen sent the BMW home and they stepped into the office. It was after midnight, but there was a human being on duty: a kid with his feet up on a desktop, eyes closed, a pile of cheese fries within arm's reach and Ram Dash's "You Must Be Dead" blasting over the office's speakers. He did not know anyone had arrived until Owen pounded on the desktop with his fist.

The kid's eyes popped open and he yanked his legs off the desk. "We called in a rental-truck order," Owen said.

The kid shook his head, pointing to his ears. He turned around and touched the gain on the stereo, but Gen did not notice any change in the volume. "HELP?" he shouted, swiveling back.

"WE CALLED IN A RENTAL!" Owen bellowed.

"BIG?"

"THREE METRIC TONS!"

"MONEY!" The kid held out his hand.

Owen handed him a cash chip. The kid slid it into his reader, punched a key on the computer and a rental form emerged. "SIGN!"

Gen watched over his shoulder as Owen filled out the name "John Smith" of 200 Sycamore Street, Bridgeport. He handed in the form. Bouncing to the music, the kid pulled a key off the board behind him and pointed out the window to the truck nearest them in the row outside.

"THANKS!" Owen shouted.

The kid turned off the music. "You are most welcome, sir," he said. "And though I am of course consumed with curiosity, and my experience in this firm's employ leads me to draw certain conclusions, I won't ask you whether the circumstances compelling you to rent a truck in the middle of the night, using cash, under a name like 'John Smith,' fall within the boundaries of those countenanced by Connecticut's legal system. But if I were you I'd get it back by dawn."

"I'll do that," said Owen.

"Nice haircut."

They went out to the truck. "I'll drive," Gen said. "You navigate."

The truck's guidance was able to get them to the bay, but from there Gen had to drive manually to Thornberry.

"Let me off at the greenhouse," Owen said. "I'll get a projectile hypo and some sedative and follow her path off the estate. Meanwhile, you drive along the river road. Cruise slowly. Stop when you get to the old fairgrounds. If you spot her before I do, blow the horn three times."

"Roger, Mr. Smith. Would it help if we brought something for her to eat?"

"Good idea." At the greenhouse Owen hopped out and ran inside. He brought out a sack of food and loaded it into the back of the truck, then dashed off across the lawn, tripping over one of the lawn geese. The goose squawked away. Owen picked himself up and set off, tuxedo, wild hair, hypodermic pistol and determined look.

For more than an hour Gen drove down past private woods occasionally broken by elaborate estates. The road was deserted. Fifty years ago this had been farmland, but had long since been abandoned to a renewed wildness. Gen peered out of the window but could make out nothing in the darkness.

She was just turning back to the road from the side window when Wilma lurched into the headlights from the opposite side. Gen jerked the wheel, and the truck dove to a stop in the ditch. Wilma thundered off into the trees. Gen sat in the suddenly still cab, trying to catch her breath. She climbed out to survey the damage. From the bush came thrashing, and Owen, muddy to his knees, burst into the roadway.

"Are you all right?" he asked.

"I'm fine. But Wilma looked like she wasn't coming back any time this century."

"Let me get that feed out of the back," Owen said. "Maybe I can coax her, once she calms down."

Owen hauled out the sack. "I should call a tow truck while she's gone," Gen said.

Owen looked at her. "I suppose so. I'll go after her while you call, okay?"

Owen shoved the hypo pistol into his tuxedo jacket, heaved the sack over his shoulder, turned on his flashlight and trudged off through the ditch into the woods. Gen used the truck's phone to call a local garage. She sat down on the back bumper and waited. The sky was clouding up. She listened to the crickets chirping.

The tow truck showed up fifteen minutes later. The driver climbed out from behind the wheel, horse-faced and laconic. "Not very practical work clothes," he remarked as he affixed a chain to the rental truck's axle and used the winch to tighten the slack.

"I was going to a party."

"Ayup." He turned on the winch, the chain snapped taut with a clink, and slowly the truck backed out of the ditch. When he had the front wheels back on the pavement, he unhooked the chain. He went around to the front and inspected the front end. "Looks like you're all right. These old dinosaurs are indestructible."

"Thanks." She fumbled with Owen's wallet. "Here's five hundred. Keep the change."

"There isn't any change."

"Then don't keep the change."

The man got back into his tow truck. As he started the engine he said, "Just to keep you outta trouble, I called in a report to the state police. Should be here in a couple minutes."

Gen ground her teeth. "How sweet of you. You deserve a tip."

The garage man drove away.

She paced the shoulder, hoping Owen would take long enough for her to brush the cop. But before she could do anything she spotted Owen's light bobbing in the darkness, and he came up to the road, Wilma surging behind him like a huge surreal cow, sniffing after Owen's trail of oats.

"Owen," she said. "The police are coming. Do you think we should hurry up?"

"Help me herd her into the truck." They got Wilma into the back, then slammed the doors.

"Okay," Owen said. "One minute more. I dropped my hypo pistol back there." He hopped back over the ditch.

"Owen, there's no time!" But he was already gone.

Sure enough, as soon as Owen was out of sight a state trooper's car came around the bend and pulled to a stop on the shoulder. It sat for a moment, blue lights sweeping over its stainless-steel surface.

Finally a voice blared from the loudspeaker. "Officials Of The Connecticut Corporation Are Your Friends," the trooper said, voice distorted by his voder. "Do Not Move As I Exit The Vehicle. For Your Protection And Mine This Entire Transaction Is Being Monitored." The passenger door flipped open and the camouflage-armored trooper got out and strode forward. His pistol was holstered, but the riot gun strapped to his left fore-arm was trained on her. The servos in his power suit whined to a stop as he confronted her. In the mirrored face of his hel-met she saw a convex reflectoin of herself in the ballgown.

"What Seems To Be The Trouble?"

"No trouble, Officer," Gen said.

"The Corporation Requests Your License," the cop droned.

Gen let him tap into her wristward. Her phony identity as Emma Zume would pop up on the cop's helmet display. Be-yond the ditch, Gen saw Owen's light moving toward them through the woods. The trooper heard rustling behind him and whipped around, inhumanly quick, pistol out as he peered into the dark. Owen struggled though the ditch and up to the shoulder. The top three buttons on his shirt were open, he had lost the cuff link on his left wrist and his tuxedo was muddy to the knees. He had the remains of the feed bag over one shoulder, and the hypo pistol in his right hand. His hair still stuck out sideways. "Good evening, Officer."

The trooper did not lower his pistol. "Please Lay Down The Weapon."

Owen looked befuddled. "Weapon? Oh, this—it's not a weapon, it's a hypodermic gun."

"Which You Will Drop For Us Right Now."

Owen bent over and placed the pistol on the ground. "Sorry, Officer."

Gen assumed the mood levelers he'd taken before his shift would keep the trooper from doing anything rash. He looked both of them over. "This Must Have Been Some Party. Hypodermic Gun?"

Gen was going to have to get them out of this, at the risk of giving herself away. She stepped between Owen and the trooper. "Filled with animal sedative. You see—"

Owen broke in. "These aren't clothes, they're uniforms."

"Uniforms."

"Elite Pet Stores. 'Let your next pet be an Elite Pet.' "

The cop fixed on Owen. "You Look Familiar. Have We Met?"

"Hard for me to tell inside that armor."

"You Would Like For Us To Remove It, Would You?" There was a silence. The cop was probably running Owen's image through an identity check. Finally he said, "Okay, Mr. Pets. Tell Us What Is In The Truck."

"In *this* truck?"

"You Have Another Truck?"

"No. This is the only one."

"Then This Must Be The One We Are Asking About."

"That's true."

"And . . .?"

"And you want to know what's in it?"

"That Seems To Be The General Drift Of Our Inquiry, Yes."

"Well . . . it's full of iguanas."

"We Beg Pardon?"

Owen nodded rapidly. "Rare iguanas. We're moving them from the warehouse in Bridgeport to the outlet in Danbury. For the exotic pet fair at the armory."

"The Exotic Pet Fair."

"Yes. We'll have exotic pets from all over New England, from aardwolves to zebus. Ms. Zume and I have cornered the market in the flesh-eating Central American iguana, the Honduran 'Nice.' Would you like to see one?"

"We Think We Had Better."

"Good. We can give you a very good price on one, show-quality."

Owen moved around to the back of the truck and began to enter the combination on the lock. His story made the film company lie he'd tried out in Jerusalem seem like sweet reason, but Gen was curious to see how it would play out.

"You probably won't need any gloves," Owen said. "Your armor should protect you. Once they fasten on your hand they won't let go. But the venom's not that harmful to most people. Only twenty percent suffer any permanent nerve damage." He snapped open the lock and grabbed the handle. Inside the truck, Wilma thumped against the door.

"They don't much like being cooped up," Owen said. "Calm down in there! Darling, will you hand me a pair of number-three gauntlets from the case in the front seat?"

"These Animals Aren't Caged?" the trooper asked.

"Cages just make them mad. Stand back a couple of steps in case one of them launches himself at you."

"Wait!" the trooper's voice boomed. "Now I Know Who You Are!"

Gen got ready to run. But Owen would never leave Wilma behind.

"I MUST CRANCH," the trooper said. He stood rigid for a moment, then lifted his hands, grabbed hold of his helmet and gave it a sharp twist to the left. The seal broke and he pulled it off. The trooper let out a shuddering breath, then brightened. "You're Dr. Owen Vannice, the paleontologist!"

Owen looked poleaxed. "Yes, I am."

The trooper smiled. His pinched face was puny inside the massive powered suit. "The iguana thing tipped me off." Deprived of corporate direction, without the voder, he had a piping New England accent. He stuck out his unweaponed hand. "Officer Emil Wheeler."

Owen took his hand, then winced from the suit's powered handshake. "Ouch!"

Wheeler let go in dismay. "Sorry! You all right?"

Owen rubbed his bruised fingers. "I guess so."

"I can get you some mousse for that hair." The unincorporated trooper bounced with enthusiasm. "What a break this is! I've wanted to talk to you for months. Paleontology is my hobby."

"You don't say."

"Sure. I've read all of your papers. See, I have this theory about the relative decline of sauropods versus ornithopods during the late Cretaceous. It has nothing to do with stomach grinding. It's all about dinoturbation. . . ."

"Really. You must send me some of your notes sometime. Call my net-simulant."

"Oh, I have no notes." Wheeler tapped his riot gun against the side of his head. "It's all up here."

"Remarkable."

"See, I was thinking I could tell you my theories, and you could write them down. With your degrees and all, you could get them published, I figure. We could do it as a collaboration. I'd be glad to share billing on the final papers."

"I'm awfully busy right now. Several experiments going at once. These iguanas—"

"Oh, it wouldn't take much time. I've got it all worked out. The key to understanding my theory is the relative abundance of ceratopian—"

Owen muttered something. Then he rounded on the cop, throwing his elbow into the man's face. Wheeler went sprawling. Nimble as a cat, Owen wrenched the riot gun out of the trooper's forearm clip, snatched up the hypo gun, and popped him in the neck with the sedative. The cop's eyes glazed and he went unconscious. Owen stood above him, swaying. The riot gun slipped from his fingers.

At this moment it was Gen's instinct to run for the hills. *What would Emma Zume do?* she asked herself.

She knelt over the supine trooper. He was breathing fine. "Owen, I don't think it's a good idea to attack police officers. What was that about?"

"Bill!" he moaned. "I was grumbling about how I'd never get rid of this guy. My AIde took over. We had better get out of here."

"And leave the trooper out here by the road?"

Owen looked sheepish. "I'm sorry. You're right," he said.

"Come on," Gen said. "Help me move him."

Owen grabbed the trooper's metal boots. "This is terrible! I should never have lied about the iguanas."

"Perhaps he'll sleep it off in the car."

Owen dropped the trooper's feet. He snapped his fingers. "And we can make a statement!"

"Pick him up, Owen."

Together they dragged the officer back to the car and propped him up in his seat. He weighed a ton.

"Go ahead, talk," Gen said, indicating the monitor.

"An unavoidable interruption in Trooper Wheeler's shift," Owen told the car's camera.

"Maybe you should use your wallet."

Owen took out his wallet. He attached it to the info reader in the dashboard and downloaded his identification. "I've got an idea," he said. Gen watched him type in a substantial contribution to the corporation's retirement fund, a bonus into Emil Wheeler's monthly paycheck, and a personal message: *Sorry about that, Emil. Call me and we'll do that paper together. —Owen Vannice.*

"What good is that going to do?"

"I'm the son of the fifth-richest family in North America, Emma. I have privileges. Let's go."

Gen reached over to the car's utility box and pulled out a tube of official Connecticut Corporation Police Mousse and a comb. She handed them to Owen. "Fix your hair."

Wilma had quieted down by the time they got back on the road again. It started to rain, heavily.

"Ms. Talikovna's leg was right," Gen said.

Owen turned on the wipers. His face was so long he looked like a horse. "My night for running into insane paleontologists," he muttered.

"Maybe there's a correlation," Gen said.

"Study the past—lose your mind," Owen said morosely. He turned to her. "I didn't mean to sound arrogant back there. I'm not really the kind of person who enjoys breaking the law."

He was so amusing when he turned naive it was hard for Gen to keep from teasing him. "What are you going to do about Wilma?"

"I need to find out who's tampering with her, and why."

"Owen, if you can't find out what's wrong with her, and if

you can't keep her safe in your lab, and if you can't keep these mysterious intruders out, maybe it would be better for all concerned if you took her back to the Cretaceous."

"If my care were not being undermined, she would be fine."

Gen decided to poke him a little more. "Lance told me the reason you thought you knew me was that you met this woman who's been impersonating me."

"She didn't claim to be you."

"You met her in ancient Jerusalem? I thought you were concerned about Wilma. Not looking for new women to conquer."

Owen kept his eyes on the road. "I was stuck in Jerusalem because of a breakdown of the time-travel stage. I was holed up in a suite with Wilma and decided to get out on a Roman tour."

"You didn't worry what would happen to the dinosaur while you were out chasing this woman?"

"It wasn't like that."

"You seemed pretty startled when I showed up on your phonescreen. Why would you expect her to even remember you if you weren't involved with her? Why would *you* remember *her?*"

Owen looked at his hands. "I admit it, I was attracted to her."

"Attracted. Did you collide?"

"She led me on. She and her father—she called him her father. But I saw through her. We had a fling, it meant nothing. It might have meant more, but she was playing me for a fool. The reason I wanted to see you is that you're the genuine article. Not a fake."

"You hardly know me."

"I know that, unlike Genevieve Faison, or whatever her name is, you stand for something more than your own self-interest. The work you're doing means something. You have principles. Genevieve may have made herself look like you, but behind that pretty face she's corrupt."

"Did you tell her this to her pretty face?"

"I told her what she needed to hear."

"She must have been shocked."

"I wouldn't know. The woman's a con artist. Everything about her, down to her appearance, is a lie. You never met her."

Well, that helped. Seeing him with his big pet, worrying about state troopers, she had almost let herself like him again. She ought to thank him for reminding her of his callousness.

Why, then, did it hurt?

"No," Gen said. "I never met her."

Chapter 7

Rosethrush at Work

The cold Andean air was a shock after the travel stage. They crouched behind the building and got their bearings. The late-afternoon sun glared down into the plaza of the Inca town of Cajamarca, casting long shadows of the four thousand brightly costumed Indian retainers and the knot of Spaniards who were parlaying with the Sapa Inca.

The tour leader had chosen the moment of confrontation for their intrusion. After waiting all day for Atahualpa to make his appearance, scared to death that he might come armed, the Spaniards were now intent on the negotiations. It looked as if their ambush might work, and they held themselves ready for Pizarro's signal to attack. They were in no shape to spot intruders from the future. It was the sixteenth of November, 1532.

In the buildings on two sides of the plaza hid the Spanish infantry and cavalrymen; on the third side the harquebusers stood by their guns preparing an enfilade.

Father Valverde handed his bible up to Atahualpa, borne on a golden litter by eight men in cloaks of green feathers. The Sapa Inca opened the book, leafed through it. He held it to his ear. He threw it to the ground at the Spaniard's feet, spat out some scornful words in Chechua.

"Ready, now," the tour director said.

Rosethrush didn't want to do it, but she felt herself switch off the safety on her gravity-feed eight-millimeter assault rifle and flip down the visor on her helmet.

The priest, face purple with rage, snatched up the Bible and stalked back through the impassive rows of Indians. "Blasphemy!" he shouted to Pizarro. "The words of Christ mean nothing to him. Attack, and I'll absolve you!" Her language mod was working well, and the archaic Spanish was transparent.

"Santiago, and at them!" Pizarro bellowed, waving his sword.

"Santiago!" the Spanish soldiers yelled, and rushed from their hiding places in the stone buildings around the square, beginning the fabled massacre that would lead to the fall of the Inca empire.

Except this time the Conquistadors were the focus of an intervener's special organized by Extreme Tours of Atlantic City. Before the Spaniards had killed their first dozen Inca retainers, the guide waved the tourists on. "Rags and bones!" he shouted.

Rosethrush dashed out into the crowd, assumed an attack stance with her weapon at her hip, and sprayed an arc of bullets into the backs of the Spanish infantrymen. Their steel armor was useless against the kevlar-coated rounds. The first one who turned on her lost his arm in a spray of bloody fragments. Her stomach heaved.

The Indians were just as shocked at the Spaniards. They crouched, they ran, eyes wide with fear; a lot of them were taking friendly fire. She dashed forward. One of the Spaniards managed to turn his sword on her; she felt the blow but the edge skidded harmlessly off her assault vest. She kneed him in the groin, shoved the rifle into his gut and ventilated him.

It looked like the tour group was going to set a new record

in the Atahualpa rescue, when Rosethrush felt a blow to the back of her head and was knocked to the ground. The rifle skittered out of her reach. She rolled over and looked up into the hooves of a rearing horse. The guide had told them the Spanish cavalry would be on the opposite side of the plaza. Instead the Spaniards were behind them.

The horse's hooves came down on her. A tremendous blow, searing, splintering pain. And then she couldn't move her legs. She lay on her back, trying to raise herself on her arms, watching the other tourists struggle against the surprise attackers. The tour director and his lieutenant sprinted for the cover of the buildings, stumbling over fallen Indians. One of the Spaniards stooped over Rosethrush, ripped open the visor of her helmet, and holding the hilt of his sword two-handed over his head, stabbed it down into her face. Everything went black.

Out of the blackness arose an ominous forty-cycle hum, then the title:

THE INCA TOURIST MASSACRE
—WHOSE FAULT?

Rosethrush fumbled for the switch, turned off the VR rig and pulled the headband off. She blinked in the light of her office, massaging her forehead where she'd just had a sixteenth-century sword driven through her skull. No matter how disgusting she found it, she had to admit it was great pix, the ideal opener for the special on time exploitation.

She had to decide whether to go with it. Certainly it would be better if such tours were outlawed. Sure they made money, but they pandered to people's worst instincts. And they were raw meat for protesters. Incidents like this massacre gave capitalism a bad name.

On the other hand, interveners' tours drew attention away

from more subtle forms of time exploitation, which would only be the next targets if extremes were outlawed.

And finally, the situation presented Rosethrush a temptation. She could count on a huge audience for the Inca Massacre exposé. The straitlaced public that would never think of indulging in such a tour could wire in and exercise its prurience and moral outrage at the same time.

The curse of the modern age was the contradiction between public propriety and private vice. Rosethrush was chair of the industry's censorship board. Did she want to profit from that contradiction? Could she afford to court a conflict of interest?

She put the decision off and turned to some more mundane work. On her desk was a quarterly statement on Harmony's pharmaceutical branch. Ralph had sunk deep money into his latest project, to create new antibiotics using microbes from the past. He hadn't told Owen, but he was counting on the Cretaceous station to provide specimens he could use.

Owen was too busy to care anyway. He had Wilma established at the College of Advanced Thought. Thornberry's gardener had fallen to his knees in prayers of delivery, and the relandscaping had begun. Owen's nighttime excursion with Wilma, culminating in the filmed encounter with the state trooper, had made a pretty good flare in the continental media. This, preceding his testimony in the Zealot trial, had renewed his celebrity.

But though Simon's trial was approaching its climax, it had not provided the juice Rosethrush had expected. She had thought that when the trial began, a public debate on time exploitation would follow. No such luck. Maybe Owen's appearance would boost ratings, but she had her doubts. Knowing her son, he would probably just answer the questions. As dense as neutronium.

His mind was completely set on convincing Emma Zume

of his worthiness. Rosethrush could not peg Emma. She had certainly charmed Ralph, for instance. For the most part she seemed the kind of idealistic, ultimately ineffectual person who would make a good match for her son. It was better for a woman to be beautiful than smart, because most men could see better than they could think—but Rosethrush suspected there was an edge of hard intelligence beneath Emma's idealism. Or was she giving Emma credit for intelligence simply because nobody could really be more naive than Owen?

Regardless, whether he realized it or not, it was inevitable Owen would pop the question to Emma sometime soon. Now if only Rosethrush could figure out some way to work Wilma into the wedding.

Her intercom buzzed. "Mr. Parker is here to see you."

"Thank you, Gracie. Please send him in."

Ralph had once described Parker as the kind of man only Thomas Hobbes could love: nasty, brutish and short. He had been one of the earliest trendsetters to go shabby, refusing to twank himself handsome. "How are you, Mrs. Vannice?" he said.

Parker's big-shouldered electric-blue lamé jacket hung to his knees, over a gold shirt and flashing red tie. He pulled a stick of Force out of his pocket, unwrapped it and popped it into his mouth. A man who chewed personality gum during a negotiation was no contest.

"Fine," she said. "How was Mars?"

"The tour broke even, and I suppose it was good publicity, but otherwise it was a bust. No nightlife. Frankly, I don't see the point of spending any resources colonizing another planet. At least if we go into the past there are people around we can use."

"That's the point about Mars—there are no people, so there are no politics."

"No politics? You should see those crazy immigrants. Ten minutes after they arrive they're calling themselves Martians, wanting to set up their own government."

"They get surly and we cut off their oxygen. That's another reason for sending them to Mars. They're going to be dependent on us for a long time."

"I thought the idea was to get rid of the dependent, not to keep them that way. History is a better investment."

"I forgot," Rosethrush said, "you're the expert on handling historicals."

The dig had no effect. Parker had been a propaganda officer in the 1775 M-U before an uprising there shut down the entire project, abandoning an oil refinery and wasting five years of groundwork. Largely because he had done nothing to insulate the historicals from cultural dislocation. Just like a man to let his appetites rule while business went awry.

But Parker had come out smelling like a rose, largely because he'd brought back with him an eighteen-year-old version of Wolfgang Mozart, who stormed the charts with his genuinely new pop sound. Now Parker headed his own entertainment cartel. The heart of it was Anachros, the supergroup. Mozart on synthesizer, with Franz Liszt keyboards, Sappho doing vocals, Jimmy Blanton playing bass, Sidney Bechet blowing sax, and an AI drummer. But Bechet has just quit, and Parker was looking for a new sax. Rosethrush had John Coltrane under contract.

"Have you been paying attention to Saltimbanque's new mystery boy, Ben Simeon?" Parker asked. "Where did they find him? He's flattened our latest album. It's not fair for them to keep him under wraps. The very fact they won't produce him is stealing our press. It's unethical."

"Maybe you need a new angle. I have a suggestion: a live percussionist. A historical giant."

"You're missing *the concept*. Anachros isn't just another time-immigrant band. It isn't about historicals playing pop. It's about *destroying the relevance* of history. It's science as sound. AI percussion is a vital part of—"

"You want science, I've got science. Richard Feynman."

"Who?"

"Richard Feynman! One of the greatest physicists of the twentieth century. And a cutting-edge drummer." The intercom buzzed again. Gracie's face came on. "Mr. Thrillkiller and that other man are here."

"Send them in." Parker wanted to keep complaining. She raised a hand. "We'll talk drummers later."

The door opened and Lance Thrillkiller came in, followed by Simon. Thrillkiller had Simon dressed in a modern suit, and his trimmed beard might have passed for contemporary, but the bright orange court-mandated wristward stood out like a fire alarm. He was dark and small and his soft brown eyes were completely unreadable.

During the introductions, Parker offered Simon his hand. Simon looked at Parker calmly for a moment, then took it. Rosethrush offered them papaya juice. "I understand you've just returned from Seattle?" she asked Thrillkiller.

"We made all the local media outlets," Thrillkiller said, "and did a mall interview. ComPP hosted a fund-raising dinner in the Space Needle."

"Good. Simon, although it's really not my place to get involved on either side, I've helped Mr. Thrillkiller meet up with Mr. Parker to cut a song."

"Wolf is very interested," Parker said. "We see this as an opportunity for Anachros to get involved in the time protection movement, a cause which deeply moves us. The band doesn't forget where they came from."

Simon's stare made Parker fidget. "I will write the lyrics," Simon said, as casual as if he were ordering lunch.

"Simon, this is a professional production," Parker said, dripping condescension. "You don't have any experience."

"It will be a blues song. Also, as I've told Mr. Thrillkiller, I want to reserve the right to direct my own defense before LEX."

Rosethrush leaned forward. "You're right to take an active interest in your defense, Simon. But you are unfamiliar with how our legal system works."

"We've got Diane Ontiveros, one of the best advocates in the business, as your lawyer," Thrillkiller said. "She's won three Darrows for best performance defending a capital case."

"Nevertheless, I will arrange a statement."

"What kind of statement?"

"Things that must be said in my behalf."

"We'll need to see it," Rosethrush said.

"You have to be honest with your lawyer, Simon," Thrillkiller said. "It's her job to lie afterward."

"I have taken God's instruction on this. If I am to be judged, it must be on God's terms."

Rosethrush had met many historicals who acted as out of their natural place as Simon, but none who at the same time seemed so aware of it and not overwhelmed by that fact. He was disarming. None of this communicated itself in the media appearances he'd made. It was too bad, for his own sake, that Simon could not meet the public en masse, in person.

Thrillkiller jumped in. "You don't understand, Simon, these things have to be carefully orchestrated. Every element of a PR-influenced trial must be thought out. In a single minute at the trial, you could undo all the hard work we've done."

Simon ignored Thrillkiller and addressed Rosethrush. "I understand you are interested in increasing the audience. Tell them that I am going to present a statement, but no one knows what it will be. This will make more people want to know what will happen, no?"

He had a point.

Parker's wristward beeped. He looked sour. "I've got another appointment. You wrangle this thing out. I'll expect you at the Astoria studio on Monday to meet with the boys," he told Thrillkiller. "Nice to meet you, Simon."

Rosethrush stood up. "Simon, I think we may be able to accommodate you. Meanwhile, why don't you step outside with Mr. Parker and wait in the reception area. Mr. Thrillkiller and I need to discuss some of the legal maneuverings we'll need to make to arrange for your statement."

Simon bowed his head. He stood and followed Parker out. As soon as the door closed, Lance spoke up. "I'm sorry about that, Mrs. Vannice. He's got a mind of his own, it's been hard for me to ride herd on him. Why did you ask me to bring him here in the first place?"

"Because I wanted to get some estimate of how this trial is going to come out."

"Maybe this song thing will work. He's very committed."

"Don't kid yourself. You haven't got a prayer."

Thrillkiller looked at his shoes. "I know."

"Public opinion polls are running seventy–thirty in favor of continued time exploitation, 'with proper controls.' Your grassroots campaign is pure astroturf. That would be all right if it were high-quality astroturf, or if there were a lot of it. Let him make some ideological rant before LEX, and the likelihood of an acquittal is slim."

"Maybe this statement he makes will show people how overwhelmed he is. He's a pretty pathetic character."

"Pathetic people are not attractive."

"Well, a conviction isn't necessarily bad," Lance said. "If you want more press, the appeals could go on for years."

"Appeals? On what grounds? This thing is so open-and-shut it'll be forgotten in a week. Plus, I happen to know that Saltimbanque is planning to drop a bombshell at the trial that will blow Simon back to the penitentiary so fast, all that will be left is his shadow on the courtroom wall. I'm going to lose a lot of cash on this first round. For the next trial, Jephthah, I want to suggest a new approach."

"What do you have in mind?"

"I don't think rational arguments are the way to do this. Who cares about the principle of self-determination? You must generate charisma. Play up the rebel leader, the dark, dangerous man of action."

"And Simon?"

"There's something more to him than pathos, but you heard him. He has a message from God? If you talk to God, you are praying; if God talks to you, you have schizophrenia. I don't think this is going to help his PR problem."

"So what happens?"

"Cut your losses. He goes up, he goes down, he goes away. We move on." She showed Thrillkiller to the door. "I trust you not to tell Simon any of this."

After he left, Rosethrush buzzed Gracie. "Gracie, give any calls in the next hour to my simulant. I'm going to be reviewing this month's VR releases for the ratings board." She rang off, fitted the headband on again and slid into the bedroom of a luxury suite at the old Plaza Hotel. She felt the tug of a cross-gendered virtuality experience; on the wall above the bed, in flaming letters, the title appeared:

THE ELIZABETH TAYLOR WEDDING NIGHTS.

She did not see how this could possibly be socially justifiable. But it was her duty to see it through.

On the way out to Connecticut Gen sampled three different mood drugs from the courtesy bar of the limousine Owen had sent for her. How would Emma Zume greet the man she was falling in love with? Should she be bright and curious? Darkly thoughtful? Gen settled on calm. Emma Zume, confident in her propriety, would be properly calm.

Evening was approaching when she drew up before the veterinary labs at the College of Advanced Thought. Owen stood in the entrance, wearing a cashmere jacket, slacks, an open-collared shirt. His mood boots gleamed a passionate red. He hurried forward to meet her, opened the limo door. "I'm so glad you could come."

"Is something wrong with Wilma?" she asked, letting him help her out.

"No, no. She's taken very well to the new surroundings. No signs of tampering with her since the move. She likes to wallow in the lake. It's no problem. The students like her: she's the new mascot. And the scientists on the faculty are ecstatic."

"So why did you ask me here?"

Owen hesitated. "I thought you might be able to guess." He took her back to a paddock off the rear of the building. Wilma looked up from a basin of oats and snorted when she saw

Owen. Owen stroked her neck. "Let's go for a walk," he said to Gen.

Owen led Wilma out, and they headed down toward the lake at the center of the campus. A number of students watched them. In the glow of the westering sun, Gen could see the inroads Wilma had already made in the pines. Wilma's head bobbed forward and back on her reaching neck as she trotted along, unearthly, majestic, deeply weird. The sunset painted her yellow sides gold. Her eyes gleamed with a hysterical light, and she lashed her tail languidly as they followed her down to the lakeside. Gen was sincerely glad that the tampering with the dinosaur had stopped.

Owen, shy as a young boy, slipped his hand into Gen's. "A beautiful evening," Emma said. "Look, there's Venus."

"You're a stargazer?"

The trick to being a convincing Emma Zume was to give Emma a little of Genevieve Faison. "I love to look at the stars. It puts everything in perspective. The only legitimate justification I can see for your Cretaceous station is the early astronomical research."

"I'm so glad to hear that. It makes me think you may not completely disapprove of me." He faced her. "Emma, there's something I need to speak with you about."

She squeezed his hand. "Yes, Owen?"

"You've got me thinking about right and wrong, Emma. You know, most people don't pay any more attention to their system of morality than to their shoes."

"I suppose that's why they're so moral."

"No, they pay *less* attention to morality than their shoes."

"Ah—but not you, Owen."

"Uh—right. You see, Emma, you've called my attention to my own behavior. I don't blame you for having the wrong impression of me at the beginning. So I'm going to show you what I'm made of. I've contacted the defense at the Zealot trial, and persuaded them to challenge the authenticity of the pix of the hostage siege. In response, the prosecution has called me in to testify. I want you to watch. On the witness stand I'll demonstrate what I stand for."

"But Owen, wouldn't you rather stay out of the public eye?"

"To prove myself to you I'd risk anything. Listen, Emma. Though some might call it unseemly, even rash when we've known each other such a short time, I have felt an instinctive understanding between us from the first moment I saw you."

"On the lawn, where you were disguised as someone else?"

"Right after that. I'm a scientist, Emma, and I know about evolution. In their times, dinosaurs like Wilma—"

Wilma, hearing her name, bumped her head against Owen's shoulder, almost sending him sprawling. Gen caught him.

"Are you all right?"

Owen pushed Wilma's head away. He showed only a trace of annoyance. "Yes. What I mean to say is . . . creatures like the *Apatosaurus megacephalos* were, during their times, the highest expression of the biological tropism toward complexity. Just as we are today. We act out these scientific truths whether we are aware of them or not. . . . I'm talking about love, Emma. Love is evolutionarily determined. A kinship exists between us that may be young and undeveloped, like little Wilma, but like Wilma—" The dinosaur swayed toward him again, and Owen ducked. "—it has in it the programming to become very large."

"And strong."

"Yes—that's right! Stronger than custom, or family—"

"Or thought. Some things are wired into our natures, and individuals can't go against them."

"Yes! That's exactly what I was trying to say! That's miraculous! How did you know?"

She turned her back to him and concentrated on Wilma,

who was now poking her head into the shallows as if to root around for lily pads. "I can read many of your thoughts, Owen."

"Then you must know what I want to ask you. Though I'm hardly worthy of the least attention—"

"Oh, I can see your sterling qualities, underneath that rough exterior."

"No, Emma! I'm not worth it."

"But you are, Owen. What you've just said about your sense of right and wrong proves it, beyond doubt. You deserve me. No one could deserve me more."

Wilma stopped, lifted her head as if to check that they were still there.

From behind, Owen put his hands on Gen's shoulders. "That's why I love you," he said. "You're so much better than I, so pure, so dedicated."

"I know."

"You're so good that I'm prepared to face Mother and demand we be permitted to marry immediately. Despite our difference in class."

She stood on her toes, her back still to him. "How big of you, Owen. How you've grown—like Wilma." She pointed at the dinosaur. "You're so large. You're such a *large* man."

"Not really."

"You *are.*"

"I'm not so large, but—"

"Well, you would know."

Owen turned her to face him. "Emma, would you—could you—might you give me your hand in marriage? A marriage, not just of bodies, but of minds—of souls!" His face was lit with nobility, as if he were posing for a statue of some pilgrim father signing the Mayflower Compact.

"This is so sudden!" she breathed. "But of course, Owen. Yes."

"Darling!"

He drew her toward him, bending to kiss her. She let him, briefly, then pulled away and lowered her chin to her shoulder, shy as a buttercup. "Please, Owen. These people!"

"Emma, dearest. You make me blush."

"There is a good deal to be said for blushing, if one can do it at the proper moment," she said. She retreated from him a few steps, and when he followed, he tripped over Wilma's tail and fell on his face.

Riding back to New York Gen flipped through the pix in the back of the limo. Kemal Night's blabshow was running another report on the Zealot trial. After the new video by Anachros, Night did an interview with Simon.

The video was adequate, a retro blues with a simple lyric. Anachros had a new drummer, a dark-haired man Gen did not recognize. The interview was curious. Simon sat quietly. In answer to the breathless vidiot's questions, he told about the planning of the assault on the hotel as if he were not ashamed of it. He did not seem out of his depth. He did not talk about exploitation. He did not stress his confusion and helplessness. At first Gen thought, what a bad idea, he's going to alienate the watchers, or bore them. What an abject political towelhead, a born loser.

But as the interview went on, Simon's directness began to grow on her. It was so against the grain of the typical flash-edited chat that it was interesting. If any viewers managed to stay tuned past their normal attention spans, this approach actually might make inroads.

It was late night when she got back to August's Greenwich Village apartment. She found her father sitting in his reading chair, a glass of scotch in his hand, an opened book on his lap. "How did it go?"

"He asked me to marry him."

He set down the scotch. "You're not going to do it, are you?"

This was harder than she thought it would be. It was so different from the last time Owen wanted to marry her, back in Jerusalem. She sat down on the sofa. "Yes, I am."

August shook his head slowly. "Remember, you're not just marrying him, you're getting the whole family."

Genevieve smiled. "Watching Owen Vannice relate to his family is like watching a man pinned helplessly beneath a huge stone. But that's just it, Dad: he's *not* helpless. He's *chosen* helplessness."

"He may be helpless, but don't underestimate his mother. Rosethrush Vannice has teeth." August drummed his fingers on the arm of his chair, watching her. Through the opened window a breeze carried the sound of street music. "This revenge is a powerful emotion, Genevieve. You can't tell when it might be time to beat a retreat."

"I'll pass on your advice to the first person I meet who can use it."

"Don't get angry," August said. "I'm worried about you. If you were marrying Vannice to scam him, I'd approve. If you genuinely loved him, I'd say you were crazy but I'd approve. But this seems seriously conflicted. You love him, you hate him."

"I hate what he represents. His blindness, his hypocrisy. He ought to be better than he is."

"So? We're not social workers, we're con artists. A mark may learn a lesson from running into us, but that's not why we con them."

"He doesn't need to be conned. He cons himself." She told August about Owen's plan to testify at the Zealot trial. "It's a perfect example of what's twisted about him. He talks to the defense, then testifies for the prosecution. He's not above being tricky, but he tells himself he's working within the system—when with all his money and connections he could simply *buy* Simon's freedom! To be an honest man he'd have to learn how dishonest he is. Break a law on purpose, and make no excuses. If he doesn't watch out, he'll become like his father, a pillar of society who makes money selling pornography as historical material."

"Again, where do you fit into this? Owen Vannice isn't unique. I never came across anyone in whom the moral sense was dominant who was not heartless, cruel, vindictive, log-stupid and entirely lacking in the smallest sense of humanity."

Gen wasn't listening "It's the same thing with Wilma. He violates the past, but claims to be against exploitation. He thinks if he feels sorry about it somehow that makes it all right. As if sympathy alone ever accomplished anything!"

The doorbell rang. August got up and checked the security camera. "It's a delivery girl. From a florist."

"Send her up."

August buzzed the girl up and Gen met her at the apartment door. She wore a yellow uniform halter and shorts, powered shoes. Bucktoothed and freckled, she had probably been indentured to the job from an employment opportunity center. The transparent box contained a dozen long-stemmed roses, with blooms as big as saucers. The cost of the flowers alone would have kept the delivery girl for a month. "How lovely," Gen said. She slipped the girl a twenty-dollar piece. "Thank you."

"Don't mention it."

Gen closed the apartment door, examined the card that came with the flowers. A tiny image of Owen spoke to her. "Emma. One rose for every sleepless hour I'll have thinking of you."

Gen closed the card. "I'm going to do this, August. I'm

going to give the Vannice clan a thrashing they'll never forget."

August sighed. "I expect the audience for that will be huge. Give the public what they want to see and they'll be sure to come out for it."

Chapter 9

Witness for the Prosecution

Ever since he had heard Owen describe to Emma Zume his planned testimony, Bill had been advising Owen against it. =This is exactly the kind of situation your parents bought me for. You'll put yourself in the way of public ridicule, if not legal hazard, for no good reason.=

"Showing Emma what I stand for isn't a good reason?"

=Trust God, not shopping; dreaming men, funny women.=

The physical courtroom, crammed into the Stamford Vannicom studios, was not large. At the front stood LEX's polished mahogany bench. Before the bench was the performance space, with its matte black floor and the dramatic stage lighting. Next came the tables of the defense and the plaintiff, and behind a rail, an arc of a dozen seats for witnesses and those spectators who were physically present. But the courtroom was wired for VR, and countless subscribers jacking in would be there watching.

Not only would they watch, but each participant's sensorium was backwired to the court. Their instantaneous judgments about the case were crunched by a computer. Home viewers could pull down a monitor that would display at any moment the state of public opinion: on the defendant's guilt or innocence, LEX's rulings, the lawyers' arguments, the lawyers' clothes, the lawyers' cosmetic surgery, whether it would be fun to sleep with the defendant, did the defendant look like a person who preferred cats or dogs, and how, if the defendant should be found guilty of a capital offense, the execution should be carried out. The same feedback was also wired into LEX's judgment program. A modern arbitration like Simon's trial became a struggle, not just to convince LEX, but to affect that invisible audience. Everything leading up to the trial was designed to prepare that audience to be sympathetic to one or the other side.

In the courtroom, the only indicator of that feedback was the large display on the front of LEX's bench. Not visible to the witnesses testifying, it gave the number of viewers participating, while a simple needle ran along a graduated scale from the green of "Acquit" to the red of "Convict." The lawyers judged from this how the minute-by-minute PR surge was running. A good advocate was a person who could wing it, adjusting his strategy from moment to moment in keeping with the VR jury's reaction, without losing track of the framework of law within which LEX would rule.

At the Saltimbanque table were Jerry Canady heading the plaintiff's team, and his two regular assistants, Lisa Yuanxin and Wanda Skolnik (who had already become a notorious figure on the worldwide net because of her demure seriousness and great legs). Plus a dark man Owen did not recognize. "Who is that?" he whispered.

=Delbert Lamont,= Bill said. =PR. He's monitoring responses and advising Canady on his closing argument. When you cross them he's going to have Canady use you for wallpaper.=

In contrast to the crowded prosecution table, at the defense table sat Simon and Diane Ontiveros. Simon wore a woolen tunic and a leather belt, a headband, sandals. "The embattled little guy," Owen muttered.

=The lone fanatic. The guaranteed loser, no matter what you do.=

"Hear ye, hear ye, the court of the honorable LEX is now in session. All rise."

The in-court spectators rose, and Owen got up with them.

The door behind the bench opened and LEX entered. Today he had chosen to be a huge black raven with a yellow beak and beady eyes. A sharp crest of midnight feathers shot up from his narrow head. He wore striped trousers, a waistcoat, a stand-up collar with jet cravat, black cutaway and brilliant white gloves. Only the fact that Owen knew it was an illusion kept him from thinking the creature was really there.

LEX settled down behind the desk. "Be seated," it said in a skirling voice that stood the hairs on the back of Owen's neck. "In our last episode, the defense challenged the authenticity of the Herod's Palace security pix. Mr. Canady, are you prepared to respond?"

"Yes, LEX. We call Dr. Owen Vannice to the stand."

Owen moved to the witness stand. The lights were bright enough that he could not see past the lawyers' tables: there might have been an army of watchers. He looked over at Simon. If Ontiveros had told him of Owen's plan, he showed no signs of either hope or resignation.

"Dr. Vannice," Canady began, "thank you for taking the time out of your busy schedule to be here. Thanks to the pix in question we've all witnessed your heroic action in the resolution of the Jerusalem hostage crisis, for which we must commend you."

"Thank you."

"In regard to those pix, in your view, are they an accurate representation of what occurred in the Herod's Palace Hotel?"

"As far as it goes, yes."

"I want you to identify for us the man who threatened to kill you at the end of that confrontation."

"Objection, LEX," Ontiveros said. "We don't know the defendant's intentions."

"Sustained. Try again, Jerry."

Canady was undeterred. "Is the man who pointed his weapon at you here in this courtroom?"

"Yes he is. But—"

"Would you point him out for us?"

Owen pointed to Simon. "There he is. But I want to make clear that he didn't shoot, although—"

Canady looked vexed. "He was standing there, with a rifle."

"Yes"

"And he pointed it at you."

"Yes, that's so. But—"

"So the tranquilizing gas kept him from firing."

"Objection, Your Honor. Leading."

"Sustained," said LEX.

Canady's eyes flicked over the feedback indicator. "Let me rephrase that, Dr. Vannice. You were there. As the pix seem to show, were you passing out from the tranquilizing gas?"

"Yes."

"Were the other hostages likewise affected?"

"Yes."

"Is it likely that anyone not wearing a gas mask would be equally affected by the gas?"

"I suppose so. But—"

"That's all, Your Honor."

Owen looked at Simon, who was watching the indicator on the front of LEX's desk. He doubted anything he'd said so far had done much to nudge it toward "Acquit."

=Nice job, boss. Now let it go.=

Diane Ontiveros got up for the cross-examination. "Dr. Vannice, when you were injured during the assault, did the defendant do anything to hurt you?"

"No. In fact, he prevented the guard from hurting me further."

"Now, in trying to understand the defendant's behavior, let me ask you—you yourself have experience with time travel to distant moment universes, is that right?"

"Yes, I do."

"You might even be said to be an expert on the effects of time travel. As a scientist, Dr. Vannice, would you give us your opinion of the effects of time travel on the present and past? What has the result been since the first cat was sent back to the 2022 moment universe by Patel in 2035?"

"Objection, Your Honor!" Canady said. "Immaterial."

"I'm going to allow it," LEX chirped. "Ratings could use a boost."

It was the opening Owen had hoped for. Bill whispered, =I don't suppose at this point you want to listen to reason.=

"Time travel's had many deleterious effects," Owen said.

=I didn't think so. I'm outta here, boss.=

"In your opinion, what have these effects been?" Ontiveros asked.

Now he would show Emma who he really was. "We're all aware of them. For instance, you go back into a two-second-old moment universe and you can pull an essential duplicate of a real person into our world. These historical duplicates have been used for fraud."

"Isn't that illegal?"

"It hasn't stopped people from doing it. But that's the least of time travel's deleterious effects. Look at the effect on the economy! How many plastic farms have gone out of business since we've started pumping petrochemicals out of the past? Plus, the psychic costs have been immeasurable! We're living by the past so much we've closed off our own future. Try to become a writer or entertainer or athlete on your own today, when you have to compete with the best of all history."

=You're in free fall now.=

Owen ignored Bill. He was enjoying this, and Bill's attempts to derail him only made it more sweet. He was acting on principle, in defiance of what his parents wanted. He felt himself growing eloquent. "What about the destruction of past peoples? The antibiotic-resistant microbes of the twenty-first century have wreaked havoc in earlier eras. Influenza killed millions in the fourteenth century alone, exceeding deaths caused by the Black Plague. How do we know the retrovirus explosion in the late twentieth wasn't a result of contamination by time travelers?"

=Without a net.=

"By entering the past we are creating whole new universes! Whole other earths, other human races, which we create and abandon. We steal their significant historical figures and leave them to struggle on, and never even know how or whether they cope."

=Wake me when you hit.=

"Then there are the theoretical questions. What about bleed-over? You can't go on burning adjacent moment universes without eventually having an effect on the fabric of time itself. You create a focused mass of altered timestreams and you're going to affect our own. A black hole of warped history, sucking us down into it."

=That noise you hear is the sound of fingernails scraping the bottom of the barrel.=

Ontiveros asked, "What about those who say that there have been no measurable effects?"

"How would we know? Once the past has been changed, the present goes along and we are none the wiser."

"Supposing all this to be true, Dr. Vannice, does it in any way justify Simon's actions?" Ontiveros asked.

"I'm not saying that. All I'm saying is that some much larger crimes have to be ignored before we presume to judge those men who took over the basement of Herod's Palace."

"Thank you, Dr. Vannice, for your frank and honest appraisal." Ontiveros swept her arm outward in a magnanimous gesture as she spun to face the gallery. "I'm sure it must have been difficult for you to speak the truth when your interests lie so strongly on the other side."

She returned to the defense table. Owen started to rise.

Jerry Canady held up his hand. "Just a minute, Dr. Vannice."

The prosecution lawyers conferred, grim-faced. Delbert Lamont's head was an inch from Canady's, whispering in his ear while Canady stared impassively at Owen. The witness stand felt suddenly uncomfortable.

"Your Honor, we'd like the opportunity to redirect," Canady said.

"Go ahead."

=Nice knowing you, Owen.=

Canady stood and came forward, a tight smile on his face. Owen tried not to feel nervous. "Dr. Vannice, are you an expert on time-travel case law?"

"I'm not."

"So you don't know that it's illegal to take doubles of living citizens, or the recently deceased, from moment universes?"

"It may be illegal, but people still do it."

"Are you an expert on the economics of time travel?"

"Not exactly. But I've done a lot—"

"In fact, it costs a lot of money to go back two seconds. So much so that the number of documented cases of illegal doubles being taken is—twelve. Should we close down a multibillion-dollar industry, one that employs hundreds of thousands of people and has beneficial effects throughout our economy, for the twelve times people have used this technology against the law?"

"Those crimes are just the tip of the iceberg."

"I didn't know you were an expert in icebergs, either. Now, you talked about 'bleed-over.' Tell us, Dr. Vannice, is your doctorate in temporal physics?"

"Uh—no."

"You are a paleontologist, is that correct?"

"Yes."

"At present, are you affiliated with any accredited college or university?"

"No. I was at MIT, but—"

"So, in fact, you don't have any scientific basis for lecturing us about the concept of bleed-over, do you?"

Owen tried to keep calm. "Well, okay. It's generally felt that those moment universes are completely separate from our own past."

"Thank you. You used the term 'fabric of time.' Is there any scientific evidence that time is a fabric?"

"Uh—not exactly."

"Do you know where that term comes from?"

"It's in common use."

" 'Fabric of time' is a metaphor that was popular in the science fiction of the twentieth century. In fact, according to contemporary physics, time is a quantum gas. Do you know what a quantum gas is?"

"Not precisely."

" 'Not precisely.' " Canady turned to the invisible audience. "We're talking about reality, not metaphysical concepts like 'bleed-over' or archaic fantasies like the 'fabric of time.' "

"Some reputable scientists speculate—"

"Isn't it true that we have visited moment universes adjacent to ours to the next second," Canady said, "and that when we do so we find no perceptible difference until we begin to make an effect on it ourselves? That according to every study ever undertaken, our present, the True Moment, has not been affected in any way by changes made to past moment universes?"

"As I said before, how would we know?"

"How would *you?* at any rate. You mentioned those petrochemicals taken from the past. How many people have been able to afford artificial hearts because of those cheap petrochemicals?"

"I wouldn't know."

"Those plastic farms were only started when we ran out of oil. Now that we have another source, we don't need them. As the son of wealth, and a cosseted academic, I guess we can't expect you to be familiar with the world of commerce, but that's the way the marketplace works. Yet you sit before us wearing a pair of mood boots made from oil piped from past versions of fields that were exhausted when you were a child."

"Objection, LEX!" Ontiveros said. "Mr. Canady is making a speech, not examining the witness."

LEX's crestfeathers waggled in excitement. "Sure. But it's a pretty good speech. Go for it!"

Owen tried to regain the initiative. "You're talking about science, or economics," he protested. "But the moral issue has not been settled."

"Precisely. Settling it is one outcome we hope this trial will have." Canady moved away from the stand, toward the viewing audience. "We're not saying time use has had no effect. It's had an enormous effect: a positive one. Our lives have been immensely enriched by the things we've brought from the past. Our children go into the park and feed the passenger pigeons, and come home to play with Rin Tin Tin—the very same loyal, faithful, intelligent dog that made all those movies in the twentieth century."

Canady pressed ahead. "If it's not beneath you, Dr. Vannice, you should go down to your local mall and walk into an art shop, where anyone of modest means can purchase an original of the *Mona Lisa, Starry Night,* or *The Persistence of Memory.*"

"But the effects on historicals—" Owen said.

"For every historical who's been harmed by a disease brought from the future, we've saved ten using modern medical science. Why see those created moment universes as a debit when they could as easily be seen as a great unintended benefit of time-visiting. Whole new universes exist. Whole new versions of history. Who's to say that the inhabitants of those alternative histories don't live better lives than they lived in our own history?"

"Ask Simon about that," Owen said.

Canady turned back to Owen, as if he'd forgotten him. "Dr. Vannice, I seem to recall that you are running an experiment on an apatosaur."

"That's true."

"A creature that's been extinct for sixty-five million years. Are you telling us that you harmed the past by bringing that creature to the present? That you're harming the dinosaur by studying it? How can you, who altered history yourself by establishing your research station and bringing her here, take a position in opposition to time travel?"

"I know things about that dinosaur that you can't possibly understand."

"So you say. In the area of paleontology I'm prepared to listen. As a witness to the assault on the Jerusalem hotel you are no doubt reliable. But as an expert on the effects of time travel you are a paranoid who would impoverish our cultural and economic lives, for nothing."

"Objection!" Diane Ontiveros said.

"I withdraw the question," Canady said. "That's all, Your Honor."

=Splat.=

"The witness is excused!" LEX crowed. "Used and abused!"

Owen looked over at the defense table. Diane Ontiveros was watching the viewer reaction indicator with a grim expression on her face. Simon sat impassive, as if nothing had happened. On the way out Owen glanced over his shoulder and saw the needle in the far red.

Owen's boots felt like they were made of lead, and he did not need to look at them to know they were a sickly green. He left the courtroom as quickly as possible. On the steps in front of the studio, he was greeted by a host of reporters. Owen brushed them aside. But as he tried to move toward his waiting limousine, a woman in sixteenth-century Japanese clothing threw herself at him. She tore apart the top of her kimono, exposing her breasts. "We're all animals!" she shouted. "We're all extinct!"

Owen gave her his coat, then ducked into the limo. "Thanks for not killing her," Owen told Bill.

=Hard work ends obsessive bed poetry laughter.=

Throughout Vannice's testimony Simon watched the indicator plunge steadily toward "Convict." At the end Diane Ontiveros was scribbling furious notes on her thinkpad. "You have to let me make the closing statement," she whispered to Simon, "or this case is lost."

"If the case is lost, then it doesn't matter who speaks," Simon said. "Allow me the dignity of choosing my own end."

LEX stood. "Next come the closing arguments. For those of you who may have tapped in late, we remind you that the defendant Simon the Zealot is charged with conspiracy, riot, kidnapping and attempted murder. In order that we may proceed without any misunderstandings, let me reiterate that I am going to allow counsels for the defense and plaintiff wide latitude in their arguments. We've seen the physical and testimonial evidence, experienced the unsuccessful raid on the Herod's Palace Hotel in the 1200 GMT 16 February 29 C.E. moment universe, and its aftermath. But from what perspective are we to view this incident? Justice is a public thing. Justice is political. Prejudice, hearsay, misinformation, ignorance and plain blockheaded stupidity all must have their say. That's where you in the participating audience come in."

LEX paused and glared down at the contending representatives like an upstart crow. "In the closing statements, as per the previously enacted coin flip, the plaintiff has first serve."

Jerry Canady stood. "We've called in a special spokesman for closing, LEX."

"Objection!" Ontiveros shouted.

"Is this going to be interesting, Mr. Canady?" LEX asked.

"I hope it will be very interesting."

"Okay, I'm going to allow it. Who is this new spokesman?"

"Our closing argument will be made by a Saltimbanque employee: Mr. Abraham Lincoln."

At that even the spectators in the room murmured. The door at the back opened and in walked a gangly bearded man. Ontiveros put her head in her hands. "Who is this?" Simon asked her.

"This is your worst nightmare," the lawyer muttered.

An untidy shock of black hair fell over the tall man's forehead. He wore an awkward black suit. Stoop-shouldered, his face deeply lined, he moved to the performance area. He lifted his head and took a good long look at LEX. If he was intimidated it did not show.

"Your Honor, thank you for this opportunity," Lincoln began. "Part of this case rests on the proper treatment of historicals. I was born in 1809. On April 14, 1865, while attending a play at Ford's Theater, I was shot by the actor John Wilkes Booth. Thirty seconds after the assault I was abducted by a team of agents from the Saltimbanque Corporation, rushed to an intensive care unit in the year 2058, and through the miracles of modern medicine experienced a full recovery. Were it not for the intervention of the people of your time, I would not be alive today. And thanks to the Saltimbanque Corporation, I have my son Will back, and my family reunited.

"I want to speak to the issue of the exploitation of the past.

"I do not pretend to understand the awful power that men have bent to the service of time travel. I do not pretend to be able to weigh, or judge, what is a people's just deserts. Certainly the defendant, a man of the Holy Land, who walked the same stones that the son of the Creator walked over two thousand years ago, has a knowledge of his own place and time that I cannot contradict.

"But I am otherwise acquainted with the people of the past, whom you call historicals. For the most part, historicals are poor. That does not mean they are helpless. We make our own world, and we have the will to affect it. Under this new dispensation, all people of all times are brothers; through the portal of your machines, they are neighbors. Commerce with people of the future offers the historical the chance to eliminate that poverty that has been the lot of most men from our fathers' times to this. Change is coming.

"But in this new world, as in the old one, it cannot be just to take up arms against one's neighbor without just cause. Fellow citizens, we cannot escape history. And history, it seems, cannot escape us. It must be therefore that the people of the past will have to learn to live in a world which contains the future. Time travel offers the poor their last, best chance to seize their own lives, to rise or fall on their merits. It offers the freedom my people fought for, a chance to work.

"It seems to me, however reluctant I may be to say so, that the defendant's actions, and those of his fellows, as well as a rebellion against duly constituted authority, were an admission that they could not rise to the occasion that was offered them. We must not rejoice in their failure, but neither should we condone it. The Saltimbanque Corporation may be an alien force in ancient Jerusalem, but it is not the corporation that rules in Jerusalem; it is Simon's people. A just God will have to decide whether this man has sinned, but there can be no doubt that he has raised his hand against his neighbor.

"In 1865 the people of the future intervened to prevent a bitter man, in the service of a lost cause, from killing me. Fervently I pray that we not establish the letting of blood in anger as a proper response to the peaceful intercourse we seek." He touched his breast, looked sadly over at the defense table. "Simon, my brother, it does my heart pain to say this."

Lincoln finished speaking, turned and, like a pine tree in a southern forest, slowly, majestically, fell over.

The spectators gasped. The lawyers rushed forward, rolled the Great Emancipator onto his back, and loosened his collar. "Call a doctor, call a doctor!" someone yelled. Lamont tore open Lincoln's shirt, and leaned forward to listen to his heart. Slowly he sat back on his heels. He looked up at LEX. "Your Honor," he said. "He's dead."

"Dead?"

"Yes. It looks like a massive coronary."

It took them forty minutes to bring in an emergency crew, remove the body and restore order. On the trial indicator, the figure listing the number of viewers tuned in tripled. Ontiveros turned fishy white. When LEX asked her to make her closing statement her mouth opened and shut several times in silence.

"I ask for a recess until tomorrow, LEX."

"Request denied," LEX said. "The air time is already scheduled. If we cut away now Lincoln will have died in vain—as far as ratings go."

"Now is the time," Simon whispered to the advocate. "Let me speak."

Ontiveros shrugged. "At least you've got an audience. I advise you to keep it simple."

Simon rose. "Given the fact that my accusers were allowed to call in this Abraham at the last minute," he said, "I would like to call in a friend to speak for me."

"We object, Your Honor," Canady said. "We haven't had this new spokesperson registered with the court. He shouldn't be allowed to spring some surprise on us."

"Mr. Lincoln's concluding rhetorical ploy here was certainly a surprise," LEX said. "I'll allow it. Mr. Simon, who is it you wish to speak for you? Is she or he here today?"

"I believe he is waiting outside. Would someone go back and see if Yeshu is ready?"

The courtroom buzzed. The doors opened again, and from the back of the room Jesus stepped forward. He was older than the Yeshu that Simon remembered. This was the one Detlev Gruber had told him about, recruited from a different moment universe. Since a brief period of fame after his retrieval, he had retreated to his privacy in Central America, his celebrity stolen by younger versions of Jesus not so burdened with personal history.

The wide sleeves of Yeshu's robe draped away from his strong brown arms. He was short, clean-shaven, balding, though a fringe of dark hair hung to his shoulders. His penetrating green eyes were wrinkled at the corners, as if he had spent a lot of time squinting into the sun without the least of cosmetic rejuvenators. He came forward, hugged Simon. The feel of his strong arms around him brought back memories that misted Simon's eyes.

Yeshu advanced to the center of the performance area. "Thank you, Your Honor, for giving me this chance to speak for this man Simon." His English was excellent, the trace of Aramaic showing through only adding to the voice's warm luster.

"Like Mr. Lincoln, I am a historical. Like him I was rescued from the point of my death, by men from an age I did not understand, for purposes I could not fathom. I remember standing before Pilate, feeling the pain of my whipped back, calm in the knowledge I would soon be dead in the service of the kingdom of God. But I did not die.

"Instead, I have lived in your world for twenty years now. At first I saw only its wonders. I was awed by its wealth. I was stunned by my salvation from the hands of the Romans. I was taken from my people, surrounded by those who called me their leader, who were not even Jews. I loved to eat, and drink, and you gave me much to eat and drink. I was lost. I lost myself.

"After a time I withdrew. I found a place alone in the wilderness, and the world went on to find another Yeshu, one that better suited its needs. I have spent all this time silent, because I did not know what to say. I did not know what I *could* say.

"Now I am back. I am back because though I could not speak for myself, I discovered I could speak, must speak, for this man. I have the advantage of knowing this world he has been forced into; he does not."

Though he had calculated this moment for months, Simon was surprised at the emotion that overwhelmed him. To hear that voice again, feel the power of that person . . . He closed his eyes, lowered his head and listened.

"Not many know that Simon is my cousin. He was a violent, an angry man. Many years ago, in a time and place so remote it seems at times like a dream to me, I went to his wedding. When the servants ran out of wine, I showed them how to drink water as wine. Simon became one of my friends, and followers. He turned from violence to peace. He strove to turn the other cheek. Let he who thinks this is easy, do it. He loved his wife, and his child. Now his wife is dead, and his son— I will tell you later about his son.

"Simon's name has significance. 'Simon the Zealot.' The zealot represents the zeal in man, the thirst for righteousness. The name Simon means 'he who hears, hearkens, obeys and understands.' He hears not just the words of other men, and the teachings of his fathers, but also an inner voice that cannot be explained. Simon is one who is receptive to the indwelling immortal life.

"Many of the things Simon has heard are sayings we have all been told. One of them is known to all Jews: 'When you cut down your harvest in the field, and forget a sheaf in the field, you shall not go again to fetch it: it shall be for the stranger, for the fatherless, and for the widow: that the Lord thy God may bless you in all the work of your hands. . . . And you shall remember that thou wast a bondsman in the land of Egypt: therefore I command you to do this thing.'

"Simon, as he joined in that band of desperate men, confronting a world distorted by powerful strangers, the Saltimbanque Corporation and its lawyers, money and soldiers, listened to a private voice. He hearkened and obeyed. He understood the parable of the sheaves left in the field.

"Does any of this absolve him of the desire to hurt, and kill? These men who persecute him"—Yeshu gestured, smiling slightly, to the plaintiff's table—"say that others are not responsible for his actions. I would ask you: what man is entirely responsible for his own actions? I do not serve violence. I do not condone Simon's actions. But I ask that you ask yourself this: in the state prison, who kills the condemned man? Who owns the death-penalty chamber? Who pays for the poison that is given there? If not us, then who?

"In this world where all things can be measured, I wonder that no one has thought to measure the rates of moral evasion among the prosperous who direct the actions of the Saltimbanque Corporation.

"I have come to understand that, among you, a corporation

is the same as a person. This is something that those of my time find it hard to fathom. If a corporation is a person, Mr. Lincoln asked you to appreciate the good that this person did in saving his life.

"Let us suppose that the Saltimbanque Corporation *is* a person. Imagine this person as a king, King Saltimbanque. King Saltimbanque has changed the lives of everyone living in that land Simon, and I, come from.

"Must we submit to the power of this alien king? A king who treats us as if we were images on a screen, to be saved or discarded as it pleases him? A king whose only concern is profit? Who gives those profits to those who do not need, and takes them from the sweat of those who work and die? A king who harvests all the fields, leaving not a single straw for the widow deprived of her husband by this king's own action, for the orphan deprived of his father by the king's own soldiers?

"I told you earlier that Simon has a son, a son he has not seen in a year, a son now separated from him by a gulf of two thousand years. Simon's son listens to the music brought back from the future to Jerusalem. He loves your music. From it he makes his own. For Samuel, music is free. It doesn't come from the corporation that records the music. It comes from that voice of God inside.

"On the way here I heard a song on the radio. If you listen you will hear it too, a song by Ben Simeon. Who is Ben Simeon? He is Simon's son Samuel. The Saltimbanque Corporation has earned millions of dollars from that song. Samuel has not received a penny for it. He doesn't expect it. To him the music is free. But Samuel's father is on trial for his life.

"A man stole the bread from his neighbor's table. Another man destroyed the neighbor's business, and the neighbor had no bread for his table. Which man is guilty?

"Simon is he who hears, hearkens, obeys and understands. Does the king Saltimbanque hear, hearken, obey or understand? Can the king hear the still, small, quiet, interior, mysterious, eternal, magnificent, powerful voice of God? Can you?

"Over the sound of Mr. Lincoln's dying words, it may yet be heard. If you can quiet the lies of the king, even at this late moment, then perhaps you can hear that voice. Perhaps you can repeat what it says back to the king, multiplied a thousandfold, a hundred thousandfold, a million times by the power of your individual voices. Let him hear the voice of justice, thundering through the world, across time itself, spoken in the words of your individual souls. The true kingdom, the kingdom of God, is inside you. It can come into the world as you speak. It cannot come into being any other way."

Chapter 10

One Hour with You

In his dream Owen searched the greenhouse for Wilma but could not find her. Something was wrong: she was growing smaller instead of larger. Now she was lost under some leaf. Instead of the smell of decay, the air was heavy with perfume. He pushed aside the fronds of a fern, and there was Emma, wearing her wedding gown.

"Don't worry about her," Emma said. Her right shoe was off, and she was unbuttoning her left. The dress was pulled halfway up her calf, and she wore fine white stockings. "Help me with this." She turned around and fumbled with the buttons up the back. Looking over her shoulder at him, she smiled. The hair curling over her ear made a question mark. Her eyelashes were long and dark. . . .

Then they were in his classroom at MIT, and she was naked, lying across the table at the front of the room. Her hips rounded up into a tight, taut belly whose curve was an invitation to a caress. Her thighs were smooth as satin. The line of her collarbone fine as a child's wish. The swell of her breasts . . .

A freight train crashed into a bridge abutment in his mind, accompanied by a voice like the gates of hell closing. =Wake up, boss.=

Owen's eyes snapped open, the dream blown into rags. "You didn't have to be quite so decisive."

=You said it was important you wake by eight.=

Owen staggered out of bed. His back and shoulders were sore, and he was as exhausted as if he had been up all night, but he had done nothing strenuous for weeks and the clock testified to a good nine hours' sleep. Bleary-eyed, he found his way to the shower.

Twenty steamy minutes later he felt more like himself. As he dressed he looked over at his wallscreen, running the paper from Emil Wheeler, the paleontology-mad state trooper. The thing was a salad of unfounded speculation and left-handed insights. Owen had been forced to agree to collaborate. But the man would not take yes for an answer, and had been pestering Owen with new drafts daily.

Still, he had not taken offense at Owen's knocking him out on the road. When Owen explained he had been decked by a martial-arts AI, Wheeler had even taken it as a point of distinction. The rich, it seemed *were* different.

Owen dressed casually and hurried down to the kitchen to grab something to eat. Thanks to the wedding preparations, he hadn't been able to get over to see Wilma in person for three days, and had to be content with remote sensing. His mother had made the wedding preparations an absolute madhouse. The ceremony would take place at one o'clock, on the lawn below the big house, with the reception in a pavilion near the pool. An army of caterers had descended on Thornberry, followed closely by an army of relatives. It was a toss-up as to which was more disruptive.

The staff bustled around the kitchen in a frenzy of preparation. The friction between the caterers and the regulars was barely concealed, and the only stable person there seemed to be Jeeves, who was decorating the sixteen-layer cake with an abstract network of fluorescent frosting. Owen breezed past and stuck his head into the big refrigerator. The regular staff tended to like Owen because he made no demands and occasionally spoke to them as if they might possibly know what they were doing. But Owen never felt comfortable around servants; there was always the chasm of several trillion dollars between them.

At least a third of the staff were wearing spex as they hustled around the kitchen, glued to the coverage of the Simon trial. LEX was expected to render his verdict sometime that morning, and speculation was rife as to what he might rule. The appearance by Yeshu was considered by some to be a coup that might get Simon an acquittal.

Owen found some milk and a bowl of cereal, a cup of coffee, and retreated to the verandah. There he ran into his uncle Suede. Suede was also wearing spex, and looked up at Owen with a dazed expression on his face.

"What ho, the groom!" he said, taking off the glasses.

"Keep quiet, Uncle. The walls have ears."

Suede Vannice was actually Owen's great-uncle. He was at least one hundred years old, but a fortune in rejuvenation treatments had kept him looking no more than forty, and he could whip the shorts off Owen in a five-set tennis match. It would be surprising if he couldn't, since he had spent his entire life doing little more than playing various games, marrying various women and avoiding any real work. Despite this he was a charming man, impossible to dislike. Blond, athletic, with a brilliant smile and an open manner, his wealth rested easily on him. He was also dumb as processed cheese.

Suede winked a bright blue eye. "Trying to dodge the pixmen, Owen?"

"As much as possible," Owen said.

"I don't think they're dodgeable. Your nuptials remind me a little of the wedding of King Charles to his first wife, eighty years ago. They had old-style video of everything except the examination to prove the bride was a virgin. Of course, pix was in its infancy then." Uncle Suede touched the spex lying on the table. On their twin screens Owen made out the tiny face of Aron Bliss, one of Rosethrush's posthuman media flacks. Over Bliss's face scrolled the tiny words of today's pretrial promo: DOES JESUS SAVE?

"Just look at this Simon trial," Suede said.

"I don't have to look at it, Uncle. I was a part of it."

"Yes. I just watched the scene where you left the studio again. Do you think those breasts were genuine?"

"One can only speculate."

"I'll tell you what I hope. I hope they nail this Zealot. Not that I have anything against him personally. I like his clothes. I'm thinking of growing a beard. What do you think?" He lifted his chin to show Owen his profile.

"I was trying to help him out," Owen said.

"Thank God you're incompetent. These historicals can't take care of themselves; they expect us to take care of them. That's why God built prisons." Uncle Suede dug into his ham and eggs.

Owen stared at the cereal in his bowl. Emma's reaction to his bungled testimony had been miraculously understanding. She gave him every credit for trying to do the right thing. "It showed completely," she said, "the kind of man you are."

=Nothing is more enjoyable than watching the privileged classes enjoying their privileges,= Bill said.

"Uncle Suede didn't mean to hurt my feelings," Owen sub-vocalized. "He's harmless."

=The very rich are different from you and me. They have more excuses.=

"What do you mean?"

=That man has never taken responsibility for anything in his entire life. Crab lice have more social conscience.=

"Where did you learn to talk like that?"

=My last upgrade gave me a new heuristic subroutine.=

"Well, you've never criticized my family before. Stop it."

=Yassuh, boss.=

After breakfast Owen excused himself and went back to his room to get ready for the ceremony. Jeeves helped him on with the wedding suit. Owen's father dropped by to give him some advice on the honeymoon.

"If I have one word to say, it's this, son: steak. The rarer the better."

Rosethrush came in to inspect him. She had chosen the tux. On the one hand Owen's mother wanted to control every aspect of the ceremony; on the other she was so caught up in the progress of the Zealot trial she could not pay good attention to details. The dramatic surprises of the closing arguments had boosted her interest to the point where she wanted to postpone the wedding. Owen refused. But the publicity! she protested. A thing like this needed handling. It didn't matter, Owen said. If she wanted a wedding, it would have to go as planned; if she didn't, it was fine with him and Emma—they would elope.

For the first time in his life, Owen prevailed on something.

After they took their shots at him, Owen's parents retreated downstairs. He chased Jeeves away, too. Then he dawdled in his room, picked up the plastic titanosaur he had played with as a child, ran his hand over the poster-sized photograph of the bright green-and-orange allosaurus that Wilhelm had taken on the first visit to the Jurassic. He paged through the text of the Wheeler paper, then turned it off. His boyhood was over now.

At the top of the stairs he hesitated, his mind filled with images of Emma. The curve of her calf, the soft indentation of her upper chest between her breasts, the light down of fair hair on her forearm catching the sunlight, the curve of her lower lip in profile, her white teeth, her hair brushing her cheek.

He went down to the entrance hall. The house was strangely

silent. The hardwood floors gleamed. The flowers on the side tables inundated the room in sweet scent. No one was there. In the south gallery the gifts were piled in high profusion. No one was there, either. The ceremony was scheduled to begin in twenty minutes. He looked out the window to the pavilion, and saw only the serving staff. He wandered through the first floor, looking for the guests.

Finally he found them in the den, lounging, standing, sitting on the arms of chairs—all watching the screen on the wall.

"What's going on?"

"LEX is going to announce its verdict."

Gen was upstairs in the room they had given her, supposedly getting dressed. She sat on the chair before the vanity, veil in hand. She had sent the ladies' maid out for help, and instead, like four hundred million other citizens, had the Simon the Zealot trial running on a window in the mirror.

Yeshu's courtroom appeal had been one of the most effective arguments for jury nullification that Gen had ever heard. It was an argument that would work as well for a murderer as an innocent. She hoped, when the boot of the law finally came down on her someday, she had a lawyer that shameless.

The bombshell that Ben Simeon was Simon's son only sweetened the sale. Netheads across the wired world, and by remote from Mars and the moon, voted their glands. The PR meters swung into the green.

But LEX had taken a long time in his deliberations. The wirehacks filled the screens with gas. Who was really behind the Yeshu appearance? Did Simon have grounds for a countersuit regarding exploitation of his son?

The host of the analysis, a way-posthuman named Aron Bliss, displayed his lethal cheekbones as he speculated. "Did Saltimbanque have Lincoln killed for effect? There has been no official autopsy on the dead historical. Lincoln was only appointed the company's Moral Spokesperson a month before his appearance at the trial. And sources have said that he was merely a figurehead for advanced corporate superintelligences. What do you think, Hiroko?"

"I think as little as possible, Aron. But I do know that the readings on the trial were disappointing up until that last day in the courtroom. First we have the comic interlude with Dr. Owen Vannice. The prime hostage double-crosses the plaintiff's lawyers and attempts to support Simon. Then the double-barreled surprises of Lincoln and Yeshu." She raised one perfectly painted eyebrow. "It couldn't have worked out better for Vannicom if it had all been orchestrated, could it?"

Bliss assumed his full moral stature—he was over two meters tall. "One thing we do know, Hiroko, this media appearance certainly has brought Yeshu back from the dead. The bandit leader, the messianic claimant, the millennial prophet, the protester, the magician, in all his lethal charisma! Vannicom CEO Rosethrush Vannice, biomother of Dr. Owen Vannice, had this to say about . . . Just a minute, Hiro. Central tells me that LEX has returned with a verdict! Let's go back to the courtroom immediately!"

The VR image zipped Bliss and his partner into the third row of the courtroom set. The lawyers were hastily resuming their positions. Behind the defense table, Yeshu sat with Simon and Diane Ontiveros.

The judge's door opened. LEX stepped out to return to the bench, no longer a carrion bird but a resplendent bird of paradise. The virtual representation of the contractually agreed-upon legal entity looked over the room, and at last, spoke.

"We find the defendant, Simon the Zealot, guilty but innocent!" LEX sang. "Culpable! But free as me, as a big beautiful bird!" It held up its iridescent-feathered hand, palm open, high above the crowd. "Peace be with you."

Yeshu held up his own hand. "And also with you."

A hundred reporters fired off their acquittal leads. Simon, weeping, fell to his knees before his cousin. Yeshu took him by the shoulders and made him rise. It was great video.

Over the image of the boisterous courtroom, Aron Bliss's voice spoke. "There you have it, folks. The verdict 'Guilty but innocent,' means that the defendant has been found guilty of the crime he is charged with, but that due to extenuating circumstances, malfeasance by the arresting authorities, extreme popularity—whatever—his guilt doesn't matter. Hiroko, in this case, what do you guess the reason—"

Gen flicked off the screen. What a coup! She had nothing but admiration for Simon. When had he contacted Yeshu? If Lance had known anything about it, he hadn't let on to her. No, it had to be Simon's own plan, and it revealed an understanding of the politics of his situation that was stunning for a man raised in the first century. Back in Jerusalem he had seemed overwhelmed by the time travelers. How had he managed to vector in on the weaknesses of the twenty-first-century legal system? Clearly she had underestimated him.

And Owen? Despite the fact that she had mocked Owen's attempt to help Simon, there was something remarkable about it. Owen came from a class of people who would not spend a second worrying about fairness to a historical, let alone a terrorist who had held him hostage. Even if his testimony was wrongheaded, it reminded her of the goofy innocent she had fallen for back in Jerusalem.

The maid returned with a helper and a paper of pins. "We need to hurry," she said. "People are gathering on the lawn!"

"I bet they're watching the trial."

"Well, maybe. But you need to get ready."

Gen let them fuss over her, and within minutes she was set, trussed up like a Christmas goose and twice as appetizing. She had to admire her figure in the full-length mirror. When he got a look at her, Owen would faint from loss of blood.

She was not disappointed. From the moment she stepped up the aisle below the pavilion awning, Owen was fish-eyed with lust. A surge of anger blew away her misgivings. As he took her hand and they stood before the ancient minister, out of the corner of her eye she noted Owen's face full of pride of ownership and fatuous self-importance.

Soon enough it was over. "By the power vested in me, I now pronounce you husband and wife. You may kiss the bride."

Gen turned her face up to Owen. He closed his eyes and bent to her. She glided to the right, and his lips missed hers. He drew back. "Excuse me," he said.

"Certainly," she said. She let him kiss her. Beneath his starched shirt, she could feel him tremble. She ran her hand inside his coat, pressed it against his breast, felt his heart thumping. She pulled back, smiled at the minister. She took Owen's hand and they ran laughing back down the aisle.

Then a whirlwind reception, flocks of photographs, hordes of relatives, magnums of champagne, more awkward dancing, the overly sweet cake, the change of clothes, the limo to the airport, the evening flight on the private plane to Palm Beach.

As they were getting off the plane in the terminal, a man rushed up to them. "Mrs. Vannice," he said. "I have an urgent message for you."

Owen looked puzzled. Gen went to a private booth, turned on the security. The screen lit up. It was August.

"Father!"

"How was the wedding?"

"Elaborate."

"I wish I could have been there. When the minister got to that part about 'If there is anybody here who knows a reason why these two should not be wed . . .' I would have brought the thing to a dead halt."

"That would have been fun," Gen said wistfully.

August was quiet for a moment. "Look, Genevieve, I've never tried to control you. But for the life of me I cannot imagine why you went and married a man you despise. You do despise him, don't you?"

"More than ever."

"Then what is this all about?"

"Don't worry, Dad. It will come clear real soon now."

"But you're going on your honeymoon!"

"It will be more fun than Owen imagines."

"Listen, I've arranged for a car. It's waiting outside the airport right now. If you hang up this call, turn around and walk out of that place right now, you'll never regret it."

"I won't regret anything. You'll see."

August looked sad. "Pretty hard on a father to have his only daughter marry and not be there." He mused for a moment. "You're not going to kill him, are you?"

"No, Dad. Don't worry."

"I mean, I wouldn't object, but I could help you with the details. . . ."

"Nobody's getting killed. It'll be more fun my way. Trust me."

"You know I do."

"I've got to go. Dr. Nice is champing at the bit."

"Good-bye, Genevieve. I love you."

"I love you too, Dad." She hung up.

Owen was waiting at the exit where the limo waited. When he saw her his face broke into a grin. "You mustn't be late. We'll have to learn to do these things on time."

"I do everything on time," Gen said. He held open the car door, and as she passed him to get in she brushed his forearm. She imagined she could hear his blood race. In the back of the limo, he tentatively put his hand on her leg.

"Look at this scenery!" she said as the car glided through

the twilight to the villa. She took his hand in hers, gently removing it from her thigh. "I'm so happy, Owen."

The villa was a two-story stucco with a red tile roof, elaborate garden, a private pool. The lamps were lit when they arrived, with the first stars coming out overhead and Venus bright in the west. The driver set out their bags in the bedroom and discreetly left. A flood of white lilies spilled over the cherry credenza. The bed was the size of Wyoming. Once they were alone, Gen retired to the bath to change.

She slipped into her negligee, doused herself with perfume, and went back to the bedroom. Owen, wearing his dressing gown, had laid himself out on the bed like a buffet.

"Darling," he said, reaching out to her. "I have a surprise for you."

She took his hands, pulled herself down to him. "A surprise?"

"You'll see it soon enough. I came down here myself, a week ago, to do it."

She could only imagine, and she didn't want to. They lay together. As she had many times before, she played the part. The badger game.

Hadn't she given up that con? What was in it for her?

She reminded herself: this was Emma Zume in bed with Owen, not Genevieve Faison. She undid his robe and ran her hand up the inside of his thigh. She kissed him, long, passionately, and they twined together on the bed. The wind rustled the trees outside their opened window. Owen moaned; she felt his feverish brow on her cheek. She ran her hand through his hair, then pulled away.

"That's enough," she said. "I hope you have a pleasant dream. I know I will."

Owen smiled at her, befuddled, breathing heavily. "Darling?"

"I asked the servants to put a blanket and pillow for you out on the sofa."

For a moment it did not register. Then his face fell as if he'd been ejected out an escape hatch. "But I thought . . ."

She took his hands in both of hers, and held them between her knees. Owen turned green. "We're off to a wonderful start. Why risk it by sharing the bed? Perhaps after two or three years, once we've come to understand one another."

"But Emma! For weeks I've done nothing else but think of you."

"And I of you."

"I thought you loved me."

"Can you doubt it? I married you, didn't I?"

"But now we're husband and wife!"

"Yes. Isn't it delicious? There is absolutely no legal or practical reason why we shouldn't make love all night, and half the day. But we won't. Think of the frustration, the longing, the passionate embraces we'll build up in our minds. The elaborate fantasies, the temptation to stray, the evasions, the sublimation! You'll throw yourself into your work. Our careers will soar on the strength of our unfulfilled sexuality. Every morning you'll struggle to teach your classes through a haze of desire. Every night I'll close my bedroom door thinking of your embrace. How wonderful, I'll imagine, it would be to run my hand down the small of your back. It makes me tremble just to say it."

"But Emma—"

"Why throw all that away just for a moment of lust? A moment not likely half as fulfilling as the ecstasies of anticipation we will put ourselves through over the years. Why, who knows? Perhaps, if we love each other enough, if we create enough of a spark between us, guard it from the winds of indifference until it becomes a roaring bonfire of passion—perhaps we'll never have to sleep together!"

"I'm not sure, in the long run, I'd like that."

"But it's what makes our relationship so special! Think of it another way, if you prefer: there is no place for entangling sexual expectations between us. I remember how you described it, 'A marriage of minds, not just bodies.' That's when I knew I would marry you."

"Yes, I remember, but—"

"But what?"

"Well, I . . ."

"You can't think this is sudden. I told you the first time we ever spoke that I was a sexual deliberationist. Did you forget?"

"No. But I thought—"

"What did you think?" She felt genuinely angry. She was Emma Zume, not Genevieve Faison, and this man had misjudged her.

Owen looked at her in dismay. He stood, fumbled with the belt of his robe, pulled it savagely tight. Jerking like a puppet, he rummaged in his overnight bag and pulled out his laptop. "I guess I'm going to have some time to work on this paper."

He closed the bedroom door behind him and left her alone.

And that was that. Gen lay back on the bed. From the other room she heard the faint sound of Owen making up the sofa. She lay there for some time, mind blank, watching the ceiling fan slowly revolve. Finally she turned out the light.

The ceiling was decorated with a spray of phosphorescent stars, hundreds of them, large and small, an entire Milky Way. Across the center a constellation spelled out *Emma's Galaxy*.

Chapter 11

The Palm Beach Story

Owen woke up with a crick in his neck that would not go away. He groaned out of the sofa and into the bedroom. Emma was not there. He avoided looking at the disordered bedclothes. While taking a shower he muttered to himself, "What a fool. What was I thinking of?"

=You were thinking about getting laid.=

Owen didn't say anything.

=What I can't figure out is why she's holding out on you. Please trust your naked poetry to eat women. Maybe she's really a man.=

"Maybe you're a figment of my imagination."

Owen's hand jerked up and slapped his own face.

=Was *that* a figment of your imagination?=

Owen gained control of his hand, rubbed his stinging cheek. "You're not supposed to do things like that."

=My value inheres in my ability to do the unexpected.=

Owen turned off the water and got out of the shower. Angrily, he began to towel himself dry. "I fail to see the advantage of you slapping me with my own hand."

=What is the sound of one hand slapping?=

"Ho." Owen pulled on his robe. He didn't even have a body of his own.

=I'm just a machine interface, Owen. But I have to say, recent events have made me question whether I can take care of you.=

"Good. I'll take care of myself."

=You're a naked obsessive dysfunctional free details man.=

"I'm not naked anymore."

Well, self-pity would get him nowhere. He wandered through the villa, out to the patio. The day could not have been brighter or the air more fragrant had it been ordered from a catalog. He found Emma at the breakfast table, fairly glowing. She had gotten some invisible staff person to prepare breakfast for them. The stunning white tablecloth was laden with covered serving dishes, toast, jam, a floral centerpiece of sunbright yellow mums. The coffee smelled beautiful. Emma's violet eyes drew him down to sit beside her. Owen's annoyance subsided.

"Last night was wonderful," she said. "I never knew it could be like that."

" 'It'?"

"Our conversation."

"Sure," Owen grumbled. He found he was ravenous. He lifted the lids on the various serving plates, spooned out some scrambled eggs, selected a croissant and a breakfast steak. The smell of the steak made his mouth water, and he dug in.

After a while he felt a little better. "You know," he said, "I think it was a good idea not to rush into the sexual part of our marriage. There's more to sex than sexual intercourse."

"I'm so glad you see it my way."

"Of course, when we decide to have children, that will be different."

"It doesn't have to."

"I mean, not that I would let them influence my decision, but my parents are eager to see some grandchildren. They've been after me about it for years."

"Don't worry. They're having grandchildren as we speak."

"Excuse me?"

"Your mother explained how you refused to do anything about fathering a child. It was one of the things that proved to me you were a man of principle. She even told me that woman at the college dance was trying to trick you into providing a sperm sample."

"I see."

"I told them how they might get one more easily, and they did. They're preparing a child in an artificial womb."

It took a moment before he caught on to what she was saying. "They took a sperm sample? How? When?"

"I believe they had your Aide produce it while you were asleep."

Owen swallowed. "Bill?"

=It was a delicate operation.=

"I'll bet," Owen subvocalized.

=It's not as if you hadn't shown me how.=

Owen turned on Emma. "Why didn't you tell me?"

Emma looked innocent as a flower. "It really was a matter between you and them. It's embarrassing. And I knew we weren't going to have children the normal way."

=Looks like we may have opportunity to collect further samples.=

Owen sighed. At least his parents would leave him alone about grandchildren now.

"Darling, I'll forgive you this time, but in the future you're not to interfere in my affairs without my permission. I may be a liberal, but I draw the line at the exploitation of my body."

Emma lowered her eyes. "I'm sorry, Owen."

Her forlorn look mollified him a little. He took another piece of the steak. Animal protein, in massive quantities. His father would be proud of him. He tried to make conversation.

"This steak is excellent. Thanks for ordering it."

Emma smiled. "Your father says it tastes like iguana. It's infant dinosaur."

Owen stopped chewing. He put down his fork. "Emma, that's not funny."

"It's no joke. Grilled Wilma, courtesy of Ralph Siddhartha Vannice."

"That's absurd! I checked Wilma through telepresence not twenty-four hours ago. She's in the campus ecologarium."

"Don't worry, Wilma hasn't been harmed. Your father had her cloned."

"Cloned? How? When did he get to *her*?"

"You did that, too."

"*I* did it?"

"Yes. While you were asleep. She wouldn't sit still for *any* of his agents, so your father had Bill sample some tissues for cloning. He told me at the wedding reception."

"Bill!" Owen said.

=It was none of my doing.=

"None of your doing! Whose was it, then?"

=Well, according to that trial summation the other day, that's sort of a metaphysical question.=

Owen balled up his napkin and threw it into his plate. "Emma—you're against exploiting the past! How can you countenance this?"

"Wilma is no longer part of the past."

"But she's a unique specimen."

"Wilma is an extinct creature yanked out of her proper era. But as far as cloning her for meat, that has human benefit. Wilma hasn't been affected one iota; you could take her back tomorrow."

"But you objected to my taking her in the first place."

"That's right. And I still do. Either Wilma should be returned to the past, or disposed of. Tampering with time is an abomination. It's an uncompromising principle with me. Didn't I make that clear from the start?"

"Of course. So why would you allow anyone to clone her?"

"I'm against interfering with the past, not cloning." Calmly, she took another bite of the fillet.

Owen tried to get his mind around the discoveries he was making. Was he being unfair? But she had told him . . . he had assumed . . . "My father is an exotiphagist?"

"He's the president of the New England chapter. Don't tell me you didn't know. He's planning a series of restaurants. Dinoburgers, dinogyros, dino salad."

He should have known. That was the worst of it. But who *was* this woman? "How could you lie to me?"

"I never lied to you."

"The Committee to Protect the Past? How can you reconcile this with your work?"

Finally she got mad. "Must I take *your* definition of my work? My actions are quite consistent with my ideals. You're the one who seems to bend your principles to the occasion." She caught her breath in a little sob. "I thought you were better than that. I must say, Owen, this is a considerable disillusionment for a girl to get on her honeymoon."

"Emma, how could you trick me like this?"

She wiped her eyes. "Trick you? Who tricked who?"

A bright yellow canary landed in the bush beside the patio, rattling the leaves in a flutter of wings. Owen thought of the bird's ancestors, a hundred million years before, in the woods outside Vannice Station. He felt bitterly used.

"I don't know who tricked who. But if you mean what you say, you're being inhumane. You can't keep the past inviolate. To try to do so is to create some sort of false virginity, like your sexual deliberation. Once you lose your innocence, you can't get it back. It's not so awful a loss anyway."

"So then you rape the past, now that it's not a virgin. You use it like a whore?"

"You're going to extremes," Owen said. He struggled to articulate what he felt. "It's—it's not that clear-cut. There's a lot of ground between virginity and rape. You can relate to the past like a lover, a spouse, a friend. You have a relationship with it."

"The Saltimbanque Corporation will love that line of reasoning, Owen. They can use it in their PR."

"You can make me look foolish. Make me? What am I saying?—I am a fool! What I'm saying isn't consistent, I know. But you delude yourself if you think right and wrong's so easy. You ought not to act like some innocent, Emma, when you're not."

She stared at him as if seeing him anew. "You think I'm not innocent?"

"You probably are. Too damned innocent."

"You're the one who was looking for somebody pure."

"I was. I was wrong."

"If you want some floozy, there are plenty in the world. More's the pity."

"Most bad people aren't nearly as bad as they seem to be. Most good ones aren't as good. Neither am I." Owen got up from the table. Emma looked up at him, as beautiful as the first moment he'd seen her at Thornberry. But it wasn't her he really loved.

Trying not to look like an ass, he strode back into the house, through the bedroom, into the bath. He sat there, his head in his hands, and thought about that last breakfast he'd had with Genevieve, on the terrace at Herod's Palace. He hadn't gotten to finish anything that time, either.

After a moment Bill spoke. =You were very eloquent there, boss. A little pompous, though.=

"Thanks."

=I don't want you to feel any worse than you do, but it seems to me your sexual frustration is driving this. But you won't admit it.=

"You're getting mighty damned psychiatric lately."

=Never trust men who eat the bed of God. Just tell me this. How did you go from your father betraying you, to a lecture on the morality of time travel? Doesn't that seem like an odd way to react to what she said? Wouldn't it be better if you just went back there and told her she hurt you?=

"I'd rather get divorced."

=You could do that, too,= Bill said. His voice sounded almost concerned. =Divorce is an ancient institution. But I suppose marriage is a few weeks older.=

Chapter 12

What Kind of Blues

Lance Thrillkiller grabbed Simon's shoulder and pulled him away from the phalanx of shouting reporters. Brushing away a hovering camera, he pushed them through the glass doors to the time-travel stage. Yeshu, behind them, remained an extra minute to speak with the press. After the madness of the last few days, it was a relief to be in a quiet room away from masses of strangers.

"I don't know why I got myself mixed up in all this," Lance muttered.

"For the money," Simon said. He adjusted the bag slung over his shoulder, which contained some books, some music and his olivewood box. At the time-travel control board Simon spotted Serge Halam talking to the technician.

"I like money, sure," Lance said. "I also like a little lower profile."

"Get used to publicity," said Yeshu, entering. "We are only beginning."

Lance looked uncomfortable.

Halam came over to them from the board.

"There'll be another press conference at the other end. They've arranged to hold it in the atrium at Herod's Palace."

It had been borne in upon Simon over the last weeks that

press conferences were going to be a fact of life from now on. Since the trial, his fame had doubled. A HISTORICAL REVOLUTION! the tabloids shouted. Pixmen recapped the raid on Herod's Palace, put viewers in the courtroom for Yeshu's summation, replayed the toppling of Abraham Lincoln from every angle, speculated over the possibility that the upcoming trials of the other conspirators might be called off, treated the curious to a tour of Yeshu's retreat in Costa Rica, gave viewer reaction to the trial and speculation about its aftermath, offered call-in numbers for Simon and Yeshu's nascent political organization. Both younger versions of Jesus had called off personal appearance tours to offer support to their older self.

Simon had become, if not the most famous historical ever brought into the present, then the most politically significant. In first-century Jerusalem, his picture was plastered on every building. Herod had retreated to Galilee, unable to show his face in the city. Mass rallies pressed for a new Sanhedrin, led by Simon, to assume the political rule. While Simon went back to Jerusalem, Yeshu would negotiate with Saltimbanque Corporation representatives in the present.

Repercussions were echoing up and down the settled moment universes. In the eighteenth century, radicals led by Paine and Danton had taken control of Paris. Across the 2062 net, a new debate raged over the practical effects of time intervention. The movement had its unexpected consequences: the Committee to Protect the Past had been raised into a position where it was forced by circumstance to play it straight. Lance was not happy.

Simon was not sure how he felt about all this. Before the hotel raid he had thought his life worthless, and had been willing to throw it away. The fight against the time travelers had seemed a simple thing. Now he could have an effect, but he was no longer the narrow Zealot he had been.

Yet he was glad to be going back home, where he could once

again see the sunlight on the Temple and hear the sound of voices speaking his own tongue. Why did he feel so sad?

Halam led Simon onto the stage. Yeshu embraced him. His eyes were moist. "Good-bye, cousin. You will see me soon."

"Once again, you have saved me," Simon said.

"Your need brought me out of my retreat," Yeshu said. "You reminded me what I am for. All of the me's." He smiled.

Yeshu went back to stand beside Lance. Halam nodded to the technician, who touched his controls. Across the room, Yeshu waved good-bye.

The room fell away, Simon's stomach lurched, the space swam about them, and a moment later the Gödel stage at Herod's Palace rushed forward to surround them. Simon swayed for a moment, then got his balance. A group of historicals came forward to greet them. How strange it was to see these people in the clothing and beards of his own time. But he guessed that it would never completely be his own time again. Never the place it had been when he was a boy.

As the men approached, Simon whispered to Halam. "I remember when you told me, back in the Hippodrome, that no matter whether the revolt succeeded, the people from the future would be here. I thought nothing could be worse. Now I know that, no matter what you do, we will be here, too."

From among those coming to greet them stepped a tall young man in twenty-first-century clothes, with curly black hair. It took a moment for Simon to recognize him. "Samuel?"

"Father."

Genevieve paid the cab and got out at Broadway and Fifth Avenue. She expected she had shaken him crossing the bridge. She hurried into the Flatiron Building, but got snarled up in security.

They checked her bag, examined her fake ID, ran an MRI

to assure themselves that she contained no explosives. "What is the purpose of your visit?"

"I'm Mrs. Owen Beresford Vannice! I'm here to meet with my husband."

The security flak checked his screen. "You're not listed as a party to this meeting."

"Call up. They'll want me there."

In private mode, the man called up to Rosethrush's office. After a moment he turned back to Genevieve. "All right. That's the top floor. The elevators are—"

"I see them." Gen took her purse and hurried to the elevator bank. She wanted this over before August could stop her.

It had been two weeks since the honeymoon. Four days after Owen had left their breakfast table and flown back to Connecticut, the call came from his lawyers.

Genevieve had spent those days discovering things. She could still see him walking away from the table, the belt of his robe jerked tight, despair in the set of his shoulders. The joy of her revenge had lasted only a moment, followed by a queer blankness. Her mind replayed the details of her triumph: first Owen's smug assurance, his pathetic attempts to conceal his desire, the way he protested as she dropped each of her bombshells, his sudden turn to arguing the opposite side of interference with the past.

It had not been hard for her to play Emma Zume's anger. Her offended propriety. Even the tears.

But after Owen was gone, instead of elation, Gen felt sadness. She had dished out to Owen exactly what he deserved, but balancing the equation had brought her no relief. She was angry, disappointed, frustrated, and worse still, unhappy with herself.

The phone call had crystallized her feelings. He was having his lawyers deal with her? Did he actually imagine he didn't love her? Did he think if he got an annulment it would be over and done with? She knew him better than that, and it enraged her that, after all this, he didn't know himself any better. Or was there some part of him she did not know, something he was keeping inside that he could not tell her?

The elevator doors opened on the top floor. There stood August, waiting for her. He pulled her aside.

"How did you get here ahead of me?" she asked.

"Never try to out-hustle a New Yorker in New York, daughter."

She looked past him to the glass-fronted reception area of Vannicom Limited. "Let me go."

"I will. But first I would like to know exactly what you are doing."

"I'm going to talk to him."

"Just talk?"

"They checked me at the door. No weapons."

"A pity. But why? You know I was against this marriage, but now that you've gone through with it I wish you'd understand that you're sitting in the catbird seat. He wants an annulment. He has no grounds for one. In such a situation you can hold out for a virtually unlimited amount of money."

"I'm not interested in money."

"Bite your tongue."

"I'm not going to ask for anything. I'm going to tell him who I am. If he can look me in the eye, as Genevieve Faison, and tell me he doesn't love me, then he can have his precious annulment." She pulled away from him and pushed open the heavy glass door to the office. August trailed behind.

A pleasant young woman looked up from her desk.

"I'm here to meet with Mr. Vannice and his lawyers," Gen said.

"They're in the office. I'll let them know you're here."

"Don't bother."

"She's a determined woman," August explained.

Gen glided past the desk and through the dark wood door to Rosethrush Vannice's office. Behind a big desk sat Rosethrush, wearing a trim business suit. Ralph Vannice, smoking a cigar, was looking over some papers with a shark-like man in an expensive suit, whom Gen recognized as Owen's lawyer Derek Choi.

"Where's Owen?" she asked.

Rosethrush stood up. "He left. When Ralph let slip that you were coming, it was as if he had rockets in his shoes."

Choi spoke up. "I don't think it's a good idea to tell this to her now. We have some negotiations to get through first."

Gen ignored him. "Has he gone back to Thornberry?"

"He's going to the New York Port Authority Gödel stage. He arranged it all beforehand. He just wanted to sign the papers and leave."

"Where's he going?"

"Back to the Cretaceous," Ralph Vannice said. Something was odd about Ralph. He had less hair, and the skin of his face and neck had a pebbly sheen, as of tiny scales. His nose was flatter, and were those wattles growing beneath his neck? "Who are you?" Ralph asked August.

"He's my father," Genevieve said.

Ralph stuck out his hand, the back of which was similarly growing scales. "How good to meet you. Emma didn't tell us she had a father."

"Don't trust him, Ralph," Choi said.

"I'm not Emma's father," said August.

Vannice looked befuddled. "But she just said—"

"This woman isn't Emma. It's Genevieve."

The lawyer spoke up. "You can't have some proxy sign these papers. That's fraud!"

"I'm not going to sign any papers," Gen said.

Rosethrush Vannice's brows knit. "I know that Owen's behavior may have seemed ill-bred, my dear, but—"

The lawyer was out of control. "Keep quiet, Rosie. Don't try to bluff us, Ms. Zume."

"Faison."

"Whatever. If you think we're going to pay you a cent, you have another think coming. This marriage wasn't even consummated."

"Yes it was. Six months before it took place. And I'm not going to annul it until I speak to Owen." She turned to Rosethrush. "Why is he going back to the Cretaceous?"

"He's returning Wilma. He says it was a mistake, she doesn't belong here. We had the devil's own time arranging for her transport. We had to get an exclusive lease on the stage."

"The trip back to the Cretaceous wasn't the problem," Ralph said. "It was the stop in Jerusalem."

"Jerusalem?"

"Yes." Ralph puffed on the cigar, a wry look on his face. "Mark my words, that boy is up to no good. It's about time."

"He said he was going to change his life," Rosethrush said. "What he meant by that, he didn't say. I'm very cross with him. How dare he run off without honorably settling with you? It's simply not the done thing."

"I bet Det Gruber knows what he's up to," Ralph said. "It's got something to do with this Historical Revolution." He poked a finger at Rosethrush as if he'd said something significant. Then he got distracted by the slight greenish tinge of the back of his hand. He held it up and rotated it to admire how it caught the light.

Gen grabbed her father's arm, "August, is your passport in order?"

August raised an eyebrow. "Where are we going?"

"You know where. Not all predators are in the Cretaceous."

If there was skepticism in his face, there was also delight at her, an expression she had not seen in a long time. She supposed, from his point of view, he'd gotten his daughter back. They headed for the door.

"What about the annulment?" Rosethrush shouted.

"Don't say anything!" the lawyer insisted.

"Good-bye," said Ralph Vannice wistfully, as the door closed behind them.

PART THREE

Jerusalem, 41 C.E.

Chapter 1

Unfaithfully Yours

Red torchlight gleamed on the sweaty faces of the legionaries, a frigid wind whistled up the Tyropoean Valley, and the last rays of the sun rose off the walls of the Temple high above their heads. On the pavement in front of the Antonia the Romans had laid out the bodies of the rebels killed in that morning's raid. They'd hoped to catch some of the conspirators when they came to claim the bodies, but only a few women showed up to weep, and those had left. Owen, dressed as a centurion, passed down the row of corpses. He found Simon at the end, his tunic dark with the blood from the neck wound that had killed him. Simon's eyes stared at the darkening skies. Owen knelt and closed them.

Owen heard the clink of armor and creak of leather behind him as a troop of Roman soldiers double-timed down the street to search the lower city. He stood and walked in the opposite direction, hoping to avoid any encounter.

It was the beginning of the first watch. Down in the streets below the Temple mount, all was deepening shadow. The articulated metal armor covering Owen's chest and shoulders did little to cut the cold wind. He had trouble moving quickly. The open tunic was drafty, his short sword banged against his thigh and the crested bronze centurion's helmet was too large and kept slipping down over his forehead. He held the helmet under his arm, slipped around a corner into a side street and pulled his dark wool mantle around him.

=This isn't your line of work,= Bill said.

"Bill, you've been undermining my confidence since I was eight. I'm tired of it. Personally, I think that I am more than competent. As of today I'm resourceful, intelligent and adaptable."

He turned the corner, stepped on a sleeping dog and fell on his face. The dog squealed and ran off.

=You're going to get yourself killed.=

A couple of soldiers on the plaza were looking his way. Owen picked himself up, jerked his cloak straight. "And if I go down, then you go down."

=You told Gruber you'd be back within three hours. There's an hour and fifty-four minutes to go. I ought to just take over and get us out of here.=

"Don't even think about it. You can take over my body, but you can't stop me from shouting."

=What would that accomplish?=

"It could get us both killed."

=It can get *you* killed. I'm hardware. I can be reinstalled in a new host.=

"In this universe, their idea of hardware is a thumbscrew. You'll be buried with me, waiting for your batteries to die out while I rot. Just help me with directions and I'll get us through this."

=Go north, take the third street on your left.=

Pilate had come to Jerusalem from Caesarea to show Roman force during the Passover holidays, always a time of political tension among the fractious Jews. He might have expected a dispute between a mystic rabble-rouser and hostile Jewish authorities, but he couldn't have imagined a raid by time travelers.

Owen was revisiting the moment universe from which Detlev Gruber's recruiting team had snatched Yeshu in the 2040s. He'd arrived on the afternoon of Good Friday, the same day that Gruber's team had run the bloody raid on Yeshu's audience with Pilate. Here was Owen's problem: to find Simon's wife Alma in the chaos of the Jerusalem night, and persuade her to come with him back to the settled moment universe a decade later.

The trouble was finding anyone at all. With sunset Passover had begun, and any good Jew was bound to his home. Tonight it was not simply the holy day that sent them there. The city was in a state of fear. The surviving apostles were in hiding.

It was a risky business.

Owen had one lead: on a map of old Jerusalem, Gruber had pointed out the location of the house in the Second Quarter where he and his crew had met with the frightened apostles early that morning, after Yeshu had been taken in the Garden of Gethsemane. But since Gruber and the snatch crew had retreated to the future immediately after the assault, he could not tell Owen what Yeshu's followers had done afterward.

=Down two buildings, then left.=

Owen kept in the lee of the west side of the street, in the shadows. At the corner he scanned the street. It was one of the better neighborhoods, lined with stone houses with stout wooden doors. Some had small courtyards and second stories whose awnings projected over the street.

=It should be that large house on the left.=

But between Owen and the house were two Roman soldiers, huddled against the cold, arguing. Owen circled around to the shadows of a nearby building and eavesdropped.

"I don't like this," said the shorter of the two, with massive forearms and several days' growth of beard. "The staff officers sit on their fat asses in the baths. And here we are, just the two of us, going house to house. I haven't had anything to eat since noon."

"Let's just keep moving."

"Those centurions around Pilate kiss butt until their lips are chapped. They don't care if they get us killed."

"What were they supposed to do? They haven't got enough troops. They had to spread us out."

"All the more reason to wait for reinforcements."

"I'm not arguing with you. But the sooner we're done, the sooner we get back."

The short one blew on his hands. He picked up the six-foot javelin leaning against the wall.

"They say that demons stole this magician away."

"Demons," the other snorted. "If they were demons, why didn't they protect his apostles?"

"I hear they shot lightning bolts that killed the guards. Lucius from Hippona got it, and Artinius. Holes blasted right through them. Commodus said these demons were dressed in black, with helmets like insects, glittering eyes."

"And once they disappeared with Yeshu, they let us tear his bandits to bits."

"So? Maybe the necromancer will come back and raise the dead. They say he's done it before. I blame Pilate. Why did he even get involved? It's all between these crazy Jews. If their priests wanted to take this Yeshu, why didn't they do it in the middle of the day, in the Temple? He was there all week."

"Surrounded by a legion of his followers. They had to do it at night."

"All the more reason for Pilate to stay out of it. He knew that if he condemned the man his followers would riot."

"He was trying to keep public order. The rebels needed to be taught a lesson. I wouldn't want to have Pilate's job, arguing with priests and magicians. And I don't know who those demons were, but I don't expect we'll see them again."

"So why don't *you* knock on the next door?"

"Shut up, you bastard."

Owen stepped out of the shadows. Learn to pretend. He was a centurion, a man of authority. He tried out his Latin. "Why are you men idling?"

The two legionaries stiffened, saluted. "Centurion!"

"You're supposed to be rooting out rebels."

"Uh—yes. We were just about to start on this street."

"Well, I'm glad I found you. I have information that they're hiding in this very block—that big house. Are there only two of you?"

"Yes."

"That's bad. Still, you look like brave fellows, ready to storm the gates of Hades for the emperor! I want you to back me up. But let me warn you, these rebels are magicians. They're protected by beasts."

"Beasts?"

"Yes. Iguanas."

"Ik-hanas?"

"Nasty things. Fierce lizards six feet long, with fangs like lions. Follow me."

The taller of the two hesitated. "We would follow you into Vesuvius. But how is it we've never met you before? We know all the centurions in our cohort."

=You are Drusus Quintillius of the cohort recently arrived from Sebaste.=

"I am Drusus Quintillius, attached to the Prefecture . . ."

The soldiers exchanged an uneasy glance.

". . . and we can't disobey the commands of the Prefect, can we?"

"Noble Drusus, everyone knows the valor of the Prefect's

staff. But should you risk your person in this perilous search without proper support? Let us return to the garrison and at least round up a troop of auxiliaries."

"There's no time for that," Owen said.

"Though you possess the guile of Mercury, the arm of Mars," the tall one said, "we may lose these rebels if we are too hasty."

Owen made a show of thinking. "Some wisdom there," he said. He clapped the short one on the shoulder. "Very well. You two go back to the garrison and fetch these auxiliaries. Bring the legion's astrologer, too. I'll watch the house. Hurry, though."

"We'll be back before you know it."

"Yes. Well, then, get along."

The legionaries saluted and hotfooted it away.

=One hour and sixteen minutes. Where'd you learn to manipulate like that?=

"They wanted no part of this search. I just gave them what they wanted."

Owen moved silently down to the house. It was a sturdy two stories, made of gray stone, with a corbeled staircase to the second-floor room. Avoiding the downstairs entrance, Owen moved as silently as possible up the outside stairs. He stepped onto the rolled mud roof of the lower story and listened at the wooden door to the top room. A pale wash of lamplight escaped from the gap beneath the door. It was colder still up here, and weeds sprouting from the corners of the roof danced in the wind. Through the door Owen heard the sound of weeping.

He pushed the door slightly ajar. In the flickering lamplight he could make out the back of a woman, crouching, and facing him, a second woman huddled over, her face turned downward, hands in her lap. Her dark hair was parted in the middle.

"Do not weep for him," the other woman was saying. "Trust in the Lord. Remember the psalm:

> *'Now I know that the Lord saves his anointed;*
> *He will answer him from His holy heaven*
> *With the saving strength of His right hand.*
>
> *Some trust in chariots, and some in horses;*
> *But we will remember the name of the Lord*
> *our God.'* "

Owen pushed the door fully open. The two women started and turned. He held his finger to his lips, closed the door and came to crouch beside them. The woman who had been trying to comfort Alma held the back of her hand to her mouth, eyes wide.

The weeping woman looked him in the eyes. "Who are you?"

He had questioned Gruber about Alma, and had a description of her rebellious character. In a world where a woman could not even speak to a man unless spoken to, her headstrong nature had kept her unmarried longer than most. She had married a Zealot and run off from her parents to follow the *nabi* Yeshu.

Now her oval face bore an expression of despair. Her tears glistened in the guttering lamplight.

"I am someone who knows your heart. A friend of your husband."

"You are no Roman. You are one of *them.*"

"Yes. I have come to help you."

"Help us? As you helped us before, and got Simon killed?"

"I am come to undo that injustice."

"How can you undo that? He's dead."

"You were a follower of Yeshu. You saw the dead rise."

"Is Yeshu here?" the older woman asked.

"I come from the place where he is now. I cannot raise the dead, but I can bring you to a Simon who never died."

"I don't understand."

"Look at this." Owen pulled a fabric television from within his cloak, shook it out, tugged it rigid. The women looked fearful. When the screen lit they backed away.

"Don't be afraid. This is only a picture."

"Pictures of men are forbidden," Alma's friend said.

"That's one of the rules the Sadducees would have used to crucify Yeshu. Does he care about the divisions enshrined in order, ritual purity, what the good people of the world say?" He ran a clip of Simon from one of the interview shows after the trial.

Alma drew closer. "What magic is this?"

"This is your Simon, alive. I can bring you to him."

"Where is he?"

"He is in Jerusalem—a different Jerusalem. I cannot explain. If you wish to see him, you will have to trust me."

"How can I trust you?"

"Why would I be here unless I wanted to help you?"

She took up her heavy cloak and shawl. "Take me to him."

"No, Alma!" the other woman said. "It's some trick!"

"I should tell you," Owen said, "in this new Jerusalem, things will not be the same."

"Simon is dead. Yeshu is gone. Things will not be the same here, ever."

Alma embraced the other woman and followed Owen out. It was the fourteenth of Nissan, mid-month, and the full moon, now risen, lit the silent street. They kept to the shadows until they reached the market plaza before the Damascus Gate.

=Fifty-nine minutes,= Bill whispered.

"We must put on a show now," Owen said to her. "Don't

say anything. Just look like my prisoner." Looking into Alma's face, he saw that it would not be hard for her to feign fear.

Owen stepped out and walked boldly to the guards at the gate, tugging Alma by the arm. The men straightened, clutching their lances.

"What is your business, centurion?"

"I need to take this woman outside the city. Let us out."

"Where are you going?"

"A special inquisition, on the hill of skulls. Something you need tell no one about." He winked. "I will probe this woman, and get what I want from her."

Alma pulled against his grasp, and he jerked her toward him. She lowered her head.

"It's a cold night out there," the guard said. "Why not take her to the Antonia?"

"Pilate does not approve of the kind of questioning I'm going to do."

The soldier's lips twitched, and he lowered the javelin. "Be careful. Who knows how many of those bandits are abroad at night?"

"I know all about bandits."

Owen and Alma passed through the gate and out onto the moonlit northern road. Behind them the walls of the city stood dark and silent. Owen hurried them a half a kilometer down the valley, then struck off the road to the copse of trees where he had left the portable time-travel unit. He'd already laid the cable out in a circle, its ends plugged into the suitcase-sized field generator. As he knelt beside the case, Alma watched him from the middle of the circle. Bill led Owen through the sequence of settings for their return. Owen touched the control and stood beside Alma. "This will only take a moment. Be prepared for a change."

They were jerked out of the Judean night, fell through

space, and reappeared in broad daylight, behind a construction shed for the new Samaria road. Detlev Gruber sat in a jeep in the shade of a palm, smoking what smelled like marijuana. He tossed aside the cigarette and got out. "About time," he said.

Beside Owen, Alma swayed on her feet. He took her arm. "Don't be afraid," he told her in Aramaic. "Look," he pointed to the south, where the city's walls peeked over the top of a hill. "Jerusalem."

She was struck dumb. From cold night to warm day, from spring to high summer. Still she shivered. The palm fronds rustled. Owen pulled back his mantle to let the sun fall on his face. She turned from the city to study him.

While Owen tore off his Roman armor, Gruber bent over the portable time-travel unit, detached the cable, wound it around his forearm and stowed it in the case. The portable looked like a medium-quality overnight bag. "I've got half an hour to get this unit back uptime before anyone misses it."

"I'll drive," Owen said. He helped Alma into the passenger's seat, took a moment to fasten her seat belt. "This will seem strange," Owen said. "We are going to move very fast."

"Let's go!" Gruber said from the back.

Owen started the engine and jolted them over the rough ground to the road. He sped past the construction area, dodging orange detour cones toward the city gate. Alma clutched the sides of her seat, white-faced.

"You drive like a maniac!" Gruber said.

"You're the one who's in a hurry."

They shot through the gate without slowing, and down a network of narrow streets toward the hotel. "Try not to get us caught with her," Gruber said. "It's not just fraternizing with a historical you're talking about here. Retrieving the dead is seriously illegal."

Owen took his eyes off the street and looked over his shoulder into Gruber's spex. "I know you've got those things recording," he shouted. "So record this: I'm responsible. I forced you into this scheme. I did the snatching."

He turned back just in time to screech to a halt behind a parked vegetable truck at an open-air market.

Gruber lurched forward. He touched the temple of the spex. "I don't think that's going to do us any good if we get caught. Money's the antidote."

"I gave you most of what I had," Owen said. "My father and I aren't talking, and my mother cut me off."

"Marvelous," Gruber said. "I think I'll get out here." He took the bag and hopped out of the jeep. "Look, I'll get this back without anyone finding out, but can you keep your mouth shut?"

"My word is my bond," Owen said.

Gruber smiled grimly, shook his head and hurried off down the street.

=Looks like you've made a friend,= Bill said.

Alma was looking around in a daze, watching the men unload crates of oranges from the truck, a dealer selling glittering wristwards and music boxes, people in both traditional and outlandish clothes swarming the market.

When Owen touched her shoulder she started. "I know you are frightened," he said in Aramaic. "But I did not lie to you. We can go to see Simon now."

He backed up the jeep and jammed it in the narrow space between two buildings. He took her hand and helped her down. They walked through the market and into the streets.

At the stone house in the Upper City that served as the headquarters for Simon's political movement, he introduced himself as Dr. Vannice. They searched him.

"What is your business here?"

"Simon will want to see this woman."

"Who is she?"

"He will know her."

They discussed the matter among themselves. Alma gazed guardedly around the room, her eyes hesitating on every unfamiliar object. But she held her chin high. One of the men retreated, then returned and led them to the back.

Simon sat before a portable computer on a table on which were scattered a number of papers, speaking Greek with a dark man in a twenty-first-century suit. He recognized Owen, and switched to English. "Dr. Vannice. I'm surprised you would bother to—" When he saw Alma, his face froze.

"Alma," he said. He stood and came around the table.

Alma moved toward him, reached out, touched his face. "You are older. Your beard is gray." She blinked her eyes rapidly, let herself rest her head on his shoulder. Simon embraced her. "I saw you dead," she said. "Not three hours ago."

"I'm not dead," Simon said. "I must be dreaming."

He looked at Owen over Alma's head. "How is this possible?"

"You'll figure it out. I'd rather not go into the details. I only ask that you keep her identity secret, at least for a while. Help her to adjust."

Simon closed his eyes, lowered his chin to Alma's hair and held her tightly. The man Simon had been speaking with stared at them, then at Owen. Owen took his arm and led him from the room. The man turned animatedly to the others in the front.

As Owen left the building, Bill whispered, =Free men always trust naked screaming bed poetry!=

"Amen," Owen said. For the first time in a very long time he felt relaxed.

=You handled that pretty well, considering, boss. I still think you're crazy. It goes against all my programming to let you do this stuff.=

"Just remember who's in charge. If I have you removed, you're twenty years out of date. Nobody's going to want to purchase an archaic personality platform. Especially one who rants about naked screaming bed poetry."

=What are you talking about?=

"Never mind."

=What I can't figure out is, why did you do all this? If anyone ever investigates Alma's reappearance, you're in trouble. It's a joke.=

Owen couldn't explain it to Bill. He hardly understood it himself. Life was a series of jokes on people like Owen, undermining their seriousness, their need for certainty about what was right and wrong, about who was in and who was out. That was the point. Simon, the epitome of the outsider, was now in. Owen, the billionaire, was out. Owen had done something for someone who could do nothing for him, an act for which he would get no recognition. It was the only thing he'd ever done in his life completely without self-interest.

=You can't even guarantee they'll get along. He's ten years older. He's had time to get used to the changes. She from another universe. She's never seen the son they had. It's too long odds. =

"Tell me about long odds between women and men, Bill."

As he wandered back to Herod's Palace, Owen planned his evening. First he needed to check up on Wilma in her special quarters in the hotel warehouse. Then a big dinner in the hotel's restaurant, the last decent food he was likely to have for some time. Tomorrow morning he'd take Wilma back to the Cretaceous. He would spend a few weeks there trying to figure out what to make of the shambles that his life had become. He had rushed into the marriage so quickly, so sure of himself. Now he was sure of nothing. Could he bring himself to go back and face Emma Zume again? What could he possibly say to her: that he had made a mistake? That she was not the woman he had imagined her to be?

Already the advent of Simon's political movement had

changed the feel of the Jerusalem streets. The historicals walked along with more confidence. The broad plaza outside the hotel was busy with vendors, rubberneckers, political speechmakers with knots of listeners. As he wove his way through the people Owen came upon Dr. David Dunkenfield in ebullient negotiation with a man in a safari jacket. Dunkenfield glanced up, saw Owen and did a double take.

"Owen? Owen Vannice!" Dunkenfield's big voice boomed over the pavement, drawing stares from passersby.

"Dr. Dunkenfield. What are you doing in Jerusalem?"

Dunkenfield was holding a primitive bow and a leather pouch that rattled as he gestured. "I'm on leave, here for the conference of the American Astronomical Society. I've got a paper on the Cretaceous dark matter measurements. By the way, boy, I've seen the draft of your paper with this fellow Wheeler on the precocial growth rates. A breakthrough! It's good to see that your time with us wasn't wasted."

Owen was trying to think of some way he could explain how the only credible scientific research he'd produced in the last year was the result of a traffic violation, when he realized the man Dunkenfield had been talking to was August Faison. August watched Owen impassively.

Dunkenfield finally slowed long enough to notice the two men eyeing each other.

"But I haven't introduced you, Owen," Dunkenfield said. "Meet Colonel Harrington, of Cambridge. He's returning from a private expedition to the Fertile Crescent human settlements in the Pleistocene." He held out the bow to Owen, spilled the contents of the pouch into his hand. It was a bunch of flint tools. "Look at these remarkable artifacts! Colonel Harrington's forced to sell these to raise some money for his research. Would it be unethical for me to take advantage of his distress?"

Owen rolled the flint razor in his hand, examined the bow. He was pretty sure the carvings on the grip had been made with a steel knife. He watched August out of the corner of his eye, then handed the artifacts back to Dunkenfield. "They're worth twice whatever you offered; Charge it to my father, through Vannice Station's account. I'll vouch for you."

"Wonderful. Did I tell you the new shower came, just as you promised?"

"Glad to hear it. We must meet for dinner when I get back to Boston." Owen maneuvered Dunkenfield away, eager to speak with August.

"I'm afraid I can't pay you right here," Dunkenfield said to August. "Can we meet in the hotel later this evening?"

"Certainly," August said. "In the bar perhaps, at eight?"

"Excellent," Dunkenfield looked embarrassed. "I say— would you mind if I held on to these until then? I don't want you to be seduced away by a better offer."

"I expect I can trust you," August said.

At last Dunkenfield left.

"Mr. Faison," Owen said. "I wouldn't blame you if you cut me dead, considering the way I treated your daughter last time. But please—give me a moment. I need your advice."

"You just did me a favor, Owen. What can I do for you?"

"Come walk with me. I need to check on Wilma."

On the way into the hotel and down to the warehouse, Owen told him the whole sad story of his involvement with Emma Zume. "The thing is, I never would have gotten involved with her if I wasn't so taken with Genevieve. I was so much in love, but my stupid pride—"

They found Wilma pacing back and forth along one wall of the warehouse room, poking her head into the steel rafters at either end. When she saw Owen she snorted and skipped toward them. She lowered her long neck and butted her forehead against Owen's chest, almost knocking him over. Owen scratched the wattles beneath her jaw, continuing to explain himself to August. "Do you think I've made a fatal mistake?

Maybe I should I try to understand Emma. But I don't want to. If you would only tell me how I could reach Genevieve, I'd try to explain all this to her. I can't help but think about her, how very much in love we were, how much better off I would have been if I hadn't let my ego get in the way. We could have been married by now!"

August shook his head sagely. "It's been my experience that it is most unwise for people who are very much in love to marry."

Owen felt a hand on his back. "What do you know about it, Father?"

It was Genevieve. She had cut her hair short, and wore dangling jade earrings. She looked a little older, a little more wary than he remembered from the night they had danced. But still beautiful, with a sly knowingness so different from Emma. Owen was overjoyed. "Gen. What a stroke of luck! You can't know how happy I am to run into you!"

"Why should I think it's lucky?"

"Please don't be angry. Though you have every right. I just didn't know. I—"

She turned to August. "Father, Owen and I are going outside to talk. You take care of Wilma for him."

"This is mighty irregular, young lady!"

"Excuse us, Mr. Faison. For now. But let's have dinner tonight, okay? Please!" Owen took Gen by the hand, pulled her away down the hall to the stairs. "I'm so sorry," he kept repeating as they ran up to the main floor and he dragged her out into the gardens of the palace. It was dusk, and high overhead the stars were coming out. They walked along the pathways beneath the trees and among the fountains, and it was very like the evening of the dance more than a year before.

Owen found himself rambling on, alternating apology with mad recitation of all that had happened in the last year. He told her about Emma. Except he couldn't make himself tell her that he was married. He'd sneak glances at Gen, find her smiling at him in the enigmatic way that had sent him into a trance the last time they'd walked together down these paths. His anxiety grew with every step.

"I hope you didn't toy with this woman's feelings, Owen. She doesn't sound like the type who plays games."

Owen colored. "No, I guess she doesn't."

"Because if you were entangled with her, I don't see how we could honorably continue this conversation. It wouldn't be right."

Owen's heart sank. He must have been dreaming to think they could go back to a year ago without any scars. A suicidal chameleon ran across the path in front of them, from flower bed to flower bed, almost beneath Owen's feet. Without thinking, Owen adjusted his stride, avoiding it. "You're right, of course. It wouldn't be honorable."

Gen sat down on a bench behind a shield of hyacinths. She drew him down beside her. He could smell her perfume. Despite himself, he found himself drawing closer to her.

"More than that," Owen said, "it wouldn't be right, because of how I treated you."

She smiled at him, her eyes glowing in the declining light. "I'm not proud of the way I acted, either," she said. She moved closer, her fingers behind his back, playing with the hair about his ear.

"I'm committed to Emma, not you. Every canon of our social polity demands that we separate right now—" Owen said.

"—and never speak to each other again," Gen breathed, resting her head on his shoulder.

Owen felt so dizzy he thought he might faint. He put his arms around her. "I might as well admit it," he said.

She turned her face up to his. Her lips were parted; her eyelashes fluttered. "Admit it."

"I only fell for her because she looked like you. But that doesn't matter, because we can never—"

She kissed him. It lasted a long time. Not quite as long as the Cretaceous, perhaps, but a good long time.

At last they drew apart, breathless. She was so warm in his arms. "I—I was trying to tell your father," Owen managed. "Some rules just can't be broken. I'm already married."

"Is that all?" she whispered. She pulled his face down to hers. "So am I, Owen. So am I."

=Timid men screaming love for a funny price,= Bill murmured in his ear.

Acknowledgments

I need to thank Bruce Sterling and Lewis Shiner for "Mozart in Mirrorshades," whose premise was too good not to steal. James Patrick Kelly, Richard Butner, Bruce Sterling and Greg Frost for hard readings. (And Greg, belatedly, for a title and a cover for *Meeting in Infinity*.) Cason Helms, Andy Duncan, Kathryn Locey, Kelly Winters, Steve Grant and Mark Van Name for SycCity. Paul Park, David Drake, Connie Willis and the participants in the 1995 Sycamore Hill Writers' Conference for good advice. Kim Church and Anthony Ulinski for the hair. My editor, Beth Meacham. Sue Hall. The real Emma Zume.

Finally, Kathryn Locey was a fount of invaluable information on the Bible and first-century Palestine. She's responsible for whatever credibility these portions of this book may have. Of course, any errors of fact or opinion are my own.

Have I left anyone out? My personal trainer? Hairdresser? All the wonderful little people who make this great industry possible?